THE EXCHANGE

A Dylan Thomas Thriller

Also by Vaughn C. Hardacker

Sniper

The Fisherman

Black Orchid

Wendigo

My Brother's Keeper

THE EXCHANGE

A Dylan Thomas Thriller

Vaughn C. Hardacker

Vaughn C. Hardacker

September 4, 2020

Encircle Publications, LLC
Farmington, Maine U.S.A.

Paperback ISBN 13: 978-1-64599-081-9
E-book ISBN 13: 978-1-64599-082-6
Kindle ISBN 13: 978-1-64599-083-3

Library of Congress Control Number: 2020944727

Editor: Cynthia Brackett-Vincent
Book design: Eddie Vincent
Cover design by Christopher Wait, High Pines Creative, Inc.
Cover photographs © Getty Images

Published by: Encircle Publications, LLC
PO Box 187
Farmington, ME 04938

Visit: http://encirclepub.com

Sign up for Encircle Publications newsletter and specials
http://eepurl.com/cs8taP

Printed in U.S.A.

Acknowledgments

IT'S DIFFICULT TO ACKNOWLEDGE ALL the people who have helped me throughout my writing career. Nevertheless, I'm going to try.

First, there was the staff at the Manchester, New Hampshire, Barnes & Noble store. It was through their relationship with the New England Chapter of Sisters in Crime that enabled me to meet many of the Boston Crime Writers. Hence, thanks are owed to Kate Flora who coordinated the SinC Speakers Bureau. I attended the crime writer events. There were many nights when I felt sorry for the writers as I was the only person there. Each and every one of them spent one to two hours listening to and answering my questions. It was these writers who led me to join Mystery Writers of America.

Then, there was the first writers' group that I joined, talk about walking into an ambush! The group consisted of Paula Munier (published author, editor, and now, literary agent), Susan Oleksiw (author, photographer, and publisher), and Skye Alexander (author of more than thirty fiction and nonfiction books). I will always remember the first meeting. I entered thinking I was going to amaze everyone with my wonderful prose. The one thing that will never leave me was when I finished reading the first chapter of my book, Susan in her soft, gentle way said, "That is a great piece of crime writing." I felt my head grow a couple of inches, then she said, "Take it out, it reveals too much too soon." My head returned to normal. That night I limped home. I was angry and believed they didn't understand my work. My late wife, Connie (gone for twelve years as I write this), walked into my office, and I vented on her. When I had finished sitting on the pity pot, she looked at me in that knowing way she had and said, "Did they give you any advice?" I replied, "Yes." She countered, "Did you write them down?" (she knew if I didn't, I wouldn't remember anything). My reply: "Yes." She said, "Well, if I were you, I'd try taking that advice. If you don't, you're wasting their time and yours." And then she left. I tried it. It was damned good! Well, at least a lot better than it was. I went upstairs and was peering into the refrigerator when Connie walked into the room. She asked what I was doing and I told her I was looking for a crow to cook, because I was eating it. I didn't know it then and only learned later that not one of those women expected to see me the next week. Not only did I go back, but I was early! The result was a book entitled *My Brother's Keeper*, the second book in my Ed Traynor series, published on July 2, 2019.

Paula Munier moved, which ended the Salem group and led to another writers group. Susan and Skye were no longer in the group due to the long commute. This group met at Paula's new home on the south shore in Pembroke, Massachusetts, a seventy-five-mile-each-way commute from my home in southern New Hampshire. To make this short, I stuck with it.

In the winter of 2009, I moved from the Boston area back to my hometown in northern Maine. I kept hammering away, and my first book, *Sniper*, was published in 2014. *The Fisherman* in 2015 (both of these were selected as finalists for a Maine Literary Award in the Crime Fiction category). *Black Orchid* followed in 2016. *Wendigo*, my first crime/horror novel, was released in July 2017 and was a finalist for the 2018 Maine Literary Award in the Crime Fiction category.

If I have learned nothing else in this journey, I have learned that if you tell people you are a writer and want to get it right, no matter what their occupation, they will help you to get it right. I've received assistance from members of law enforcement (both police and Maine Warden Service), professionals in law and medicine, and from other writers. I believe that writers are like Marines. Both of them will go to the limit to assist one another; Marines work as a team, and the vast majority of writers will gladly assist other authors, published or unpublished. I can honestly say that I have never encountered a group of people who all do the same thing but don't consider others in the trade as competition. As a Marine, no longer on active duty, I believe no one but another Marine can appreciate what you have to go through to be able to call yourself a Marine. Likewise, no one knows what a struggle it is to write a cohesive book or short story but another writer. Marines and writers are, I believe, kindred spirits in that they are always willing to offer a helping hand.

Some of the people who have made it possible for me to keep going:

Connie Hardacker (July 20, 1951 to October 16, 2006), my late wife, and for more than thirty-six years, my best friend.

Al Blanchard (May 13, 1945 to November 14, 2004), President of the New England Chapter of MWA and founder of the New England CrimeBake Conference, who took me under his wing and taught me about the business of writing.

Leslie Jane Hartley, my current partner, first reader, and best friend. She patiently waits when I'm working on a novel and keeps at me to attain my daily goal of one thousand words so she can read them.

There are so many members of law enforcement who have taken time to review my work for proper procedure. Brian Thiem: commander of the Oakland, California PD Homicide Section, and author of the Detective Matt Sinclair Mystery Series. Bruce Coffin supervised all homicide and violent crime investigations for the Portland, Maine, PD, and is the author of the John Byron Mystery series. Lee Lofland, former law enforcement officer, established the Writers' Police Academy, blogger at *The Graveyard Shift,* and is the author of *Police Procedure & Investigations*. Thanks to various members of the Maine State Police and the Maine Department of Inland Fisheries & Wildlife. John Cormier: a friend since junior high school, and retired Maine state homicide detective and polygraph expert. Dr. D. P. Lyle: for assistance in all things forensic; author of *Forensics for Dummies* and *Forensics*. Have a story related question? Ask Doug at thelab@cox.net, he'll get back to you with an answer, and he's a mystery writer to boot.

Penny Celino and Linda Hamilton, who read my first short story (when we were class mates in Caribou Junior High School in Caribou,

Maine) and had not seen nor heard from me until we met the evening of our fortieth high school reunion, and they said, "Why aren't we seeing your books in bookstores." I looked to my wife for support and she said: "Why aren't they?" I returned home after the reunion and got serious about learning the craft.

I have been fortunate in my life. I've had two women who support me, take no bull from me, and make me feel secure. What can be said other than: "Thank you, Connie and Jane; I will always love you both." As I'm writing this, I realize just how important women have been in helping me achieve whatever success I have—but then haven't they always been the driving force behind most men?

Finally, there are you, the readers, without you, none of this matters.

—Vaughn
Stockholm, Maine, March 2020

Dedication

To Connie and Jane—the two best friends I've had in my life.

To my grandsons,
Nickolas and Ryan (September 23, 1994 – September 3, 2017) Kaad.
To Nick, I hope your life is as fulfilling as you have made mine.
To Ryan, the Lord took you from us way too soon.

To all of my fellow Marines, past and present, wherever they may be,
especially to those in harm's way.

Adoption today has become a business that sells children as commodities with a disregard for children's human rights and with the moral indignity of selling children to meet the need of some adults to parent and others merely to make money.

—Kenneth J. Herrmann, Jr., Associate Professor, Department of Social Work, SUNY

It is illegal in every state for an adoption that requires exorbitant amounts of money be paid upfront to go forward, specifically if the money must be paid either directly to the birth mother or to a third party or agency acting as a go-between. Any requests for large sums of money in this manner is an excellent sign that the adoption is a scam or other type of illegal activity. This illegal adoption itself will probably not be legally recognized even if it is completed.

—family-law.freeadvice.com/family-law/adoption_law/illegal_adoption.htm

Saturday: Day One

WHEN DYLAN THOMAS WALKED ONTO his deck at four in the morning the thermometer read thirty below zero and steam spiraled from the hot coffee in his mug. The moon had not set and rested on the horizon as it awaited the rising sun. The wind blew snow across the icy surface of the lake and sent an involuntary chill through him. He finished off his coffee and said, "It's going to be a nice day to stay in the ice fishing shack." His telephone rang breaking his reverie. The phone rang again and he thought, *nothing good comes from a phone call at four a.m.* He returned to the warmth of his cabin, picked up the telephone, and said, "this is Dylan."

He was surprised to hear his sister Caitlin say, "Dylan I… we need your help."

Thomas immediately knew that whatever his sister needed was serious—serious enough for Caitlin to call him at this hour. If there was anything his *baby* sister was not, it was an early riser, nor was she compulsive enough to call about something not requiring immediate action. "Calm down, Caitlin what is wrong?"

"Sandy is missing and the police think we have done something to her. They've taken Oreille (she pronounced her husband's name Orell in the French way) and won't tell me where. You have to help us."

"Sandy… little Sandra?" Dylan almost dropped his phone. "*Your* daughter has gone missing?"

"Yes. She disappeared from her bedroom two days ago."

"And you didn't call me then!"

When there was no response from Caitlin other than the sound of her soft sobs, Dylan took a deep breath. The last thing Caitlin needed at that moment was for him to point out any mistakes she had made. When his momentary anger subsided, he asked, "Have they given any indication why they think you and Oreille have done something?"

"They haven't actually said anything. But the way they are talking and acting scares me. Should we tell them we want to call a lawyer?"

"Caitlin, you have, I'm your lawyer."

Her relief was obvious when she said, "So you will come?"

"Are you at home?"

"Yes."

"I'll be there in less than an hour."

"That soon, aren't you at home in Gray?"

"No, I'm at my camp on Cross Lake. I came up for a few days of ice fishing. I know you're upset, but listen to me carefully. Do *not* go anywhere with the police until I get there and more importantly don't say anything to them until I get there."

"I know, say nothing to them. But what if they ask me questions?"

"You tell them that under advice of your lawyer, you won't answer any questions until he arrives."

"All right."

"I'm on my way..."

When she said, "Please hurry," Dylan thought she sounded like a frightened child.

"Caitlin, I won't get there if you keep me on the phone."

It took Dylan fifteen minutes to close up the cabin and get on the road. He maneuvered his F-150 Lariat 4X4 along the icy surface of the private unpaved road that circumvented the north shore of the lake, connecting his cottage to State Route 161. It took all of his concentration to keep his wheels aligned with the frozen ruts created by the sparse traffic that used the country lane. Several times he almost lost control, barely avoiding jumping the road, plowing through the towering snowbank that lined the road, and crashing into the dense woods beyond.

His headlights cut through the predawn blackness. It had been a long, cold winter, *not like there was any other type in Maine's northernmost county*, he thought, and it wasn't even half over yet. It was early February and even though the calendar said spring was six weeks away, residents of Aroostook County knew there would be at least ten more weeks of cold weather before they would see leaves on the deciduous trees. Whoever it was that described the climate of Maine's northernmost county as *nine months of winter and three months to get ready for it* had nailed it. He saw the red stop sign in his high beams and started slowing as he approached the intersection with route 161. He eased the nose of his truck onto the paved road in order to see beyond the eight-foot-high snowbank that the Maine Department of Transportation plows had created. He saw the glow of headlights to his left and backed up so that his truck was out of the road.

An eighteen-wheeler, with logs piled high, raced by creating a mini-blizzard in its wake. Dylan shook his head. This section of Route 161 was famous for two things, black ice and moose in the middle of the road; the truck was doing at least seventy-five in a fifty mile-an-hour speed zone. Had Dylan not taken the action he had; he would be splattered all over the road. The wreckage would be so extensive that rather than try and determine truck from him, they would bury him in the wreckage in lieu of a coffin. He put his truck in gear and repeated his approach to the pavement. Seeing no sign of traffic, Dylan entered the road and turned left, in the direction of Fort Kent.

Caitlin and her husband, Oreille Dufore, lived in a house overlooking Eagle Lake, and what always impressed Dylan was how palatial it was. He believed that in the fall when the foliage was at peak color it was one of the most beautiful places on Earth. He turned off the highway and followed the twisting narrow lane that led up the side of the bluff before giving way to a large plowed area abutting the western face of the building. There were three cars in the yard: a white 2017 Lincoln MKC, a pale blue Ford Interceptor, which was easily identified as a state police patrol vehicle by the emblem on its doors, and a flashy, highly polished, burgundy Mustang that needed no signage or light bar for him to know it was an unmarked state police cruiser—the government license plate did that for him. *They sure as hell didn't have anything like that when I was on the state police,* he thought.

As Dylan entered the parking area, a motion activated light turned on cutting through the primordial darkness. He parked alongside the Mustang and stepped out of the warmth of his F-150 into the frigid air. His boots made crunching sounds as he walked across the packed snow and ice to the front of the house and pressed the doorbell.

The door opened and Caitlin stood in the threshold, her appearance so disheveled that it surprised him. His sister was meticulous when it came to her appearance; not so much as a single hair was ever out of place. However, that was not the case this time. He immediately knew that she was upset because her auburn hair was in disarray; her clothes looked as if she'd slept in them, and her eyes were red from crying. Caitlin was five feet nine inches tall but still had to stand on tip-toes when she kissed her six feet three inches tall older brother on the cheek. She smiled at him and stepped back, allowing him to enter into the living room. The room was immense; Dylan never ceased being amazed by its dimensions, which he believed to be a minimum of forty feet by fifty feet. To the left a fire burned in a granite fireplace that took up half the wall. The room was furnished with expensive mahogany furniture and the floors were an expensive hardwood imported from South America—Caitlin had once told him that it was called *bocate*.

Dylan wiped his feet on the mat that was centered in the tile square in front of the door and debated whether or not he should remove his boots. Caitlin must have sensed his uneasiness and said, "Don't worry, Dylan. People have been walking everywhere for two days."

Dylan hugged his sister and said, "Have they been interviewing you?"

"Right after I called you, they tried, but once I told them that my lawyer was on his way, they stopped."

Dylan scanned the room. "Where are little Orrie and Gloria?"

"Since we discovered Sandy was missing, they've kept themselves occupied in their rooms. Thus far we've been successful at keeping them out of this."

"The police haven't interviewed them?"

"They've talked to them, but not in any detail… I suppose it's just a matter of time before they do though."

"When they get around to them do not leave those kids alone. One of us—preferably me has to be present."

Caitlin nodded.

"Don't be surprised if the cops don't try to keep you and Oreille away so you can't influence what they say. Speaking of Oreille, have they told you where they took him?"

"No, they haven't said anything, but it wasn't the state police who took him."

"Who took him?"

"It was a county deputy sheriff. Do you think they're arresting him?"

"No… at least not yet. Most likely they want to separate you to see if your stories match. They must have taken him to the county jail in Houlton."

Two men stood in the far corner of the room and when they heard Dylan and Caitlin speaking, they had looked their way. The taller of the two was in plain clothes, but there was no need for him to wear a uniform; his very demeanor and bearing was like a neon sign flashing *cop*. He was over six feet tall, about six-three, his hair was buzz-cut so close to his scalp it was impossible to tell its color, and he wore an expensive suit and shoes. The plainclothes cop crossed the room, showed his credentials, and held his hand out. "I'm Detective Jean-Paul Thibodeau, Maine State Police—and you are?"

"Dylan Thomas, I'm Mr. and Mrs. Dufore's attorney."

"Do you have something that verifies that?" Thibodeau scrutinized Dylan's appearance and apparently found him to be out of tune with he believed a lawyer should look like. The cop was about the same height as Dylan, whose dark brown hair looked as if it had been electrified with static and stood up pointing in every direction; in his haste to get to his sister, Dylan had not even taken time to comb it. The stubble of three days without shaving covered his face and his hazel-colored eyes were red from lack of sleep. His clothing was not what people usually associated with a lawyer either, he had on an old brown leather coat, red and black plaid flannel shirt, blue jeans with ragged cuffs, and a well-worn pair of L.L.Bean hunting boots. Dylan took out his wallet and showed Thibodeau his Maine driver's license and his American Bar Association membership card.

"What are you charging my clients with?" Dylan asked.

"At this time, we aren't charging Mr. and Mrs. Dufore with anything. However, we are considering them to be *persons of interest* in the disappearance of Sandra Dufore."

"Where is Mr. Dufore now?"

"He's being transported to the Aroostook County Sheriff's Office for questioning."

"Would you be so kind as to contact the sheriff and request that they refrain from doing anything until I get there?"

Thibodeau shrugged. "I could do that."

Dylan waited for the cop to say something more; when he realized nothing was forthcoming, he said, "Would you do it now, please?"

Thibodeau took a cell phone from the inside pocket of his suit coat, turned his back to Dylan and Caitlin, and in short time was speaking with someone in the Aroostook County Sheriff's Office, or so Dylan assumed. After several seconds he turned back to Dylan and said, "Done." A quizzical look came over his face and he added, "Are you the same Dylan Thomas who was a state police detective?"

"Yes, after I left the force, I went to law school."

"So, you went from solving crime to helping the bad guys?"

"Not quite. I went from solving crime to ensuring that everyone—even the bad guys—gets a fair trial. I'm also a private investigator and licensed to perform investigations in the states of Maine, New Hampshire, and Massachusetts."

"A lawyer who is also a P. I.? Now that's one strange combination."

"Well I have to pay the bills. If one job is slow the other will take up the slack. Now, if you are not charging Mr. Dufore with a crime, why is he being transported and not questioned here?"

Thibodeau refrained from answering.

In rural Aroostook County it's not easy to get from one place to another; all of the major highways ran north and south with state, locally, and privately maintained secondary and woods roads the primary east-west routes. From the Dufore house Dylan had to follow a series of substandard roads through the small town of Ashland and into Presque Isle where he would pick up U.S. 1 through a number of one-horse towns (a couple of which the horse had left for greener pastures) forty miles to Houlton, the county seat of Aroostook County.

It was just after eight-thirty in the morning when he walked into the Sheriff's Office and stopped in front of the deputy, whose name tag read William Dow, manning the desk. "I'm Dylan Thomas, Oreille Dufore's attorney." He showed his credentials to the officer. "Is Sheriff Turner in?"

The deputy glanced at the wall clock and said, "She's probably over at the diner having breakfast... she usually gets in around nine."

"Alright, I'll see her then. In the mean time I'd like to see my client."

"Have a seat." The deputy pointed to several chairs lined against the wall. "I'll have him brought down."

Dylan nodded and dropped into one of the chairs. He spent the time thinking about his relationship with his brother-in-law—it was not a good one. Oreille Dufore and his sister, Albertine, were the primary heirs to Dufore Lumber. At one time the family controlled the cutting rights to most of the timber in the North Maine Woods. People like Dylan were allowed to lease lakefront property and build cottages and camps on the water. However, they had to obtain permission from Oreille the First to cut any trees on the property. In the late twentieth century, Oreille number one opted to terminate the ninety-nine-year leases and offer the land to the leasers for purchase. He made millions and then sold the cutting rights to more than a million acres of woodland to a major Canadian corporation and made even more millions.

Oreille number two, Dylan's brother-in-law, was the youngest child of first's sole surviving son, Georges, and had been pampered from birth. He met Caitlin Thomas while they were attending college at the University of Maine in Orono. Oreille number two had no intention of ever working and majored in English with a Creative Writing concentration, nor did he ever intend to pursue writing as a career. He once told Dylan that it was the easiest way for him to go; he hated math and had no desire to teach or do anything technical in his life—truthfully, he confessed that he only read when he had to. His lack of interest in anything literary didn't surprise Dylan because Dufore had not so much as an inkling of knowledge about writers and/or the business of writing. If he had he would have realized that his mother-in-law, Sandra (whom Oreille's daughter was named after) was enamored with the Welsh poet Dylan Thomas, whose most famous work was his poem "Do Not Go Gentle Into That Good Night," so much so that she named her son after him and her daughter after his wife Caitlin.

It took a half hour before the deputy's phone rang. He listened for a moment and then hung up. "You wanna follow me?" he asked Dylan.

Dylan stood and followed Deputy Dow deeper into the county jail. Dow took a key card from his pocket and swiped it through the slot of an electronic lock. When the lock disengaged with a loud CLUNK, he opened the door and stepped back. "Go on in. They've already brought your client down."

"I was told that my client was sent here to answer some questions."

"That's correct."

"Then can you explain why it took thirty-five minutes to bring him here? It sounds as if you had him in the lock-up."

"Mr. Thomas, I just work here. I let other people, those of higher rank make the decisions."

Dylan entered the small ten-by-ten room. Oreille Dufore sat behind a table with an inverted metal U welded to its surface to which he was handcuffed. The only other furniture in the room was three chairs, two of which were on the side across from Dufore. A uniformed deputy sheriff sat in one.

"Deputy, I'm Mr. Dufore's attorney, this interview is over."

The cop stood up and said, "If he's innocent, why did he lawyer-up?"

"He didn't *lawyer-up*. A state police detective named Thibodeau told me that Oreille was brought here for questioning. When I heard that, I had the detective call here and *lawyer him up*. What I want to know is why did you people bring him here to be interviewed? His home is more than adequate to find a private place to talk."

There was a tap on the door and Sheriff Lois Turner walked in. Turner was best described as being lean and, when necessary, mean. Her face showed the effects of a life spent out-of-doors; her complexion was ruddy from exposure to the sun, she wore no make-up, and there were fine lines at the edges of her eyes. Her gray hair was cut short and she wore a tan uniform with brown piping on the blouse and matching stripes on the outside of her trouser legs. Tall for a woman, she could be the model in a law enforcement recruiting poster.

She nodded at Dylan and said, "Well, look what the cat dragged in and the dog wouldn't take back out." The stern look on her face suddenly gave way to a broad smile. "Dylan Thomas, what's it been, six or seven years?"

"All of that Lois."

"You come for him?"

"I have."

"I haven't a goddamned clue why they brought him here."

"Only reason I could think of is they wanted to intimidate a confession out of him."

The officer who had been conducting the interview started to speak but Turner stopped him with a raised finger. "Who told you to talk to him, Floyd?"

"No one, I just thought—"

"We'll discuss this later." She turned to the door. "Good seein' you again, Dylan."

"Been a pleasure, Lois."

Turner removed a key ring from her pocket, flipped through the keys until she located the one she sought, and removed the handcuffs from Dufore's wrist. She nodded to Thomas and said, "Why don't you take your client the hell out of here?"

Dylan motioned for Dufore to rise, smiled at the sheriff, and said, "Consider it done."

In five minutes, Dylan and Dufore were out of the sheriff's office, in Dylan's truck, and headed north on U.S. 1. "Caitlin call you?" Dufore asked.

"Yes."

"Well, I don't need any help from you."

Dylan glanced at his brother-in-law. "Say the word and I'm out of it. But if I walk you better prepare yourself to be the primary suspect in a murder investigation. They don't have a body, or it's almost a given they'd be looking at you and Caitlin for homicide. That's life without parole and I won't tell you how inmates treat pedophiles and child killers." He turned right and accelerated toward Presque Isle. "If I had left you to handle this alone, you'd still be waiting for your high-priced lawyer in Bangor to find time for you and then he probably has never handled a criminal case. So, if I was you, I'd get off the fucking pity pot and tell me what in hell happened? From what I've seen and heard, you're up to your ass in alligators—and they're snapping."

Dufore's head dropped forward. "Stay."

"I need you to sign a retainer contract."

"Hah, now we get down to it, don't we? How much are you charging?"

Dylan felt his face warm with a surge of anger. "This isn't about charging anything you frigging dolt. In the event they indict you it gives me access to whatever evidence and/or witnesses the state plans to use in court. Without it I won't be able to do shit. Now, I'm going to ask you one more time—do you want me to represent you or not? Like I said, just say the word and I'm out of here. But keep in mind that Sandy is my niece and you and Caitlin won't be just another client to me. An outsider will look at this as just another case… it's goddamned personal to me."

Dufore stared out the side window and without turning his head, said, "Yes, damn it!"

"Then when we get to your place you and Caitlin will sign the damned contract." He opened the center console of his truck. "There's a small tape recorder in there, would you take it out please?"

"You gonna tape this?"

"Yes, seeing as how I'm driving, I can't take notes."

Oreille removed the recorder and placed it on the dash.

"There should be a couple of new tapes in there, get one and load the recorder."

When Oreille had the recorder ready Dylan said, "Start recording."

When the recorder was operating Dylan said his and Dufore's names and the date and time of the recording and then said, "The first question I want to ask is the most crucial one of all."

"Which is?"

"Did you harm Sandra?"

Dufore slapped the dashboard with his free hand and shouted, "Fuck no!"

"Good, I'd be careful about watching my temper going forward if I were you. Let's get down to business. What have you told them?"

"Just the truth."

"Which is?"

"Yesterday morning Caitlin went to wake Sandy up and saw that she was gone. She searched the inside of the house and when she couldn't find her, she came and got me."

"Where were you during this time?"

"In the living room watching one of the cable news channels while I drank my morning coffee."

"What did you do when Caitlin came to you?"

"I was still in my pajamas, so I ran up to the bedroom and got dressed."

Dylan listened to his brother-in-law for a moment and then asked, "Did you go into Sandy's room?"

"Yes."

"Any signs of forced entry?"

"No."

"Then what?"

"I checked the outside of the house."

"Any footprints in the snow by her window?"

"Just the ones I left when I checked it."

"Go on."

"After we looked everywhere, we called the police."

Dylan placed his pen on the pad. "You searched everywhere?"

"Everywhere."

"Even your storage shed?"

"Especially the storage shed. Sandy was fascinated by the stuff I store in there. Several times when we couldn't find her that's where she was. So, I looked around the snowmobiles and the ATVs... there was no sign of her."

"Oreille let's put everything on the table, okay?"

Dufore nodded.

Dylan said, "They're going to try and prove that Sandra is not missing, but dead—and that you, Caitlin, or both of you did it."

Dufore looked confused, pondered his answer for a few seconds, and said, "No. Goddamn it, Dylan, we didn't hurt her! She was our baby… our youngest child."

"What about someone other than the family? Have you noticed any signs of someone prowling around your property?"

"Nothing. Who'd want to hurt a baby like Sandy? You'd have to be one sick son-of-a-bitch."

"It's been my experience," Dylan said, "that the world is full of sick sons-of-bitches.

"So, what's next?" Oreille asked.

"I find out what they've got. If they think they have enough for an arrest, they'll go to the grand jury for an indictment. Once they do that you and/or Caitlin will be arrested and arraigned. At that point it's my job to convince the judge to grant bail. However, I wouldn't get my hopes up if I were you. They don't usually allow bail on a capital murder charge. You both may be wearing orange for a while."

"Dylan, you've got to convince the judge to let us out on bail. I can pay any amount they want."

"That might work against you. You have more than enough money to run a long way and to pay someone to help you disappear."

"You got to be kidding."

"I'm afraid not. If you lived in some shack and were financially insolvent, they might consider it. It won't surprise me if they ask for millions in bail."

"But," Oreille said with a hopeful look on his face, "all I need to put up is ten percent."

"That's why they'll jack it up as high as they can. Our one saving grace is they have no body. It's difficult to prove murder without one. Now I'm going to take off my lawyer hat and put on my investigator one. Can you think of anyone who would do this to you… maybe someone who has a major hard-on for you or Caitlin?"

"Are you saying that Caitlin or I may have pissed someone off enough that they'd kill a three-year-old?"

"As hard as it may be for you to believe, there are scumbags out there that kill kids for no other reason than they get off on it." Dylan paused for a moment to let his words register. "Do you think that someone may have kidnapped Sandy?"

"Why would a kidnapper kill her?"

"Maybe he won't. Do you have any idea how much a pretty little girl child will bring on the open market?"

Oreille's head dropped forward and he ran his hands through his hair. When he looked at Dylan there was no doubt how desperate he was. Either that or he suddenly realized how grim his situation was. "Jesus Christ, Dylan you've got to help us."

"That's why I'm here Oreille."

Dufore's eyes widened as if he'd just had an epiphany. "Maybe the cops will find her."

"Oreille, face the facts. The cops think they've got their perpetrators. They will be looking for ways to hang your ass—not to prove you innocent. If we want to beat this then we've got to find the real perp and find out what did happen to Sandy."

"How much time you think we got?" Oreille inquired.

"Not much. If she was taken, they'll be looking to sell her fast."

"Holy shit, Dylan. Who would sell a baby into white slavery?"

"At her age, I don't think she was taken to be turned into a prostitute. There is a booming market for young white children. It can take months, years even, to adopt a child through legal means and then small white children are in short supply and great demand."

"Are you fucking serious?"

"Whoever has Sandy may already have a client waiting. On the positive side, the cost is way beyond what the average person can afford. Whoever is looking to *adopt* her has to have deep pockets."

An hour after leaving the interview room Dylan and Oreille arrived at the Dufore house. Jean-Paul Thibodeau walked out of the garage. Thibodeau saw them and waited. "I see you got your client." he said.

"I did. I have to say that I'm concerned about the way this was handled."

Dufore cast a menacing look at the officer and then left them and entered the house.

"How so?" Thibodeau asked.

"Oreille should never have been taken there for questioning. I can only assume that it was done for only one reason, to intimidate him into confessing that he and/or his wife murdered their daughter."

"Follow me," Thibodeau said. He led Dylan into the garage. "We'll talk in here out of the weather."

As soon as they had entered the garage and the door closed behind them, Dylan asked, "What do you have?"

Thibodeau turned to face Dylan. "Okay, let's take this one point at a time. First, the child was last seen in her bed at eleven p.m. Second, at eight a.m. the day before yesterday, the county sheriff was notified of the child's disappearance. In turn, the state police, warden service, and a deputy from the Aroostook County Sheriff arrived..."

"The warden service?"

"Who better to organize and conduct a search for someone who may or may not be lost in the woods?"

"Understood."

"Third, upon arrival your client said that he believed that someone must have abducted the child. Subsequent investigation showed no signs of forced entry and we believe that the only footprints found outside the child's bedroom to be those of your client."

"I agree, let's take this one step at a time, okay?" Dylan responded. "I don't have to tell you that there are three requirements for considering someone a suspect. First, motive, what possible motive could a father have that would make him kill his child? Do you honestly feel that a father with no history of violent behavior would murder his three-year-old child? Second, means, any parent has the means to harm his or her child. The child lived in my client's home. Third, method, let's get serious here. You don't even have a body. It's always been my belief that with no body there's no murder. Come on, detective, you're not a rookie. You know you have no case against my sister and her husband."

"Mr. Thomas, you are correct in saying I'm no rookie, that's why I make no judgment about things beyond my purview."

"Okay. Who else are you looking at for this?"

"Well, we can't overlook the possibility that the child's mother is either an accessory to or possibly the perpetrator of the crime and her husband is covering for her."

Dylan stared at Thibodeau. "You're really grasping at straws, aren't you?"

Thibodeau stood up, walked out the door, and then turned to Dylan and said, "Then your job is easy. All you have to do is prove me wrong." He got into his car and started the motor.

When Thibodeau left, Dylan remained in the garage listening to the snow and ice crunch beneath the tires of the departing Mustang. He took out his cell phone and dialed the Aroostook County Sheriff's Department. When Sheriff Lois Turner answered she said, "Dylan it was great seeing you again."

"It has been a while."

"I heard that you're a lawyer now. I would guess that you gave up your P. I. job."

"I still have my P. I. license."

"That's a strange mix, ain't it now?"

"Well, it's unique that's for sure."

"What are you doing defending a scumbag killer?"

"C'mon Lois, he hasn't been convicted of killing anyone yet."

"Who's he supposed to have murdered?"

"His three-year-old daughter."

"Why would you want to represent some piece of shit that would even be suspected of doing something like that?"

Dylan was not surprised by Turner's colorful language; she had a reputation for being profane. "He's my sister's husband."

"You know that I got no patience when it comes to pedophiles or any form of child abuse for that matter."

Dylan leaned back against the garage wall. "For what it's worth, Lois, if Oreille Dufore is guilty of doing anything to a child, it's spoiling them rotten. You can't find a more dedicated and devoted father."

"I'll have to take your word for it."

"There is no way that either of the Dufores killed that child."

"Any physical evidence?"

"The only finger prints found in the child's room were those of family members. I assume they've sent any DNA evidence they have to the lab in Augusta."

"It will be three or four weeks before the DNA test results come back. I gather that you're not going to sit back and wait for the trial?"

"I'm still an investigator and I doubt the state police are going to keep investigating, except to find more evidence against Oreille."

"I have no control over what the state police do or don't do, you know that," Turner said.

"One last thing before I leave you to go about your day. What do you know about a detective named Thibodeau? I don't recall him from my days as a state cop."

"Jean-Paul? He's from *away*. He grew up in Portland—in Riverton."

"That's a tough neighborhood."

"He's a straight shooter. If you're innocent he'll go to the ends of the earth to prove it, but if you're guilty... well, then he'll do whatever it takes to put you away."

"I gather then that he's not the type to go on a witch hunt?"

"His reputation leads me to think that."

Dylan pushed away from the wall. "Thanks, Lois."

"You got it." Before he broke the connection, Turner asked, "What's it like?"

"What's what like?"

"After five years as a cop and putting scumbags away, you're now defending them..."

"I don't know. I've never defended a scumbag."

Once Dylan was inside the house Caitlin closed the door and guided him to the large leather sofa that faced the fireplace. He placed his briefcase on the floor beside the sofa then sat back. His eyes immediately settled on a large photo of Caitlin, him, and their parents hanging above the mantle. "I remember when that was taken," he said.

Caitlin looked at the photograph, which was so old that the paper had yellowed. "Yes, six months later Dad was dead and Mom started on her downward spiral."

Dylan thought back to that time, before cancer took their father and grief and alcoholism their mother. "Yeah, that was the last time I saw him alive—the last of the good times."

Caitlin sat quietly for a few moments and then said, "Where do we stand?"

"I don't want to mislead you, but the police think they've got a strong case against either you or Oreille or the both of you."

"That's ridiculous." Caitlin looked her brother in the eye. "What recourse do we have?"

"Only one that I can think of…"

"And that is?"

"We find out what really happened to Sandy."

"Okay… where do we start?"

"Right here. I need to look at her room."

Dylan saw his sister's jaw tighten and he knew what that meant. Caitlin was not going to let the authorities tear her family apart—not without one hell of a fight.

She leapt to her feet and said, "Let's get started."

Caitlin led Dylan down a hallway, her determination evident in the rapid pace she set—in no time she led Dylan by fifteen feet. Reaching the end of the hall, Caitlin stopped and turned left. When Dylan caught up with her, he saw her standing in the threshold of a pink shrine. He heard Caitlin whisper, "She loves pink."

Dylan gently guided her to the right and stepped into his niece's room. The entire room was pink, even the walls. Mounted on three of those walls were shelves on which sat enough dolls and stuffed animals to make the owner of a toy store turn green with envy. Along the far wall, beneath a window, was a single bed with a pink spread with a white bear stitched in the center. The bed was made and the room looked as if it had never been occupied; at least not by a hyperactive three-year-old girl.

He walked to the bed, studied the window, paying particular attention to the wooden frame and sill. He saw no signs of forced entry. He straightened up and scanned the closet. It too was neat and orderly, not so much as a single piece of clothing was on the floor. "Caitlin, have you cleaned this room?"

"Yes, I didn't want the police and their people to see it in disarray—what would they think about us? I vacuumed, made the bed, and dusted."

Shit, Dylan thought, *so much for learning anything in here.* Knowing that searching the room would be futile, Dylan walked outside of the room, past his sister and continued down the hallway.

When Caitlin caught up with him, she asked, "Did I do wrong?"

Dylan didn't want to add to her anguish and refrained from saying anything.

"Dylan I can tell that you think I screwed up. I'm sorry if I did."

Knowing that he could not successfully bullshit Caitlin, he said, "You should have left it, if there was anything to be learned in there the crime scene people would have found it."

He took her in his arms and held her tight for a moment and then released her. "Cait, if you did anything wrong, I know it was unintentional and it was being a mother. But from now on you have to keep in mind that the authorities are going to look at anything you and Oreille do with a suspicious eye. They could interpret your cleaning Sandy's bedroom as an attempt to cover up something."

She wiped at a tear and walked into the living room. She grabbed several tissues from a box, wiped at her eyes, and blew her nose.

"Am I in trouble?"

"Possibly, but nothing I can't deal with."

"I know you're saying that because you think I needed it. Thank you, Dylan."

"I said it because I believe it, Sis."

Caitlin's remaining children walked into the living room. He approached trying to decide how he was going to ask the one question that was on his mind with the kids present.

Caitlin saved him. When she saw his facial expression she said, "Guys, why don't you go down to the den and watch TV or something while Uncle Dylan and I talk."

Oreille the third and Gloria said hello to their uncle and left the room.

When they were out of sight, he asked, "How are they handling this?"

"They'll need some professional help, but I think they'll eventually be fine."

Dylan reached down, picked up his briefcase, and opened it. He took out the contract and placed it on the coffee table in front of her. "I need you to sign this for me."

Without reading it, Caitlin asked, "What is it?"

"It's a contract retaining me as your and Oreille's attorney."

"Has Oreille signed it?"

"He will. Where is he?"

"I think he's lying down for a while." She read the contract for a few minutes and then said, "Do you have a pen?"

He took one from his case and handed it to her.

She handed the signed contract to her brother and asked, "What do we do now?"

"You, Oreille, and the kids don't do anything. I want you to stay home and don't talk to anyone about this—especially anyone from the media."

"What will you be doing?"

"Trying to develop a strategy."

The woman walked into the tiny kitchen and dropped into a chair across from her male companion. "She finally went to sleep."

"Good, her fuckin' wailin' was gettin' on my nerves."

"She'll adjust." She got up, filled a mug with coffee and returned to her chair. She sipped the coffee, then took a cigarette from an open box, and lit it with a plastic disposable lighter. She stared at her boyfriend until she held his gaze. "Did we do the right thing?"

"At this point it don't fuckin' matter. We done it and there ain't no way to undo it."

"The neighbors are gonna notice that we got a different kid."

"You think I don't know that!" He reached over and tapped her on the crown of her head with an open hand. "Time we moved on anyways, the work around here is dyin' out. I hear there's lots of work down around Belgrade Lakes."

Dylan joined Oreille and Caitlin as they were finishing breakfast in their dining room. He sat at the table, grabbed an empty mug, and filled it with coffee. "The cops have finally left," he said

Oreille looked sheepish when he said, "Thank you for everything, Dylan."

"I didn't do anything, yet," Dylan replied. "We could still have a tough road ahead of us."

"Nevertheless, if you hadn't come for me, I'd probably be in jail."

"That's what you signed the contract for," Dylan said. "Our first priority is to find Sandy. Now I need you to think. There was no sign of forced entry—that means someone had a key to this house and used it." He looked at the wall beside the front door. "You don't have an alarm system?"

"Never needed one—at least not until now," Oreille said. "But you can bet your fortune that I'm getting one installed first thing Monday morning."

"We need more coffee," Caitlin said. She walked toward the kitchen. "You guys sit and I'll get it."

Dylan and his brother-in-law sat across from each other at the large dining room table. Dylan saw his reflection in the glass-like surface and wondered how much a table like that cost. He raised his head and looked at Oreille. "Look, I know that if you had your way, I wouldn't even be on your Christmas card list. Nevertheless, I'm a trained investigator and you'll get a more thorough investigation from me than you will from the cops, any private investigators you hire, or some other lawyer. I've got a personal interest in finding my niece."

Suddenly exhaustion from the long night caught up with Oreille. He hadn't shaved in several days, his eyes were blood-shot, and his hair greasy-looking and matted. The only way Dylan could describe him was that he looked as if he'd been rode hard and put away wet. Oreille said, "I know I can be an ass…"

"Only when you drink," Dylan interrupted.

"Trust me," Oreille said, "I don't need to drink to be an asshole. However, I know when I'm out of my depth and right now I'm in one hundred feet of water. I… no… Caitlin and I need your help."

"That's the most truthful thing you've said all morning," Caitlin said. She placed a carafe of coffee in the center of the table.

"Well, I haven't been all that easy to get along with either," Dylan said.

"And that's the most truthful thing you've said all morning, big brother," Caitlin said.

"Okay," Oreille said, "now that we got our confessions out of the way, what do we do?"

"Let's start by you two thinking back, is there anyone you've given access to… maybe given a key to use?"

Dylan saw their faces take on a blank look.

"Have you had any work done on the house? Someone you may have given access to?"

"Felicien," Caitlin said.

"Who?" Dylan asked.

"You hired that deadbeat after I told you not to?" Oreille said.

"Well, you were out of town and after that last heavy snow the roof needed to be shoveled off. I was afraid it was about to collapse—I didn't know who else to call."

"Save that argument for later," Dylan said. "Who is Felicien?"

"Felicien Paradis," Oreille said. "He's a lowlife, never had a real job in his life. Whenever he needs money for a bottle of whiskey or some dope, he does odd-jobs around the area."

Dylan turned to Caitlin. "Did you give him a key?"

"Just to the door to the garage."

Oreille shook his head and said, "Hon, I told you I had the locks redone so that one key fits every door to the house."

"Did he return the key?" Dylan asked.

"When he got back from Fort Kent," Caitlin answered.

"He went to Fort Kent?" Dylan asked.

"Yes, he wanted some of those pellets that melt snow. You know, the ones you throw on the roof and it melts the snow and ice."

"Where did he get the pellets?"

"Collins Hardware, he brought me back a receipt."

"Where's that receipt, Hon," Oreille asked.

"It's in the kitchen."

"Did you look at it?" Oreille responded.

"Only to look at the amount so I could reimburse Felicien. He paid for it out of his own pocket. Drink your coffee while I get it."

When Caitlin was out of sight Oreille looked at Dylan and said, "Are you thinking what I'm thinking?"

"I'll reserve my thoughts until I see the receipt."

Caitlin returned and placed a cash register slip in front of her husband. Oreille glanced at it and then handed it to Dylan.

Dylan read the slip and asked, "What's this item at the bottom?"

"I don't know, but I'll find out." Oreille got up and walked to the wall phone. After a few seconds he said, "Hardware, please." Then he asked, "Is Willy working today?" There was a brief silence and then, "Oreille Dufore." Another period of silence and then, "Willy, Oreille. The other day my wife sent our maintenance man in for some snow melt. I see another item listed on the receipt would you be able to tell me what it was for? The date?" He scrutinized the receipt. "Yeah, it was on Tuesday before last, the eighteenth..." He seemed to be listening for a few seconds and said, Thanks, Willy, I appreciate it."

Oreille returned to the table, sat down, and ran his right hand through his hair. "Willy remembered him. He bought the snow melt and had a key cut."

Caitlin's face lost its color, her lower lip quivered, and she began to cry. "I'm so sorry, Oreille." She turned to look at Dylan. "He's worked for us off-and-on since last summer. I thought I could trust him."

Dylan remained quiet. She had always been a bit naive and saw people in a favorable light. For years Dylan had known there was going to be a time when she would pay a price for being so trusting. However, he had never thought that the price would be this high.

"You got a picture of him?" Dylan asked.

"No," Oreille answered, "never had a reason to take one."

Dylan turned to Caitlin. "Describe him to me." He took a lined legal pad out of his brief case to take notes.

"Maybe five feet nine or ten inches tall, and looks like he's missed a lot of meals. If he was female, I'd think he was anorexic," Oreille said.

"Dark hair and a beard—both of which could use a good trimming," Caitlin added.

"Eye color?" Dylan asked.

"Don't recall," Oreille said.

"Dark," Caitlin added.

"He's a heavy smoker," Oreille said, "always had a cigarette in his mouth."

"His hair—long or short?"

"Has a mullet, you know short on the top and sides, but long at the back. It was popular with pro hockey players a few years back."

"Any identifying features—scars or things like that?" Dylan asked.

"His canine teeth are missing," Caitlin said. "You can see the gaps when he smiles."

"Anything else?" Dylan queried.

"No," Caitlin said, "he looked kind of average."

Felicien Paradis peered through the driving snow, trying to keep his pickup on the highway. The shoulders and center line were gone and the road was covered with a white blanket of snow. He ventured a quick glance at the woman sitting beside him and the crying toddler she held. "Goddamnit, Claudette, can't you make that kid stop bawling? I got my hands full just keepin' us on the road and that fuckin' cryin' is drivin' me nuts."

Claudette Beaupre held the crying child against her bosom and gently stroked the little girl's hair. She placed her mouth near the child's ear and whispered, "Shhh, little one, Daddy needs you to be quiet so he can concentrate."

"H-he's not my Daddy. I-I w-want my *real* mommy and daddy," the girl blubbered between sobs. "I want to go home."

Claudette rocked back and forth and said, "Mommy and Daddy are here and we're going to our new home."

Sandra Dufore struggled to free herself from the arms of the woman. She did not like these people. The woman smelled of cigarette smoke and the man was mean. The woman's arms tightened, imprisoning Sandra against her. "It's gonna be okay, little one, you'll see."

"B-but I want to go to *my* home..."

The nasty man yelled, "Quit cryin' or I'll give you something to cry about!"

The small girl tried to put as much distance between him and her as possible and snuggled closer to the smelly woman. The woman said, "Rest little one, everything will be alright."

"N-no i-it w-won't," Sandra stammered. She inhaled deeply between sobs.

The rusted truck struggled on, its windshield wipers beating a synchronized rhythm in their losing battle against the heavy snowfall.

"Where does this Felicien Paradis live?"

"I haven't a clue," Caitlin said.

"We always called him," Oreille said. "I have it written down someplace."

Oreille walked toward the living room.

"Hon, I think his number is written in the address book in the drawer under the phone," Caitlin called to her husband's back.

In minutes Oreille returned holding a spiral bound book. He sat and flipped through the pages. Finding what he sought, Oreille slid the book across the table and spun it 180 degrees so that Dylan could read it. "Do you recognize the exchange?" Dylan asked.

"I think it's a cell phone," Caitlin said. "When I called that number, he answered from his truck."

"It's probably a burner," Dylan said.

"What's a burner?" Caitlin asked.

"It's a cell phone that you can buy with a set number of minutes on it. Once you use up those minutes you can either buy more or just toss the phone in a trash can."

"So, there's no way to find him," Caitlin said. Her tone showed her fear and frustration.

"Don't give up hope yet," Dylan said.

Dylan removed his cellular phone from his pocket and punched in a number. It was answered on the first ring.

"What now, Dylan?" Lois Turner said.

He chuckled. "You must have caller-ID, Lois. I need you to run a check on a name."

"Is there a reason you want this?"

"It's possibly connected to my niece's disappearance."

"Which means it may have something to do with your brother-in-law's problem."

"Possibly…"

"Which also means that you should be talking to Jean-Paul Thibodeau."

"Before I do that, I want to make sure this is good."

"Alright, what's the name?"

"Paradis, Felicien Paradis. I need this as soon as you can get it to me."

"I can give you what you need right now. That one is a real hemorrhoid. We've had run ins with him on several occasions."

"What sort of problems?"

"Drunk and disorderly and a couple of domestic violence incidents."

"He's married?"

"If he lived in Iowa, Rhode Island, or Washington, D.C. he and Claudette Beaupre would be common law. But Maine has never allowed it. While we're on that topic, Claudette's no angel either."

"Where do they live?"

"In Wallagrass Station Village, they rent a mobile home there."

"In case this pans out, do you have a number for Thibodeau?"

"Yeah, his cellular is (207) 999-9077. I know he'll be thrilled spitless to hear from you."

The southernmost edge of Wallagrass Township is actually what remains of the old settlement of Wallagrass Station, even though anything even resembling a railroad station ceased to exist years ago. Dylan turned off route 11 onto Station Road and crept along until he came to a mobile home that was about two years past the time when it should have been sent to the crusher. Once upon a time, the outside had been painted a pale blue; now the paint was faded and rust showed through. Attached to the outside was a covered porch, which consisted of wooden planks that were crumbling with rot. Dylan parked in what vaguely resembled a driveway, of which the only proof was the black patches of old oil and grease that had leaked from any number of vehicles.

He walked around to the back of the structure and saw a wooden mud room had been added to the trailer. The steps leading into it didn't look as if they were in better shape as the rotten front porch. He climbed to the top step and knocked on the door. There was no answer, so he knocked again, this time harder.

"They ain't there."

Dylan turned and saw an old woman standing in the back yard of a neat cape-style house. She wore slippers and an old bathrobe. Her hair was white and thinning; it looked as if it hadn't been subjected to a combing for quite some time. He descended the steps and walked to her. She sucked on the end of a cigarette and when she took it out of her mouth, he saw yellow nicotine stains on her fingers.

"Hello," he greeted her. "Do you have any idea where they went?"

"Nope."

"Do you think they'll be back soon?"

"Don't think they's comin' back… ever."

"What makes you say that?"

"They loaded up their pickup and them and the child took off. I watched them, they went south on route 11. I was glad to see them go."

"Why's that?"

She ignored his question. "You the police or just plain nosy?"

"A bit of both." He took a business card out of his inside pocket and handed it to her.

"She held it close to her eyes and squinted as she read it. "Says here that you're a lawyer and private investigator. Which is it?"

"I'm both a lawyer and a licensed investigator."

"Hmmph, I guess that explains why you ask so many questions. I was glad to see them go 'cause that man is evil."

"Evil?" Dylan didn't think he'd ever heard anyone described as evil before.

"He's a drinker. I don't know why Claudette stayed with him. 'Twas me I'da dumped that man long ago." She leaned forward as if she was about to relate a deep, dark secret. "I think he beat them."

"Them?"

"Claudette and the girl."

"Really? I didn't know that Felicien had any kids."

"Yes, a girl. Strangest thing though. I ain't seen that young'un in a while. Cute thing she is, beautiful blond hair—I know about them things. I owned my own shop for years… until I got so damned old I couldn't work on my feet all day." She took a drag on the cigarette and added, "Strangest thing though I think the girl they had with them this mornin' wasn't Phyllis. Like I said, she was blond. The one I saw go with them this morning had light brown hair, looked to be smaller too."

Dylan reached inside his coat and removed a photo of Sandra Dufore. He offered it to the old woman.

She scrutinized the picture for several seconds. "I seen her. This child is the one that they had with them when they left."

"Who was Phyllis?"

"Claudette's daughter. She was about the same age as this girl." She handed the picture back to Dylan. "That child, Phyllis that is, was scared to death of him. I think he beat her a lot."

"You sure you don't have any idea of where they may be headed?"

"Well, he has family downstate."

"Downstate? Like Portsmouth?"

"Not that far, round the lakes."

Dylan gritted his teeth in frustration. There were thousands of lakes and ponds in Maine and ninety-eight percent of them were *downstate*, which he knew folks up here considered anyplace south of Aroostook County.

"One time I heard Claudette say that they was goin' to visit his folks someplace near Augusta."

That narrows it down a bit, Dylan thought.

"Thank you, Ms., —"

"I ain't no mizz, I'm Missus. Mrs. Sadie Watson."

"Who owns the mobile home that they rented?"

"Brian Carton. He ain't gonna be happy about losin' a renter. Took him most of a year to find Claudette and that deadbeat."

Dylan backed up a step and said, "Thank you Mrs. Watson."

She looked at the sky. "You don't want to dally young fella, TV says it's already snowin' to beat Jesus down 'round Ashland. They're callin' for sixteen to twenty inches for us."

"I have four-wheel drive."

She made a snorting sound. "All that means is if you get stuck, you're stayin' stuck." She wrapped her robe tight around her body and disappeared inside her house.

Sunday: Day Two

THE WIND PICKED UP AND snow and sleet clicked as it bounced off the windows of the GMC pickup truck. The headlights reflected from the falling snow making the flakes look like white moths. The sun had set hours earlier and driving was a challenge. Felicien lit a cigarette and bent slightly forward as if being an extra inch closer to the windshield would give him a better view of the road.

Claudette leaned against her side window and had been chain-smoking for the past hour. In an unconscious display of nerves, she patted the child that was curled up in the seat between the two adults. "Baby, we need to stop someplace and wait this storm out."

"Stop someplace?" Felicien's voice was hoarse with fatigue and hours of chain-smoking. "You gonna squat down and shit out some money? We need what we got for gas and cigarettes."

Claudette crossed her arms in front of her breasts and said, "The baby is probably hungry too."

"You fuckin' deaf or somethin', woman? I clearly heard me say the money was for gas and cigarettes."

"But we got to eat."

"Shut up, just shut the fuck up so I can concentrate on the road."

Flashing yellow lights suddenly appeared out of the storm and Paradis jerked the steering wheel to the right. A snowplow raced by in the northbound lane throwing a tsunami of snow that obscured everything for several tense seconds. "Son of a whore!" Felicien swore. "That bastard almost wiped me out."

"Baby, we got to stop or we're going to be killed," Claudette said. Her voice broadcast her angry fear.

"All right... the next rest area or gas station I see we'll stop."

At two-thirty a.m. they finally came to a small convenience store and gas station combination. Felicien pulled in and stopped beside the gas pumps. "Stay here and keep that kid quiet." He got out of the truck and a gust of wind hit him full force, driving him back against the open door. He bent his head into the wind, stepped forward, and slammed the door shut behind him.

He opened the fuel hatch and removed the gas cap, setting it in the back of the truck. He removed the nozzle from the side of the pump and inserted it into the fill pipe. He turned to start the pump. But when he raised the switch nothing happened. A voice from the speaker that was mounted on a pillar beside the pump said, "After nine you got to pay inside before you can pump."

Paradis waved toward the building and then opened the truck door. He reached under the seat and picked up a nine-millimeter pistol.

"What do you need that for?" Claudette asked.

"Shut the fuck up and stay here."

"I got to pee. You haven't stopped in over four hours."

"So, go piss, take her with you." He pointed at Sandra.

As they walked toward the building another plow raced by and Felicien stopped and watched the snow swirl and spin in its wake.

Once inside, Claudette asked the attendant, "Restroom?"

The clerk appeared to be in his late teens pointed toward the back of the store. "Down that corridor."

Felicien stepped up to the counter and laid a credit card on it. "Lemme have three packs of Camels."

The clerk laid the cigarettes on the counter and picked up the card. "That's twenty-two fifty."

"Fine, don't run that card yet, I wanna fill up."

The kid propped the card above the keys on the cash register and activated the pump.

"Be back in a jiff," Felicien said.

"It's bad out there, huh?"

"You go to school kid?"

"Yeah, I go to the Community College down Bangor."

"What you do, take a course in askin' stupid questions?"

The kid blushed which made the acne that covered his cheeks turn a darker shade of red. "I was just sayin' that's all." Felicien ignored the clerk and walked outside. In his wake, snow and cold blew in as the door struggled to close against the nor'easter.

Ten minutes later, Felicien walked back inside and Claudette and Sandra walked to the counter.

"Get yourselves somethin' to eat," Paradis ordered. "And get me a coffee."

In no time Claudette had the counter covered with pastry, chips, and drinks. The attendant rang everything up and bagged the items. "Take it to the truck," Paradis said.

When the door closed behind Claudette and Sandra, the kid asked, "That it?"

"Yeah."

The youngster ran the credit card, gave the screen a quizzical look, and then scanned it again. "I'm sorry, but this card is no good," He said.

"I know," Felicien said.

When the attendant looked up, he saw a pistol pointed at him. "Whoa, mister."

"I want everything in that cash drawer."

"No problem there." The kid scooped all of the bills out of his register and handed them to Paradis.

"Under the tray too, that's where you guys always put the big bills."

"They only leave me the minimum."

Felicien rounded the counter, pushed the kid aside and raised the tray, "What's this?" he held up three one hundred-dollar bills. "WHAT THE FUCK DO YOU CALL THIS?"

"Honest I didn't know it was there."

Paradis grabbed the kid by the collar and guided him toward the back of the store.

"I don't want to hurt you kid, but you seen my face. I'll try to make this as painless as I can."

The sound of the storm drowned out the sound of the gunshot. Before walking out, Paradis located the breaker panel and switched circuit breaker to the off position. He saw a cardboard sign in the window of the dark store and turned it so that it read *CLOSED*.

After waiting out the storm and spending the night in a small motel in Wallagrass, Dylan stopped into the town's sole store. Upon entering the establishment, he saw that the business was divided into three distinct areas: immediately inside the entrance was a small general store, to its left was a shop which was a sporting goods store, selling hunting and fishing supplies, and to the right was a diner. Dylan turned right and walked to the small window situated beneath a board which was the menu. He studied the kitchen and was impressed with its cleanliness. A young woman walked from the back where she'd been washing dishes. She dried her hands with a towel as she approached the window and placed the towel to one side of the window. "May I help you?"

"Coffee, please."

"That all?"

"For now."

She looked past his shoulder at the snow that was once again cascading from the slate-gray sky. "This one's gonna dump on us."

Dylan turned and looked through the window. "That's what I hear."

She placed a sixteen-ounce take-out cup of coffee on the sill of the foot-wide window. "Cream and sugar?" she asked.

"Black is fine. How much do I owe you?" He reached for his wallet.

"Pay the cashier in the store on your way out," she said.

"Thank you," he said as he picked up the coffee and sat at one of the six small tables that served as a dining room. He took a drink of the hot beverage and was startled by its scalding temperature. Placing the cup on the table he took out his cell phone, ensured that he had service, and then entered in the number that Lois Turner had given him for Jean-Paul Thibodeau.

In spite of it being seven o'clock on Sunday morning, the phone was answered on the third ring. "Sergeant Thibodeau."

"Sergeant, this is Dylan Thomas. I think we should talk. Where can we meet?"

"Right now, I'm at the Troop F barracks in Houlton."

"I'm in Wallagrass… to be precise I'm having coffee in the store at Soldier Pond."

"Roads are pretty shitty," Thibodeau said. "Is this important?"

"Does the name Felicien Paradis mean anything to you?"

"Sheriff Turner told me you were asking about that piece of shit. So, yeah it does."

"Yesterday afternoon I went by his house in Wallagrass Station. The next-door neighbor told me that he, his woman, and a child tore out of there yesterday, apparently heading south."

"That's interesting."

"Not as interesting as when I showed the old woman a picture of my niece, she identified her as the child they had with them."

"You don't say?"

"The best the old woman knew was that Paradis has family downstate, near some lakes in the Augusta area."

"Belgrade Lakes."

"What?"

"Belgrade Lakes, that's where he has family living. I've been looking into him too."

"Where can we meet?"

"Nowhere this morning. This storm is supposed to let up around noon and I'll head toward Bangor. We'll coordinate by phone."

"Alright, I'm heading down route 11."

"There is," Thibodeau said, "a restaurant off exit 264 in Sherman Mills. I should be there by two o'clock. Wait there for me."

Dylan glanced at his watch. "That gives me eight hours to travel less than one hundred miles."

Thibodeau chuckled. "You ever drive route 11 in a snow storm?"

"No."

"Thought so—see you at two."

His cell phone rang. "Dylan Thomas."

"Jean-Paul here. Where are you?"

"I'm headed south on route 11."

"I'm ahead of you, in Sherman, a convenience store and gas station on route 11, about five miles north of Sherman."

"Dylan glanced at the clock in the truck's radio display. "You're about four hours early… why the change in plans?"

"Our boy was busy last night. How soon can you get here?"

"Shit, I'm just north of Patten. Give me an hour."

"I need you to get here as soon as you can."

"Where exactly in Sherman?"

"Just north of the first Sherman exit on I-95 south. Trust me, you'll know it when you see it. Look for all the police cars—you can't miss us."

"What happened?"

"A homicide. It seems Paradis has moved up to major crime. See you when you get here."

The storm had abated and the sun, reflecting from the pristine white snow that covered the trees that lined the road, was brilliant. Dylan donned a pair of sunglasses and hoped the road to Sherman was clear and there would not be many drivers going to work. He had about fifty miles to travel and he had to do it fast.

He passed a hunting lodge, nestled among the trees and noticed streams of snow flying upward as people dug out their cars. A Ford

F-350 pushed snow out of the lodge's parking lot and across the highway, pile-driving it into the snowbank. Snow slid from the sides of the plow leaving two trails of snow on the road and Dylan felt his truck bump over a pile that was left behind the plow truck. In his rear view, Dylan saw the plow driver back up across the lot and then race back toward the road. The plowed snow seemed to explode and the rear wheels of the pickup rose off the surface when once again he rammed into the snow bank.

Sergeant Thibodeau was correct when he said it would be easy for Dylan to locate the crime scene. The store's unplowed yard was filled with local, county, and state police cars. There was an ambulance by the front door and Dylan hoped that he was not going to find Sandra's body inside.

He was stopped at the door by a uniformed state police officer. "I'm sorry sir, but this is an active crime scene I can't allow you in."

A voice from inside the building said, "He's okay, give him a pair of booties and let him in." When they were handed to him, Dylan put the white cloth booties on his feet and then stepped into the store's interior. He saw Thibodeau and another police officer bent over a video monitor. "There," Thibodeau said, "stop it there."

He turned, saw Dylan, and motioned him over. When Thomas reached Jean-Paul's side, Thibodeau pointed at the screen and said, "Is that your niece?"

Dylan studied the screen for several seconds. The quality of the surveillance tape was not the best, nevertheless he easily recognized Sandra. "Yes, is she…"

"The victim? No that was a local kid, only eighteen. We won't know what the cause of death is until after the autopsy, but looks like a nine-mill shot to the head. Death was probably instantaneous."

"Are you still going to be the assigned detective on this case?" Dylan asked. "You're in Major Crimes North. If Paradis is in fact headed for the Belgrade Lakes Region, it's in Central's district."

"I can follow the case."

"Okay, I'll wait outside. I don't want to contaminate your crime scene."

"I'll come with you. The crime scene people don't need me to process the scene."

Once outside, they stood in the crisp morning air. "Colder than a well-digger's ass," Thibodeau said. He reached into his pocket and took out a pack of cigarettes. He offered the pack to Dylan. "Smoke?"

Dylan held his hand up. "I gave them up two years ago."

"I keep telling myself that I'm gonna quit."

"Why don't you?"

"Because I enjoy it and I'm a nicotine addict."

"If you don't really want to quit you won't. It's good you don't play games with yourself. You got any idea when this went down?"

"The assistant M. E. says based on the degree of rigor and the body temperature, he estimates between eleven last night and one this morning. The time stamp on the surveillance camera shows 2:45 a.m. but sometimes those times aren't correct."

"You got any idea where Paradis may be heading?"

"My money's on Belgrade Lakes. There are a number of lakes and ponds there with hundreds of camps and cottages that are empty for the winter. With his relatives to help and support him, he could hide there for quite a while."

"Like the hermit you guys hunted for years?" Dylan referred to a Maine man who had been living as a hermit in the woods of Maine for the last twenty-seven years, supporting himself by burglarizing camps and cottages. "Doesn't he hang out around North Pond, which is part of the Belgrade Lakes?"

"That was one way of his haunts."

"If Paradis drove straight through, he's most likely there by now."

"Yeah, we're only a mile off I-95. What with last night and this morning's storm, there wouldn't be much traffic and the plows keep the interstate pretty clear."

Dylan walked toward his truck. "I'll head that way. I can't do anything here."

Thibodeau nodded. "I'll be along shortly."

"You want I should book a couple of rooms?"

"I got friends in Augusta. It's only an hour away, an easy commute."

"Then I'll see you in Belgrade Lakes. I'll call you once I get settled."

"Dylan?"

"Yeah?"

"His family lives around Great Pond. I'd like you to wait for me before you start after him."

"You got my word. I'll wait for you to get there."

"Don't take him lightly. He's bound to be pretty desperate now and we know he's armed."

Paradis stopped in front of a weathered and worn single story house. A woman appeared in the door of the mudroom. She was barely taller than four feet, her long gray hair was pulled back into a ponytail that ended between her shoulders, and her faded blue jeans and man's flannel shirt she wore was well past its prime. She rested her right arm on the door jam. She held a cigarette between the index and second fingers of her right hand and she peered at the rusted and salt covered Dodge truck. When he got out, she stared at him for a second and then her mouth twisted into a smile that exposed her lack of teeth. Her accent was heavy French-Canadian when she called out, "Is that you, Felicien?"

"*Oui,* Jeanine (he pronounced her name Jah-neen)."

Jeanine Boutot looked at the truck. "Who that you got wit' you?"

"Claudette."

"I know who *she* is," the old woman answered, showing her dislike of her son's answer. "Who's the kid?"

"That's Claudette's daughter, Sandra."

Jeanine took a drag on her cigarette. "Well, don't stand there gawking at me, c'mon in." She turned and disappeared into the dark interior.

Felicien turned toward the truck. "You gonna sit there all fucking day?"

Claudette got out and reached inside picking Sandra up.

"If the old bitch asks you that's your daughter, Sandra. You got that?"

Claudette nodded. "How we gonna explain that she don't look like you?"

"We ain't. She's your kid with some other asshole. Leave it at that."

"She don't look like me neither…"

He sighed. "I got to explain ever' thing to you, don't I? She looks like her fuckin' father." He turned toward the house. "C'mon let's get inside before I freeze my balls off."

The contrast between the brilliant sun reflecting from the newly fallen snow rendered them blind for the few seconds it took for their eyes to adapt to the transition from bright sunlight to the ramshackle house's dark interior. The air stunk with the odor of cigarette smoke and stale coffee. When they were able to discern their surroundings, Claudette saw a living room that looked as if it had been furnished at the local landfill. Cigarette smoke drifted across the light that filtered through the filthy windows and looked like a flat cloud as it undulated in the air. The recliner chair in which Jeanine Boutot sat was so old and worn that the wood frame showed through the ripped fabric that formed its arms. Beside the recliner sat a small table that was scarred with scratches, gouges, and cigarette burns. The ashtray in front of the lamp was overflowing with cigarette butts and ash and held a smoking cigarette. The smoke spiraled up the lamp and through the top of the shade as if it was a smoke stack.

"Set your asses down," the old woman said. Her voice croaked, no doubt the result of years of smoking cigarettes and she no sooner ground out a cigarette than she removed another. She extracted a cigarette from the box with a generic brand printed on it and broke the filter off. When she saw Claudette watching her, Jeanine said, "All the cheap cigarettes got filters. If there's one thing I can't abide it's a filter cigarette. I read that the fiberglass in the filter can get into your lungs and cause cancer." She coughed and a phlegmy pop came from her chest.

Claudette sat on the couch, which was as worn out as the recliner, and felt broken springs causing the seat cushion to sag. She found herself hoping that their stay in this dump would be short. She felt Sandra pull tight against her and then lightly squeezed the child trying to help her feel secure.

Felicien did his part to keep things unbearable by lighting a cigarette and letting the smoke add to the already oppressive atmosphere. "We need a place to stay for a while."

"What you done, boy? You kill someone this time?"

He started, but quickly recovered. "No, I ain't killed nobody."

Jeanine saw the nervous look on Claudette's face. "Well, her goddamned face says you done somethin' just as bad."

"Would it be possible for me to use your bathroom," Claudette said.

The old woman turned her head to her son's woman and said, "You ain't comp'ny no more, you bin here more than twice so you should know the way."

When she heard the bathroom door close, Jeanine turned to her son. "You stop your goddamned lyin'. I may be old but I ain't got that Al'timer's disease. Her daughter wasn't named Sandra, it were Phyllis. Her daughter was blond and one thing that kid ain't is blond. So, stop blowin' smoke up my ass. Where'd you get that kid?"

"Alright, you're right. She's Claudette's other child. The kid came out the same hole, but was put in there by a different pole."

The old woman struggled out of her chair. She stood before her only child and slapped his face. "You don't want to tell me where you got that kid, that's your business, but stop your lyin'."

He rubbed his cheek where she hit him and felt his anger peak. It took all of his willpower not to hammer the old bitch into the worn linoleum floor. He swallowed his ire and said, "You gonna let us stay here for a while or not. I got money to pay you..."

Jeanine's face suddenly illuminated and when she smiled at Felicien her toothless mouth opened like the entrance to an abandoned coal mine. "How much you got?"

Dylan arrived in Belgrade in mid-afternoon. The blizzard of the previous night had missed the middle part of the state and there was considerably less snow than up in *The County*. The snow alongside the road was anything but white. It was coated with sand, gravel, and salt used by the state or town's department of transportation to clear it from the paved surface and looked dingy and gritty. He pulled into the parking lot of a motel on route 27. Exiting his 4X4, Dylan saw where the sun and above freezing temperatures had melted the snow and the resulting water had refrozen when the temperature returned to below freezing, lining the snow banks with a strip of ice. It was a minor thing, but he stored it to memory because one never knew what could become a problem later on.

He entered the lobby and stopped in front of a small desk. "I'd like a room, please."

The desk clerk was an attractive woman whose smile was the sort that could light up a room. She was one of those young women who made men in their forties, Dylan's age, wish they were twenty years younger. "For how many nights will you be staying, sir?"

"I'm not sure. I'll have a better idea by tomorrow."

"You're lucky," she said.

"Oh?" Dylan looked at her name tag, "How's that, Danielle?"

"The ice fishing tournament and winter carnival end today and we've had a number of guests check out. Yesterday we were full up."

"Well, I guess I am lucky."

"Would you like two queens or a king?"

"Beg your pardon?"

"Your room, would you like two queen-sized beds or a single king?"

"Oh. It doesn't matter, I'm not expecting company."

"A single King then." Danielle gave him another smile. "I don't know about you, but I like a lot of room when I'm in bed."

Dylan grinned. There was no way in hell he was going to pursue that line of conversation.

"That'll be $89.00 plus tax." She leaned toward him and said in a conspiratorial whisper, "I gave you the *Senior Citizen* rate." This time her smile had an impish quality to it. "I'll need a credit card for incidentals."

Dylan stifled a laugh and placed his American Express Card on the desk's shiny surface.

Danielle scooped it up and placed it in the card reader. Dylan heard a printer whine and then she placed a sheet of paper, his charge card, and a folder containing an electronic key card on which she wrote the number 118. "I've placed you in room 118. It's outside all the way to the left. It's far enough away from the stairs and ice machine so you won't be bothered by a bunch of noise."

"Thank you." Dylan picked up the items from the desktop and walked toward the door.

When he was halfway across the room, he heard Danielle call after him, "Don't hesitate to let me know if there's anything else I can do, Mr. Thomas."

It was another line that Dylan was not going to touch. He raised his hand and said, "Thank you, Miss…?"

"Stevens, Danielle Stevens. Don't hesitate to call—for anything…"

"Thank you, Ms. Stevens." He did not turn toward her so she didn't see the broad grin on his face.

Dylan walked into his room and knew he needed to do some shopping. He hadn't planned on a road trip when he left his camp on the lake and he hadn't had the opportunity to grab some personal hygiene products to bring with him. He was at the end of two days without changing clothes. Realizing he was not in one of Maine's larger cities such as Portland or Lewiston, he was afraid it would be sometime the next day before he could find a store that was open. He called Jean-Paul Thibodeau and arranged for them to meet at the motel in the morning. He located a small bar and grill in the center of the village and ate dinner. When the server placed his meal on the table, he asked her if there was an open store close by. She directed him to a Walmart.

Two hours later he'd bought a pack of disposable razors, shaving lather and after shave, a tube of toothpaste, a tooth brush, a pair of cargo pants, a pair of jeans, a couple of plaid wool shirts, a pack of three pairs of socks, a package of boxers, a three-pack of tee-shirts, and a small overnight bag in which he could carry his purchases. He returned to his room, took a shower and lay on his bed in his boxers and a tee-shirt. His thoughts returned to the light flirtation he'd had with Danielle and he chuckled.

He was starting to drift into sleep when there was a knock on his door. He bolted to his feet, wondering who it might be. Once he had his jeans on, he opened the door. Danielle stood at the threshold, holding up a six pack of Pabst Blue Ribbon. "Care for a nightcap?" she asked.

Dylan stood back and let her in.

She stepped across the threshold and said, "I see you went shopping."

Dylan wondered how she could know that—then he saw the tags were still on the jeans.

Jean-Paul Thibodeau hung up the phone and walked into the Major Crimes Unit—Central office located in the State Police Headquarters in Augusta. He saw an old friend sitting at the desk. As he approached, the detective saw him and said, "Hey! If it ain't Jean-Paul Thibodeau… to what do we owe the honor of your presence?"

"Hey, Barry."

"What's pulled you away from Bangor?"

"Felicien Paradis…"

"What in hell is a Felicien Paradis?"

"A piece of shit who I believe robbed a convenience store up in Sherman last night. He's also believed to be responsible for killing an eighteen-year-old kid in the process."

"We heard about that. How can we help you?"

"I need anything we can find on him and any family or acquaintances he may have in and around Belgrade Lakes."

Barry spun around his chair and logged into the state police computer network. "How you spell that first name?"

Monday: Day Three

WHEN DYLAN WOKE UP IT was still dark. He looked at the digital display on the clock radio that sat on the end table on the far side of the bed. Danielle had left sometime during the early hours of the morning with a promise to return if he was still in town on Monday night.

He sat up and wanted a cup of coffee. He took the small pot that was provided with the single cup coffee-maker, filled it with water in the bathroom sink, and poured it into the small coffee-maker. He took the coffee packs out of the small plastic holder and fanned them. Of the four, three were decaffeinated. He looked at the bags of decaf and thought, *why bother?* He opened the pack of regular coffee, removed the coffee-filled sack that was inside, placed it into the drip basket of the machine, and turned the brewer on. After shaving, showering, and brushing his teeth, Dylan studied his reflection in the mirror paying particular attention to his hair, mustache, and goatee, checking for gray hair—there wasn't a lot of gray, but there was enough. He ran his fingers through his hair and thought about the previous night… and Danielle. *There's no fool like an old fool,* he thought.

The smell of coffee drew him back to the coffee service. He poured a cup and sat in the room's single chair. He turned on the TV and tuned to a channel out of Portland-Bangor and watched the early morning news. There was nothing about the Saturday night robbery in Sherman. *Doesn't surprise me,* he thought, *these people think everything north of Augusta is Canada.*

Claudette was awake and staring at Felicien when he woke up. He stared back at her for a few seconds and said, "What?"

"She hates me."

"Who hates you?"

"Your mother hates me."

"She probably does. She hates me too—hell, she hates everyone equally, there ain't a prejudiced bone in that old bitch's body."

Claudette sat up and picked up the box of Camel filters that sat beside the bed and lit one. She took a drag and handed the cigarette to Felicien. While he inhaled his first hit of smoke and nicotine, she asked, "How long are we stayin' here?"

"I don' know. A few days anyway, maybe a week," he laid on his back, staring at the ceiling. The corners were crisscrossed with spider webs and black cob webs hung down from numerous spots. "What makes a cob web turn black," he mused.

"Dirt," Claudette answered, "Dirt and burning wood. The carbon gets into the air and sticks to the web."

Felicien handed her the cigarette and sat up. "You know," he said. "You're one fucking smart woman. In fact, you're so goddamned smart that sometimes it drives me bug-fuck." He spun around, got out of bed, and pulled on his jeans. "I hope the old woman has left some coffee for us."

Claudette placed the cigarette in an ashtray, got up, and flipped her nightgown over her head. She hooked her bra in front, then spun it around, and slipped her arms through the straps. She bounced her breasts to settle them in the cups and then grabbed a pair of panties.

"Why do you dress that way?"

She paused. "What way?"

"You always cover your teats before you cover your ass."

"I don't know. I've always done it this way. What's it to you?"

Felicien waved his hand as if he was dismissing her. "Forget I said anything. It ain't worth starting a fucking argument over."

She slid the panties up her hips and then put on a pair of jeans. "How much did you get?" She asked while buttoning the top of her jeans.

"What you talking about?"

"The store you robbed on Saturday night. How much money did you get?" She pulled a sweater over her head and then flipped her hair to settle it on her shoulders.

"I dun know, three hundred, maybe three hundred fifty."

"Doesn't seem like enough to kill someone for."

"Where in hell is that comin' from? Nobody killed nobody."

"Felicien, don't act as if I'm stupid. Didn't you just tell me that I was smart?"

He stood quiet and watched her sit on the edge of the bed and pull on a pair of wool socks before slipping her feet into a pair of moccasin style L.L.Bean boots.

Claudette was not about to let him ignore her questions. "The wind drowned out the gunshot, but I saw the flash of light when you shot that boy. Besides, if he was alive why'd you turn off all the lights to make it look like the place was closed?"

"So, what if I did shoot him? He could recognize me."

"If they catch us, we're going to jail for life."

"Why would you get life? You and me will both testify that you weren't there when the kid was killed."

Claudette pointed toward the living room, where they had left Sandra sleeping on the couch. "What about kidnapping? That'll get us twenty-five to life in any state. We're screwed, Felicien. Our only hope is to deliver the kid and once we get the money get the hell out of New England—maybe even the country."

"Where the fuck would we go?"

She turned to face the mirror mounted to the top of a scarred dresser and patted her hair until she decided that it was as good as she was going to get it. "I dunno, California maybe, or Canada, it's closer? But that's down the road, we got other fish to fry."

"I suppose you're gonna tell me what that is." His sarcasm didn't impress her.

"If they connect us to that robbery and we put one foot outside Maine, it's interstate flight—that means the FBI can come in."

"We'll do Canada. I always wanted to go to Vancouver."

"Then you got the fucking Mounties to deal with. Let's face it, either way we're up to our asses in pissed off rattlesnakes."

Claudette took a final drag off the cigarette and ground it out in an ashtray. She immediately lit another and threw the box to him. "We got to go off grid."

"What's that mean?"

"Disappear for a while. We need to go someplace where there ain't any people."

"The only place I can think of to do that is the deep woods." He lit another cigarette and as he smoked appeared to be deep in thought. After several moments he said, "I know a place we can go, my Uncle Lucien had a cabin. It ain't far from here but it's in a place where no one will find us."

Claudette was quiet for a moment and then said, "*Had* a place? Doesn't he have it now? He might be using it."

"Naw, the old bastard died two years ago. Nobody but me and Lucien ever used it. When he croaked, he kinda, sorta left it to me."

"Kinda, sorta? What in hell does that mean?"

"Ain't nobody else wanted the place. So, it kinda, sorta became mine." He pulled his keys out of his pocket, selected one, and held it up. "This here's the key to it."

"Does it have an indoor toilet and bathroom?"

"Yup."

"Running water—hot and cold?"

"It's got a water heater and sink, too... all that type of shit. There's only one problem."

"What" she asked, "might that be?"

"We can't have a TV, or electricity, and especially no phone... we can't have nothing that gives us a bill. They can track us that way," he said.

"How's the water heater and pump... I assume that's how the water comes in... going to work if we don't have electricity? What if we have an emergency?" Claudette said, "We'll need some type of phone—maybe we can get a cell phone?"

"There's one of them GPS things built into most of them and anyone with half a brain and the right app can find us. As for electricity, once we're settled in, I'll buy us a generator."

"You're talking about living like they did two hundred years ago." Claudette was not sure that she could live like that, she was certain that she had no pioneer blood.

"So? People lived that way right up to the nineteen-fifties. We can do it."

"What about food?" She asked.

"We'll use the money I got to buy enough to last us until spring."

"You're talkin' about me livin' like a pioneer woman. Ain't no fucking way."

"Then it's only a matter of time before they catch us. Think about it."

Jean-Paul walked into the diner at nine a.m. and saw Dylan sitting at a table near the front window. As soon as he sat the server placed a cup of coffee in front of him and asked, "Are you eating?"

"Just coffee, thank you." When the server had moved away, he turned his attention to Dylan. "I ran some checks on Felicien Paradis last night."

"You learn anything of interest?"

"There are several people with the Paradis name living in the area, but I couldn't find a connection between them and our guy."

"So, we do it the old way and knock on some doors."

"Unless you know of a better way."

"Can't say that I do."

"Then we need to head up twenty-seven toward New Sharon. That's where the closest Paradis lives."

Dylan crumpled up his napkin and threw it onto his empty plate. "Your car or my truck?"

"Be best if we go separate. It may not go over too good if it was to get out that I let you get involved in a case I'm working."

"Okay, I can understand that."

"If I'm going to let you work this case with me you got to agree with one thing."

"What's that?"

"You share everything you learn with me—even if it involves your brother-in-law."

"I thought we'd already cleared Oreille of any involvement?"

"You might want to recall that I didn't say that. You assumed it—and you know what they say."

"Yeah, there's three words in assume."

Felicien and Claudette drove through the Carrabassett Valley, following the two-lane road that twisted along the banks of the Carrabassett River. As they passed Sugar Loaf Mountain Claudette said, "Exactly where are we headed?"

"The cabin is west of here, up around Tim Pond Township."

"Are you sure it's still there?" she asked. "You said that it's been two years since your uncle died. It may have collapsed under snow or something."

"I asked Jeanine about it this morning. She told me that the cabin is still there, only ain't nobody used it but my Uncle Germaine. She said he was up there hunting last fall and it's still there and it's in pretty good shape. It'll be a good place to hide out until things cool off."

Claudette laughed; it was a hard, sarcastic one. "Sweetheart, ain't no way things will ever cool off—we're murders and kidnappers—remember?"

He took his eyes off the twisting road and ventured a glance at her. "How in the hell can I forget with you bringing it up every five goddamned minutes?" He glanced at the kid. She was sitting between them, staring at the dashboard and looking like she was retarded. *At least she ain't wailin',* he thought.

Claudette lit a cigarette and cracked her window to allow the smoke to drift out. "Wonderful."

Felicien gave her a scathing look. "Shut up, just shut the fuck up."

Dylan and Jean-Paul sat in the neat kitchen, savoring the smell of fresh bread baking. They sipped on coffee and listened as the old man and woman spoke, each trying to speak over the other.

"Don't surprise me none that you fellers can't find him—" Herbert (he pronounced it the French way, *Air-bear*) Paradis said.

His wife, April, cut him off, "That bunch is trouble. The next decent thing that boy and his mother do will be their first."

The old man chuckled. "They ain't exactly the type of people you want folks to know you're related to."

"Anyways," April added, "that boy never had no respect, called his mother by her first name."

"What might that be?" Dylan asked.

"Jeanine," Herbert said, looking at Dylan as if he thought he was a log or two short of a full load. "Who else you think it would it be?"

Rather than retort that no one had mentioned that Jeanine was Felicien's mother, he held his tongue and sat quiet.

"Jeanine Paradis?" Jean-Paul inquired holding a pen over the open page of his notebook.

"Her name is Boutot now, she stopped bein' a Paradis six, maybe seven years ago. She moved in with Jasper Boutot. They never married—"

"Lived in sin, they did," April said.

"Now don't be so judgmental," Herbert told his wife.

Dylan listened to their banter and smiled at Jean-Paul. He wondered where the old man had heard the word *judgmental...* probably in church he decided. He and the state police officer let the old couple talk.

"—anyway," Herbert continued, "married or not, she took on the name Boutot. Probably so no one would know she was related to that lazy, no-good son of hers."

"Where might we find Jeanine Boutot?" Thibodeau asked.

"Up near Stratton, on Rangeley Road," Herbert said. "Lives about two maybe three miles down. You'll recognize it, place should have been torn down years ago."

"It's on the left-hand side," April said.

Claudette stood by the side of the road, staring at the old cabin. It was buried with snow two thirds of the way up its walls and what looked to be another two feet of snow still on the roof. "How we supposed to get in?" She asked Felicien.

"Probably have to pay someone to clean it out so we can get to the door."

"That kind of defeats the purpose of coming out here, doesn't it? If you hire someone to plow us out, they'll know we're here."

"Jesus Christ, woman! Just once I'd like to say something without you smart-mouthing me." He cocked his arm as if he were about to hit her.

Claudette backed away and cowered. "Don't… Remember what happened the last time you hit someone."

He lowered his hand. "That was an accident—and you know it."

She straightened up and her temper got the best of her; she risked his wrath when she spat out the words, "You killed that kid. Do you know how much money you cost us?"

He pointed at the truck where Sandra was peering out the side window on the driver's side. "And I replaced her, didn't I?"

She hesitated and then in a low voice said, "Yes, you did. But the other night you may have sent us to prison for life doing it. Killing that kid in the gas station was stupid."

Felicien spun around and looked down the logging road. He changed the subject. "I'm surprised they plow this road."

As if on cue, a muddy logging truck came down the road, its sides white with road salt, mud, and snow. The brakes made a sound similar to a death moan and the engine's RPMs increased as the driver down-shifted to use the engine as a brake. The logs he was transporting were stacked over twenty feet high and the trailer swayed side-to-side so much that Paradis thought they would topple over. After several tense seconds, the load seemed to settle and the trailer ceased swaying and stopped beside their pickup. The window lowered and a bearded man wearing a dirt encrusted baseball hat called out, "You folks okay?" He spit a dark stream of tobacco juice at the road, leaving a dark brown splatter where it landed.

"We just inherited this place from my uncle," Felicien said. "Thought we'd live in it, sort of get away from all the hassles of living in town."

"I hear that. I got a loggin' operation about five miles further in and ain't got nothing goin' on today. How about I bring my plow truck up and bust you a way in?"

"That'd be great," Felicien said. "We ain't got much money to pay you though."

"Not to worry," the logger said. "Maybe you can do me a favor down the road." The gears ground when he forced them into action and with a wave drove down the road.

Felicien turned to Claudette. "See I knew things would work out."

Jeanine Boutot stood in the threshold of the mud room door. Her ever-present cigarette in her right hand and her body language made it clear to the two men that they were not getting inside her home.

"We're looking for Felicien Paradis," Thibodeau said.

"What? Does he owe you money or something?"

Thibodeau reached inside his coat and brought out his identification card and badge. "I'm with the state police."

"What's he done?"

"We just need to talk with him, that's all."

"Well, I ain't seen the son of a bitch in three years or more—don't care to see him either."

"You *are* his mother, aren't you?" Dylan asked.

"Yes, and Satan was his father. Once he turned fourteen, there was no way I could control that boy. I throwed him out when he was eighteen, that'd be..." She paused as if doing some mental arithmetic. "Twelve or thirteen years ago. Last I heard he was living up in The County... around Fort Kent. You may want to check up there."

"We know," Thibodeau said, "that he left there on Saturday. He hasn't been here?"

"No. If he had come here, I wouldn't let him in. Trouble follows him like stink follows a skunk. Now, if you ain't got any more questions, I got things to do." She backed up a step and shut the door.

"Charming sort, isn't she?" Dylan said.

"Yeah, but I'll bet dollars against donuts that she has either seen him or knows where he is."

"Maybe both," Dylan said.

Thibodeau's mobile phone chirped and he answered. He listened for a few seconds and said, "Thanks." He broke the connection, put the phone in his pocket, and said, "That was Augusta. They did an autopsy on the convenience store clerk. As I thought, he died from a nine mill in the head."

"I guess that seals it," Dylan said. "Paradis is your perp."

"Looks that way. As for him being a kidnapper, seeing your niece on that video sealed it for me."

"I'm not a big fan of my brother-in-law either, but I've known all along that he hasn't got the guts to kill anyone, especially his own child."

Thibodeau turned and walked to his car. "Doesn't mean that he wouldn't sell one though—especially if the price is right," he said.

The logger returned in a half hour, this time driving a small one-ton dump truck with a plow on the front. He quickly busted through the hard snow bank at the entrance of the cabin's drive and in a matter of minutes had a wide area cleared. He backed out of the yard and stopped beside Felicien and Claudette. "That ought to get you inside."

"Thanks, Mister—?"

"Cole, Vernon Cole."

"I'm Julien Gagnon." Felicien lied. "You any relation to the Coles that used to own the trucking company in Bangor?" Felicien asked.

"Don't think so. Hard to tell though—ain't it? You don't have to go back too far to see that we're all connected some way or another." Cole looked past Felicien and said, "You got a shovel to clear a path to the door?"

Felicien looked in the back of his pickup truck. "Damn, don't think I do."

Cole pointed to the back of his truck with his right thumb. "Should be one in the back. Just stick it in the snowbank when you're done and I'll grab it on my way by."

"Appreciate that. Who maintains this road? The county or the state?"

"You're looking at him. If I want to stay in business through the winter, I got to plow it. If you're lookin' for work, I can use a man around the place."

"That's mighty nice, Mr. Cole. I'll keep it in mind. But I think I'll be busy settling the little woman and the kid into the cabin."

"Call me Vern, everyone else does. The offer will be open if you want it."

"Thanks again."

Cole nodded to Claudette and said, "Afternoon, ma'am."

"Claudette answered, "We can't thank you enough, Mr. Cole."

"Vern…"

"Vern," she corrected herself.

Cole touched the rim of his greasy Boston Red Sox cap and said, "Well, this ain't gettin' 'er done. I'll be on my way." He spit another mouthful of tobacco juice, backed up, and the drove back the way he'd come.

"He seemed nice enough," Claudette said.

"Just so he doesn't get too friendly," Felicien replied. "Let's get the truck off the road and check out the inside."

Claudette leaned inside the cab and gathered the child in her arms. "Want to see our new home, baby?"

"I want my mommy and daddy," Sandra Dufore said.

"We're right here, hon," Claudette said.

Sandra started to argue, but when Claudette squeezed her and said, "Shhh. You don't want to make Daddy mad." Sandra gave Felicien a wary look and went quiet.

The sun was setting on the peaks of the mountains when Jean-Paul dropped Dylan off at his truck. "You sure you don't want to come into Augusta and have dinner?" Thibodeau asked.

Dylan thought of the possibility of Danielle dropping by his room and said, "No, I'm still dragging ass from the weekend. I'll see you in the morning."

"Okay, get some rest."

"You got a plan for tomorrow?"

"We still got some doors to bang on… the Boutot woman isn't his only relative around here."

Thibodeau pulled out of the motel yard and turned left on route 27. Dylan wondered if Danielle was working and walked over to the lobby. He entered and saw an elderly man working the front desk. "Is Danielle working tonight?" Dylan asked.

"Nope, she only works weekends. During the week she goes to school over in Farmington, about twenty miles away. Can I do anything for you?"

"No, thank you. I had a question I wanted to ask her."

As Dylan walked outside, he thought, *What the hell did you expect? She's half your age.* He got into his truck and drove into the village to get something to eat. His cell phone rang and startled him. He glanced at the display but didn't recognize the number displayed. "Hello?"

A familiar voice said, "Hi."

He felt a smile cross his face. "Hey, Danielle..."

"I was wondering do you have plans for tonight?"

"No, in fact I was just getting ready to go into Belgrade Lakes and eat."

"At the diner?"

"For want of another place, yeah."

"I'm leaving Farmington, it'll take me a half hour to get there." There was a moment of silence. "There's this place I know in New Sharon. It's about a ten- or eleven-mile drive for you. Want to split the distance and meet there?"

"Sure."

She gave him directions.

Danielle was standing in front of the door when Dylan arrived. Even though she was bundled up in a heavy parka and wool pants he recognized her immediately. He parked and walked across the parking lot. When she saw him and smiled, he felt warm inside. *Stop it you old fool,* he thought, *you're just a passing fad to a young woman.*

"Hey, you," Danielle said.

He gave her a quick kiss on the cheek and said, "Let's get inside before we freeze to death. Have you been waiting long?"

"Just got here," she said.

The inside of the restaurant was warm and inviting. The decor was rustic with a lot of dark wood and sedate lighting. To the right of the entrance was a cocktail lounge and the dining room was to the left. The dining room was dark so they entered the lounge. They were greeted by the bartender, who said, "On Mondays we don't open the dining room, but we serve the full menu here in the bar. Will that be alright?"

Dylan looked at Danielle and, when she nodded, said, "The bar will be fine."

The bartender walked out from behind the bar and met them halfway across the room and asked, "Would you prefer to be by the fireplace or away?"

"Fireplace," Danielle said.

The bartender smiled and seated them at a table in front of a gigantic granite and marble hearth in which a wood fire burned. "I hope this is satisfactory," she said.

"Very," Dylan answered.

Menus were placed in front of them and before leaving she said, "Rebecca will be right with you."

In a matter of minutes, a server in black pants and white blouse was at the table. She was shapely and even with glasses, very attractive. "Would you like a cocktail while you look at the menu?"

"I'll have a glass of Chablis," Danielle said.

"Bourbon on the rocks with a twist," Dylan interjected.

"Our specials are Yankee Pot Roast, with potato and a vegetable or a nice broiled salmon." She smiled at them and said, "I'll be right back with your drinks."

When they were alone Dylan said, "I have to confess your call surprised me. I don't recall giving you my number."

She gave him an impish smile. "Oh, but you did."

"When?"

"When you checked in, you put it on your registration."

"Are you stalking me," he joked.

"Possibly." Another smile. "Was that the only reason you were surprised?"

"No. I figured last night was just… I don't know, a fling with an older man."

"Does that bother you?"

"To a degree. I'm pushing forty."

She sat back and laughed. "How old do you think I am?"

"The old fellow working the desk tonight said you were going to school—I assumed it was college and not high school—so I estimated maybe early twenties."

"Thank you for the compliment. I'm thirty-five. I hope I'm not too *old* for you."

He laughed. "Not in the least."

Claudette found several candles on a shelf above the cabin's sink and she lit them and placed them around the kitchen. She carried one into the bathroom and was not happy with the woman that stared back at her from the small mirror mounted on the wall. Her hair was oily looking and her dark roots were showing. Her brown eyes were underscored by dark crescents and she knew she needed rest. What disturbed her most were the crow's feet that were at the corners of her eyes. She scanned her body and saw the beginning of a beer belly and wondered when she had first lost her trim petite cheer leader shape.

"You gonna use the crapper or spend all day starin' at that goddamned mirror?"

She returned from the bathroom and lit two more candles. One she placed on the small table that was against the wall and one she carried into the miniscule living room. "Why'd your uncle build this place?" she asked.

"Lucien used to run a trap line through here. He stayed here when he was checking his traps and when he was hunting."

"I never understood why people would build something like this in the middle of the woods. Why didn't he build it on a lake so that the family could use it year-round?"

"Because Uncle Lucien didn't want no family, he never even married. If he had any kids, he didn't know nothing about them. That's why he left this to me when he dropped dead."

Claudette glanced at Sandra who sat on the floor playing with a Raggedy Ann doll in front of the wood stove. "Don't get too close to that stove, Baby."

Sandra looked at Claudette and then went back to her doll.

"Kid don't say much," Felicien said, "That's a good thing. Usually takes eighteen months to teach them to talk and the rest of their lives to teach them when."

Claudette walked into the living room, picked up Sandra and moved her back from the fire. "I always meant to ask you something."

"You're always askin' me shit. What this time?"

"Why do you call your mother Jeanine and not mom or ma or whatever?"

"Because that's her name."

"But it's disrespectful."

"You ast a question and that's your answer," he said. "Come out to the kitchen, we got to put together a shopping list."

"Did you tell your mother where we were going and that we might not be back to her place?"

"Nope."

Claudette was becoming exasperated with his blunt short answers. "Why not?"

"Because sooner or later the cops are going to find out about her and the less that crazy bitch knows the better. If they ast her when she was drunk and she knew we was here, she'd tell them in a heartbeat. Now come on, we got shit to do."

"What exactly is it that you do?" Danielle asked.

"The uncomplicated answer is that I'm a lawyer."

"And the complicated answer is?"

"I'm also a licensed private investigator."

"Now I don't think I've ever heard of anyone being both before."

"I hear that all the time," he said. "I was a state cop for five years and didn't like the strict rules and regulations, so I quit, got my P. I. license, and went to law school at night. I got my law degree from the University of Maine Law School in Portland but kept my investigator license. It's come in handy more than once."

"You live in Gray and have a cottage on Cross Lake in Aroostook

County so what brings you here?"

"A case."

"It sounds as if you won't or can't talk about this case."

"Oh, there's no reason I can't talk about it. Four days ago, my niece was abducted from her parents' home. My sister, the girl's mother, asked me to help. We' know that our suspect has family in this area, so here I am."

"A child?"

"Yes, she's three years-old..."

He related the rest of the investigation to her.

"Your three-year-old niece is missing? That's terrible. You believe the person who has her also killed someone else?"

"Yes, an eighteen years-old gas station attendant. This guy is desperate and dangerous."

Her eyes sparkled in the flickering light from the fireplace. She finished her wine and said, "One last thing, your name is not a common one. How did your mother come up with it?"

"She was a fan of the Welsh poet Dylan Thomas. Our surname is Thomas so she named me after him. She also named my sister after his wife, Caitlin."

"I believe I've read one of his poems. Didn't he write 'Do Not Go Gentle into That Good Night'?"

"He did. It was written to his father who was dying and seemed resigned to his fate. He was dead at thirty-nine."

"His father?"

"No, Dylan Thomas—he was an alcoholic and it damaged his liver, among other things." Dylan sat back and asked, "So what are your plans for the rest of the evening?"

Danielle smiled, "I don't know. Do you have anything in mind?"

Tuesday: Day Four

FELICIEN HELD THE DOOR TO the truck open. "Get a move on, woman! We got a lot of shit to do today."

Claudette came to the door and when he saw that she was not wearing a coat Paradis shouted at her. "Why ain't you ready, goddamnit."

"You gotta go alone, the kid is burning a fever. She shouldn't be dragged all over hell."

"Jesus Christ," He mumbled, "I gotta do every fuckin' thing around here."

Felicien slammed the door as he stormed into the cabin and looked around. "Where is the goddamned kid?" He looked at the couch where Sandra had spent their first night in their new home.

"I moved her into our bed," Claudette answered.

He stomped across the room in the direction of the cabin's single bedroom.

"Felicien, you hurt that child and you and me is finished, you got that?"

He stopped and turned toward her. "I ain't gonna hurt her. When the last one had her accident, didn't I take care of her and bring you this one?"

"Don't you mean stole her?"

"Hey, c'mon, babe. Them people can get by without her. They're rich, have two other brats, and..."

Claudette clenched her fists and said in an ominous voice, "Go on say it. You know you want to throw it up in my face. *She can have another kid and I won't!*"

"I wasn't gonna say that at all."

He turned and entered the bedroom. His body language softened as he stood beside the bed and looked at the tiny girl. Her face was red and there was a thin sheen of sweat on her skin. He reached out and placed a hand on her forehead. *Claudette is right, this kid is burning up*, he thought. He tucked the blanket around the tiny chin and walked into the kitchen.

Claudette sat at the table, her arms resting on the table. He sat down beside her. "I'm sorry," he said.

"For what?" she snapped at him.

"For being an asshole."

She rested her head in her hand and started to cry.

"Hey, babe, c'mon now. I said I was sorry."

Claudette raised her head. "What the hell are we doing, Felicien? We're on the run. We got a sick child who we're takin' to Boston to sell…"

"We'll make her better."

"After we sell her, what then? What kind of life are we gonna have? Always on the run. By now they probably got pictures of her, and us, in every newspaper, TV and radio station, and there's probably an Amber Alert out."

"What's an Amber alert?"

"There will be flashing signs broadcasting her name and ours on all the major roads in every New England state. Our picture and probably the license number of your truck will be in every toll booth, service station, and public building. Sooner or later someone will recognize one of us and then we'll really be fucked."

In his usual state of denial, Felicien lit a cigarette and said, "We'll deal with that when the time comes. Now give me a list of what you need for her."

"She'll need clothes too."

"Write it down."

Claudette gave a sheepish smile, bent forward, and kissed him.

"I love you when you're like this."

He blushed. "Now don't go getting all girly on me."

She wrote out a list, handed it to him, and said, "It'll probably be easiest if you go to a Walmart or something like that, they'll have everything in one store."

"There's gotta be one in Farmington or Skowhegan. It'll take me some time. You want I should bring in some wood from out back?"

She shook her head. "You should get going. I can get wood if I need it. For God's sake get some coffee, creamer, and sweetener—and a coffee pot—one of them percolator ones that will work on top of that wood-burning cook stove."

The sound of a plow scraping the parking lot outside his window woke Dylan up. He opened the blinds and blinked at the brilliance of the day. Last night's snowstorm had moved away and left clear skies and the pristine, white puffy snow that calendar pictures depict. Across from his motel room was an open expanse of field, its surface unmarred by anything human, animal, or mechanical. The scene was pure and pastoral. He walked around the bed, taking care not to disturb Danielle on his way to the bathroom where he turned on the shower.

When Dylan saw Jean-Paul's car turn into the parking lot, he walked outside and waited until the detective parked in front of the motel. Dylan jumped into Thibodeau's car. "Damn, it really turned cold."

"I heard the windchill index is twenty-five below."

"What are we doing today?"

Jean-Paul was absentmindedly staring through the window when Danielle walked out of Dylan's room. She slid into a silver Volvo S60, started the motor, and then drove away. He watched her exit the parking lot and then looked at Dylan. "Now I know why you didn't want to join me in Augusta."

Dylan smiled, "What can I say."

Jean-Paul said, "Nothing to say. Getting back to business... Paradis is on the run with a woman and a child. Sooner or later he'll have to show his face at either a department store or a grocery store."

"Or a Super Walmart, that's a one-stop shop."

"The closest two are in Farmington and Skowhegan."

"Where to first?"

"Farmington is closest. Follow me in your truck."

Felicien finished loading his purchases into his truck when a burgundy Roush Performance Ford Mustang drove past him. He saw the blue State of Maine license plate and immediately knew it was the cops. He strolled around to the opposite side of his truck and got in. He lit a cigarette and watched the Mustang, its 710-horsepower motor rumbling as it parked two aisles over and he recognized the car's driver, a cop named Thibodeau. Another guy got out of a pickup and met the cop. Together they walked inside the Super Walmart and he noted the cop was carrying papers of some sort. He decided to wait and see what was going on.

By the time that the cops walked out of the store, the interior of his truck had cooled. They walked at a rapid pace wanting to get into their cars and out of the frigid weather as soon as possible. In short time they left and Felicien returned to the store. There was a bulletin board in the cart area and on it were two posters one of him and one of the kid. He looked around and then ripped them off the wall. Rather than walking through the store and risking someone recognizing him, he went outside and walked to the second entrance. There was another poster in that cart lobby too. He repeated the process and ripped those down as well. He exited the store and got in his truck and as he waited for it to warm up, thought: *Claudette's right they're gonna wallpaper the state with these fucking things!* He backed out of the parking spot and headed home. He decided that he had to change his appearance somehow. *A shave would do it. I'll shave off my beard and get me a haircut.*

Thibodeau and Dylan were midway to the Walmart in Skowhegan when Jean-Paul's phone rang. He listened for a few seconds and then turned into the parking lot of a gas station.

Dylan pulled up alongside the burgundy Mustang, the nose of his pickup facing in the opposite direction so that their windows faced each other. "What's up?" he asked.

"Paradis has been seen."

"Where?"

"Where we just left."

"The Farmington Walmart?"

"Yup."

Thibodeau turned on the flashing blue emergency lights that were inside the grill in the front of the Mustang. "Put your emergency flashers on and keep up," he said. "You wouldn't want to get a ticket." He pulled out onto the road and stepped down on the accelerator pedal.

Dylan heard the high-performance motor roar into life and pulled out after it. The truck responded to his pressure on the gas pedal. As he kept pace with the Mustang, Dylan felt his body sinking back into his seat. "That Mustang's got some punch," he commented.

Thibodeau and Dylan stood behind the store manager and stared over her shoulder. "There!" she said while pointing at the screen.

Although the resolution of the screen was not of the highest quality, it was better than most and there was no doubt in their minds that they were looking at Felicien Paradis. The camera picked him up as soon as he entered the door and followed him as he approached the recently hanged posters and ripped them down. Dylan noted the date/time stamp in the screen's lower right corner and said, "The son of a bitch must have been in the parking lot, watching us.

"No doubt."

They watched him exit the cart lobby and the manager switched the camera. "He repeated his actions in the other door. That got me curious so I looked at some earlier videos. I found him entering the store just after ten. He checked out on register seven, paying in cash."

"Can you tell me what he bought?" Thibodeau asked.

"All sales are captured by our computer for inventory purposes. I had an idea that you might ask that so I checked with the cashier. She told me that she remembered him because he paid in hundred-dollar bills, which we don't see many of. We also screen all twenties and hundreds for counterfeit bills."

"That must be a pain," Dylan said.

"Well if the counterfeiting is intended for international use the hundred is the most often denomination counterfeited, domestically it's the twenty. We're less than one hundred miles from Canada so we watch both."

"Did you find out what he bought?" Thibodeau reiterated.

"Mostly groceries, camping equipment, and children's clothing too. The child may be sick."

"What makes you think that?" Dylan asked.

"He also bought baby aspirin, children's Benadryl, and a digital thermometer."

Thibodeau asked for a copy of the videos and when the manager handed him a DVD, he said, "Thank you. You've been a great help."

Once they were outside the building, Dylan commented, "That proves that while Paradis has gone off grid, he and the woman are still in the area."

"Unfortunately, the area covers a lot of ground. About all we can do in the meantime is wait for him to surface again."

The sun was down when Paradis returned to the cabin. He unloaded the truck carrying in the camping equipment first. He placed two multi-fuel lamps on the table. He filled them with gas, pumped the tank pressure up, and lit them. The lamps hissed as they ignited filling the cabin with light. He walked outside and returned with a small camp stove. "At least we'll be able to cook food," he said.

"Obviously, everything went okay," Beaupre said.

She stared at him for a few seconds. "You shaved and got a haircut. How come?"

"We'll talk about that when I get everything unloaded."

Paradis had just carried in the last of the supplies when headlights flashed through the window. He immediately strode to the living room window and looked out. He recognized Vernon Cole and relaxed. They heard a door slam and then the heavy thump of Cole trying to knock snow off his boots as he climbed the stairs.

There were three heavy knocks on the door and Beaupre looked at Paradis; there was fear on her face. "It's okay," he said. "It's Cole. Answer the door."

She opened the door and when the warm inside air collided with the below zero outside air a thin mist of steam formed. She stepped back, "Come in, Vern."

The burly logger entered, closing the door as he stepped into the small kitchen. "Saw your lights and wondered if you got electricity." He looked at the gas lanterns on the table and added, "Looks as if I was wrong."

Felicien walked into the room and said, "Hey, Vern. What brings you this way?"

"I got an old generator on my truck. I thought you might be able to put it to use. Like I said, it's old but works like a charm."

Once again, Beaupre looked at Paradis and he saw her pleading look, realized she was asking him to accept Cole's offer. He said, "That'll be great, but I don't know if the place is set up for it."

"The original owner was a tough old buzzard name of Lucien."

"My uncle," Paradis said.

"Anyways we wired it for a generator hook up ten years or so ago. C'mon, help me get it off the truck and we'll have some lights and a refrigerator running in no time."

True to his words, Cole and Paradis had the generator hooked up and the light fixture in the kitchen ceiling lit. There was a humming sound as the small refrigerator began running all in less than twenty minutes. "This place ain't that large," Cole said. "So, you shouldn't have any problems running the lights, fridge, and television."

"We don't have a TV," Claudette said.

"Sure, you do," Cole said.

"We do?" she asked, "where is it? I've been all over this place and didn't find one."

"It's in my truck." He laughed.

Minutes later Cole had set a thirty-three-inch flat TV on the small table against the outside wall in the living room. "Even got an antenna," he said. He reached down under the table and pulled out a coax cable which he connected. "There you should be able to pick up Portland and Waterville. On a cold clear night, you can sometimes pull in Bangor, too."

"We don't know how to thank you," Claudette said.

"Tell you what. Since the generator's old and I don't need that TV you can work for me for, let's say a week, and you'll own them. How's that sound?"

Paradis said, "Okay."

"Good you ever worked at loggin'?"

"I have."

"Well next week I got a wood lot to harvest, how about bein' over to my place at six on Monday morning?"

Paradis said, "Sounds good."

Cole smiled; his teeth looked brilliant through the black beard that covered his face. "See you then." Before exiting he stopped and turned back, looking at Paradis. "Nice look," he said. He stroked his beard and said, "Been thinking of doin' the same thing."

When Cole was gone Beaupre said, "What a nice man,"

"Maybe he's too fuckin' nice." Paradis replied. "How's the kid?"

"She's still running a fever, but I think she's better."

He turned away and said, "Let's get this shit put away."

Wednesday: Day Five

DYLAN TURNED INTO JEANINE BOUTOT'S drive and she met him at the door again. "Where's your friend with the fancy cop car?"

"He had to spend today in Augusta."

"Why are you here?" She asked between drags on her cigarette.

"Mrs. Boutot, it's important that I find your son."

"I told you t'other day I don't know where he is and I don't give a good goddamn neither."

Dylan tried another tactic. "I believe that Felicien knows who has my three-year-old niece. Her parents are going crazy. All I want is the child back."

"Don't know nothing 'bout no kid. Whyn't you just get your ass out of my dooryard?"

"If I do that my friend will get a court to issue a search warrant and then you'll have to let us in. It'd be easier all around if you just cooperated."

"So, tell your friend to get his warrant. Until you got one you ain't enterin' my house. Now get, before I turn a shotgun on you."

Dylan turned to his car. "Have it your way, but we're going to keep coming back. Sooner or later you'll talk to us if for no other reason than to get us out of your life."

"I got a twenty gauge that says you'll get out of my life real quick. Now go."

Dylan got in his truck and backed out. He drove into the village, bought coffee at a Dunkin' Donuts drive through, and then drove to a plowed area near Great Pond and watched a couple of snowmobiles race back and forth on its frozen surface. He glanced at his dash and saw a temperature reading outside the truck, it was minus 18. A gust of wind tore across the frozen surface of the pond pushing a cloud of snow before it. A small spiral cloud formed over the frozen pond reminding him of the white tornado television commercials for Ajax cleanser. *When were those… was it the 1970s or 80s?* He altered his thoughts and tried to decide what his next move would be. *Maybe it's time I visited the local cops*, he thought.

The two snow machines tore across the pond again. Dylan was at a loss how anyone could go sixty or seventy miles an hour in conditions like today's: he thought, *the wind chill at the speed they're riding must be horrendous.* He drove out of the rest area and headed back into town. He stopped at the town hall and walked into the town clerk's office. "Where can I find your police department?" He asked the matronly woman sitting at the desk.

"Can't we don't have a police department. The Kennebec County Sheriff handles that for us." She gave him a lop-sided grin. "Helps keep our property taxes down."

Dylan stood silent for a moment.

"You need help? I can call a deputy if you'd like."

"No, it's not like that, I'm looking for someone."

"Maybe I can help with that. I know just about everyone in town. Sooner or later they got to come in here."

"Well, a while back I met a guy from here named Felicien Paradis. He said he was some sort of handyman and I need someone to shovel the snow off my roof. The house is pretty old and I'm afraid it will collapse."

"That could be a problem," the woman said. "There's been a lot of snow this year. Only a few weeks left in the winter though."

Dylan realized that as long as he stood where he was, she'd continue talking. "Felicien Paradis," he reminded her.

"I know him, haven't seen him for quite a while though. I heard he was up north in Aroostook County, somewhere around Fort Kent."

"What about relatives? Any aunts or uncles around who might know of his whereabouts?"

"There's his mother, Jeanine, but she won't help you, contrariest person in the entire area." Her face seemed to light up as if she'd just had a great epiphany. "He's got an uncle. What was his name? I know he's a Chianchette, at least that was his mother's last married name. She's a relative of the Chianchettes over in Pittsfield through marriage. Germaine, that's his name. Yuh, yuh, Germaine Chianchette is his name."

"Great, do you have an address for him?"

She turned toward her computer terminal and began typing. Her fingers walked across the keys so fast that Dylan thought that she might be the fastest typist in New England, if not the world. "Here it is," she said. "3275 Augusta Road. It's south on twenty-seven, that's Augusta Road, this is 990, 3275 is toward Belgrade just past Minot Hill Road. It'll be on your right… you can't miss it."

"Thank you mizz…"

"Doris Carter, you take care, now. Some of them Chianchettes are known to be touchy about their privacy."

After his encounter with Jeanine Boutot, Thomas had no problem believing her. He said, "I'll remember that."

"Where was it you said you lived? You don't look familiar…"

Thomas raised his hand in farewell as he exited the building.

A short, stocky man looked up at Dylan. "Can I help you?" he asked.

"Mr. Germaine Chianchette?"

"Do I know you?"

"My name is Dylan Thomas…"

The old man stepped back two steps. "Name don't ring a bell, but come in. I can't afford to heat the outdoors."

Dylan entered the neat, split-level house and stomped his feet to remove as much snow as he could. Chianchette turned and climbed a short flight of stars. "Come up to the kitchen. The Missus is making fresh donuts. We'll have some coffee and talk."

The aroma of donuts cooking in hot grease greeted Dylan as he climbed the stairs. He entered the top floor of the house, turned right, saw an inexpensive, but fashionably, furnished living room to his immediate right and, at a forty-five-degree angle to the left, a kitchen equally as large as the living room. Behind him a hallway led to what he assumed were bedrooms. Germaine waved for him to come in to the kitchen.

The kitchen was immaculate; in fact, Dylan realized that the entire house seemed to be. Everything was in its place and rather than crowd the house with knick-knacks and unnecessary decorations, there was a minimum of clutter. He wondered if they actually lived this neat or was the house for sale and prepped for showing. He dismissed that idea; he'd not seen any Realtor *FOR SALE* signs when he drove in. He noticed that the living room walls were adorned with photos of a young man. Chianchette saw him looking at a picture of the young man in the dress blue uniform of a U. S. Marine Corps officer. Dylan started when the old man said, "That's Roland, our son. He's in Afghanistan now. He's on his fifth..." He paused as if trying to think of the correct word. "Madeline, what is it that Roland calls it when he goes overseas?"

A female voice from the kitchen answered, "A deployment."

"His fifth deployment," Germaine said.

"You must be proud of him."

"Yes, we are. We would have liked for him to get a job... he's an electrical engineer, but he wants a career in the Marines." A wistful look came over the old, wrinkled face. "Well, maybe when he gets home, he'll change his mind. Come, let's get the coffee and donuts while they're fresh."

Dylan took a final look at Roland's photo and thought: *If he gets home. Five deployments! It seems to me he's pushing his luck.* He turned toward the kitchen finding it hard to believe that these people were related to Jeanine Boutot and her son.

The kitchen was warm and Dylan unzipped his parka. A woman,

even shorter than her husband reached toward him. "May I take your coat?"

"Yes, please." Dylan slid out of his blue North Face Triclimate coat and handed it to her. Rather than drape it over a chair, she opened a closet door and hung it using a wooden coat hanger.

"Please," she said taking him by the arm and guiding him to a wooden captain's chair at the table, "sit down."

Once he was settled, she asked, "Coffee? I know you'll have some donuts."

"Yes, black please."

"Ahh, you guys. You all think that black coffee makes you men."

When she placed a cup on a saucer and filled it from a drip coffee maker, Dylan tried to remember the last time he'd been served with a cup and saucer—he couldn't recall exactly, but knew it had been quite a while.

Before he could say *thank you*, there was a plate with three fresh donuts in front of him.

"This," Germaine said, "is Madeline, the love of my life and mother of my son."

Dylan turned to the short, raven-haired woman. "How do you do."

He thought it was special when she blushed at her husband's compliment. He estimated Germaine Chianchette to be five feet tall; Madeline was at least six inches shorter. She wore a cotton house dress that covered her from just below her knees to her neck, but did nothing to hide her ample breasts. She sat beside her husband and up-close Dylan knew that when she was young, she'd been a beauty.

"My name is Dylan Thomas..."

"Like the poet?" Madeline asked.

"Why yes, you're familiar with him?"

"Oh yes, I was an English teacher for many years. He was gifted but battled his demons—especially alcohol."

"I am impressed, Mrs. Chianchette."

"Please, Maddie. Madeline is so stuffy sounding."

"Okay, Maddie."

"How can we help you, young man?" Germaine asked.

"I'm trying to locate Felicien Paradis. I'm told he's your nephew."

Germaine looked at his wife and then turned back to Dylan. "He is. However, I must admit that we don't have much to do with him, or my sister Jeanine."

Dylan replied, "At the risk of insulting your family, I must say that I can understand that."

"What has he done?" Maddie asked.

"My niece is with him and I want to bring her home."

Madeline shook her head. "It amazes me some of the men young women run off with."

"Well, she didn't exactly run off with him. Sandra is only three years old."

Maddie placed a hand on her chest and said, "Oh, my Lord!"

"Maybe," Germaine said, "You should tell us the entire story."

Dylan talked, drank coffee, and ate donuts and told them what had taken place, holding nothing back. As he finished talking, he ate the last of his donuts, hardly aware of the fact that he'd eaten a half-dozen.

Maddie refilled all their cups and then turned to Germaine. "Lucien's camp."

Dylan looked at her and then at Germaine. "What's Lucien's camp?"

"Felicien ain't the only member of my family—"

"Isn't, Hon," Madeline said. "Felicien isn't."

Germaine sat back looking as if he was angry at her intrusion. But when she placed her hand over his and patted it, he leaned forward and relaxed. "Felicien *isn't* the only bad boy in the family. My older brother Lucien was one mean son of a…" He looked at Madeline and she patted his hand again and smiled at him. "…gun. He used to trap, hunt, and fish during the season and poach everything when it was out of season. Heck, he carried a concealed weapon before it was all right for anyone to do it. Fact is he wasn't supposed to have firearms—he did time in Thomaston… must have been in the early seventies."

"Did he have much to do with Felicien?" Dylan inquired.

"I guess the phrase *taught him everything he knows* fits them," Germaine said.

"What did Lucien do time for?" Dylan asked.

"He did twenty-five years of a twenty-to-life sentence for robbing a twenty-four-hour store, killed a clerk in the process."

"Sounds as if the apple didn't fall far from the tree. He got out in the minimum? How'd he do that?"

"Lucien had a gift," Madeline said. "He could talk the devil into sending him to heaven. I can imagine how repentant he sounded to the parole board."

"You're speaking of him in the past tense. I'm assuming that he's dead."

"He is," Germaine answered. "He was out poachin' and took a shot at the wrong warden."

"The warden shot him?"

"Right between the eyes."

"Where's this camp?"

"It's on a remote woods road, about fifty miles up toward the Canadian Border." Germaine walked to a cupboard beside the kitchen sink, "I'll write down the directions for you." He turned with a pad and pencil in hand and added "I'll only give them to you on one condition."

"That I take him alive?"

"Hell, no. He's not going to go willingly and you may have to kill the stupid son of a bitch. The condition is that you don't go after him alone."

Dylan promised.

While Germaine wrote the directions Dylan said, "I have to admit I expected a much more hostile greeting."

Germaine chuckled, "You must have been talking to Doris in the town office. If you asked where the local Pentecostal minister lived, she'd tell you to be careful that he can be dangerous."

Madeline stood, walked to the coat closet and brought him his parka. "Be careful and come back and visit sometime."

Dylan glanced at the photo of the young Marine captain and said, "I hope your son gets back alright."

Madeline gave him a kiss on his cheek. "Thank you."

Dylan started down the stairs and she called after him, "You drive careful young man, there's black ice on the roads."

As Dylan drove back toward Belgrade Lakes Village, he touched his cheek and smiled. "I need to come here more often," he said out loud. "Between Danielle and Madeline, I've gotten more kisses from more women than I've had in two years."

Felicien sat at the table listening to a country music station on the old AM radio that sat on a shelf in the kitchen, and played solitaire with a deck of cards he found in the cabin. He heard Claudette talking to the kid and wished he had a bottle. His favorite liquor was bourbon, but at that moment he'd settle for rotgut gin.

Claudette walked into the kitchen and poured a mug of coffee. She turned leaned against the counter, held the mug before her mouth, and said, "I'll bet if we're still here in a month, six weeks from now the insects will drive us out of here."

He kept flipping the cards, ignoring her.

"Her fever broke, she's over the worst of it."

He flipped another card.

"Felicien are you listening to me?" She turned the radio off.

"Yeah, the kid's gettin' better. Great, maybe I can get off that fuckin' couch and sleep in the bed again."

"Is where you sleep all you care about?"

He slammed the cards on the table spilling half of the deck on the floor. "No, it ain't. I care about bein' cooped up in this goddamned shithole of a cabin. I care about the cops hunting me like I was a fuckin' rabid dog. But mostly, I'm thinkin' that we should get out of here. Leave the kid here and run."

"After all this you'd desert her? Just take off? Well, asshole, there's the door. Step lively as you leave and don't let it hit you in the ass!"

She poured the last of her coffee in the sink, set the mug down, folded her arms against her chest, and stared out the dirty window at the snow and leafless trees. "If you want to go, go. I won't try to make you stay. I'll find some way to deliver the kid."

"You don't know nothin' about what I'm thinking."

"You're right and right about now I really don't give a flying fuck."

"Maybe if I take off, I can find some way of being spotted by the cops, they'll come after me and forget about you. Then you can deliver her."

"You gonna walk? We only got the one truck. Felicien, as long as that kid is with us, they're gonna keep on looking. If you haul ass it won't make it any easier. They may not know me by sight but it's only a matter of time until someone gives them one of those drawings they do. Then they'll paste my face all over the country. You leaving won't amount to a piss hole in the snow." She lit a cigarette and stood before the window feeling as desperate and alone as the single leafless maple tree that stood in the back yard; she thought of a song she'd heard, something about being a rock or an island because an island never cries. She looked at Felicien and suddenly realized that as long as she stayed with him, she'd be alone. "Maybe you're right," she said. "Maybe it would be best if you got the fuck out." She ground out her cigarette and walked into the living room. After a few seconds the sound of Drew Carey on *The Price Is Right* came through the door.

Felicien got up went outside. He stopped and then reentered the cabin. "Don't get up in arms, okay? I'm just goin' over to see Vern and make sure he still needs me next week."

"Right now, I don't care where you fuckin' go, so long as you go."

He turned and walked out the door. A minute later she heard his truck start and through the window saw him drive out of the yard. *Which way is he going to turn?* He turned toward Cole's place.

Jean-Paul Thibodeau sat across from the senior officer in the Maine

State Police Major Crimes Unit—South, Lieutenant Edward M. Roberts. "I know you got this child abduction and gas station homicide case, but I'm between a rock and a hard place. I already talked to Lieutenant Saucier and she's authorized me to use you if I can."

"I'm kind of free right now. We've hit a wall."

"We?"

"I've been working with a lawyer-detective on this one. He used to be on the job, he was one of us…"

"You wouldn't by any chance be speaking of Dylan Thomas?"

"Do you know him?"

"We went through the criminal justice academy together. He was assigned to the southern part of the state and I was assigned to Bangor. I heard he left after three or four years. I know that while he was on the job, he was taking some law courses at the U of M Law School. I gather he stuck it out and finished."

"After he left the department, he got a P. I. license which he's kept current."

"Well, that's a bit odd, but Thomas was a guy who I always thought to be a bit odd." Roberts changed the subject. "What's the latest on your case?"

"We've narrowed our search down to the Belgrade Lakes and Carrabassett Valley areas."

"I don't know if I'd call that *narrowed it down*. That's an awful lot of area to cover."

"Yeah, but it's not all that populated."

"During the season, the population doubles on weekends and during school vacation weeks, what with skiers, snowmobilers, and all."

"As I said earlier, we're at the point where all we can do is wait for him to come out of whatever hole he's hiding in and show himself."

"This perp has any support in the area?"

"His mother would make a terrific poster child for dysfunctionality and some aunts, uncles, and cousins. None of them seem to have anything to do with him."

"Well, somebody's helping him. Getting back to the reason I called you in. I'd like you to go to the Skowhegan facility and see Sergeant Arlene Doody. She's short a detective and has a hot one you may be able to help her with. Skowhegan is a short run to both Belgrade and Farmington, if anything develops. Is Thomas down there?"

"Yes, he won't leave until he finds that little girl, one way or another—she's his sister's kid."

"Well, I should tell you to tell him to keep out of it, but I doubt he'd listen."

Thibodeau stood and said, "So far he's been a valuable asset. He's calm, cool, and collected."

"Well, off you go, we both got shit to do."

Vernon Cole's shop was a hive of activity. Felicien counted four men, all busy working on late model cars and SUVs. The first words that came to his mind were: *chop shop*. He had no doubts that all of the cars he saw were stolen.

Vern Cole came out of a small glass enclosed office and saw Felicien. At first glance he did not look happy, but as he got closer his stern look turned into a smile, albeit forced. "Hey, how you doing?"

"Okay."

"What brings you here? The generator shit the bed?"

"No, it's fine. I was sittin' around the place, doing nothing and thought I'd come over and see if you were around." Felicien looked around the interior of the large metal building. There were several wood stoves located along the walls, each with a fire blazing. He counted six cars, three SUVs, two Cadillac sedans, and a Volkswagen Beetle, all being worked on. "You run a car repair business?"

Cole hesitated for a few moments and then said, "Come in the office with me."

The office was small, barely large enough to fit a desk and two straight-back plastic chairs, the type many people buy at a big box store for use on their lawns. Felicien sat in the one closest to the door and Cole circled his desk and dropped into a worn office chair.

"First off, I know your name ain't Gagnon, it's Paradis. I remember you coming here with your Uncle Lucien. How is the old bastard?"

Felicien stared at Cole, uncertain what Cole was getting at. "You got me. Uncle Lucien died a few years back."

"I don't know what you done, but I think you're on the run, you do some serious shit." He opened the center drawer of the desk and took out a folded paper. "I was over to the Hannaford's yesterday and in the entrance they have this bulletin board where people advertise shit. Stuff like puppies and kittens they either want to sell or give away, teenage girls looking for babysitting jobs."

"And?"

"I saw this and thought that I'd take it." He handed the piece of paper to Felicien.

Felicien glanced at the paper and then threw it on the desk. "Alright so you know who I am. You gonna do anything about it?"

"Don't get your balls in an uproar. When I saw that I said: Hey I know that guy. So, tell me just how big a badass are you? You enjoy kicking ass?"

"Only when I'm pushed."

"That store clerk in Sherman push you?"

"No, but he could identify me."

"How would you feel if I told you that you killed that kid for nothing? That picture proves they had you on video the whole time."

"Well, I guess that kid was in the wrong place at the wrong time."

"You got no remorse over popping a cap in that kid?"

"Like I said—"

"I know. He was in the wrong place at the wrong time." Cole reached into the drawer and took out two cigars. He offered one to Felicien and said, "Let's you and me talk. I can use someone with your talents. You know what's going on out in the shop?" Cole asked.

"Yeah, I got an idea."

"Which is?"

"You're running a *chop shop*."

Cole laughed. "Ain't no one puttin' anything past you, are they?"

Major Crimes Unit—Central's Skowhegan facility shared space with Troop C which had Troopers who worked in the field. Field Troopers patrolled all the municipalities in the state of Maine who do not have their own police departments. Along with the county sheriff's departments, they enforce laws throughout their district. Field Troopers investigate traffic accidents and respond to a wide variety of criminal complaints including domestic violence, burglary, and assault. Troop C handled an area that went from Augusta to the Canadian Border and then north to Aroostook County's western most southern border. The troop consisted of a lieutenant, three sergeants, three corporals and twenty-two troopers who provided law enforcement services; each troop is supported by a single administrative assistant.

Thibodeau arrived at the state police facility in mid-afternoon. He saw a woman, whom he assumed to be the administrative assistant, seated at a desk that was separated from the front door by a glass window and a wall; to the left was single door. She typed on a keyboard; her attention focused on a computer screen. He stepped to the window and after a couple of seconds, she noticed him. He heard a click as she spoke into a microphone that was suspended from the window frame on her immediate left. "Can I be of assistance?" her metallic voice asked.

Thibodeau slid his credentials into the small access tray at the bottom of the window and said, "I'm Sergeant Jean-Paul Thibodeau, where might I find Sergeant Doody?"

She looked at his identification, returned them to him, and said, "I'm Rose, actually it's Maureen Rose Marx, we were told to expect you. I'm glad to meet you. Arlene is through the door, the first office on the right."

"Thanks."

He walked toward the door and heard a buzz followed by the

loud *CLICK* of an electronic lock activating. He entered a large office space and almost bumped into a tall uniformed officer who was standing by a xerographic copier.

"You the Detective from MCU—north?" the trooper asked.

Thibodeau noticed that the officer wore lieutenant's bars on his shirt collar. "Yes, sir, Detective Jean-Paul Thibodeau." He held out his hand and the lieutenant grasped it.

"Lieutenant Theodore Nykriem, but you can call me lieutenant." His broad smile let Thibodeau know that the senior officer was joking. "I go by Theo, please don't call me Ted, my father called me that when I screwed up."

"Thanks, I'll keep that in mind, Theo."

Nykriem grinned. "Who'd you piss off to get sent here?"

Nobody… at least no one I can think of."

"How's things in *The County*? My first assignment was with F Troop, being the new guy, I got to patrol Hainesville and I-95 south to Sherman."

"It's March, which means there's only eight weeks of winter left up there."

"What case are you working that brought you here?"

"I've been working a case out of the Eagle Lake area for the past week. We followed the perp down here. Right now, we're at a bit of a stand-still so they thought I could help Sergeant Doody out. That way if something breaks on the other case, I'll be close by."

"Not if you have to go up to Jackman."

"That a hotbed of crime?"

Theo laughed. "Jackman ain't even a hotbed of population. Sergeant Doody's office is first on the right—I suppose Rose has already told you that."

Jean-Paul turned toward the office and said, "It's been a pleasure meeting you, Lieutenant."

"Theo."

"Theo," Jean-Paul corrected himself.

"If you hang out around here for a while, I imagine we'll cross paths again."

Jean-Paul reached Sergeant Doody's open door in five steps and knocked on the doorframe.

"Enter."

He stepped inside and Sergeant Arlene Doody was standing beside her desk. She offered her hand. Thibodeau shook it. "I overheard you talking with Theo. Have a seat," she said.

Even in uniform, Thibodeau found Arlene Doody attractive. Her blond hair was short, fashionable, and within regulation. She was a tall woman, Thibodeau estimated her height to be at least five feet ten inches, and her uniform was ironed with her shirt's military creases crisp. "I understand that you're working a murder-kidnapping case from up in The County."

"I am."

"Give me the bird's eye view of the case."

"Deputy Sheriff Fred Albair of the Aroostook County Sheriff's Department was assigned to look into a missing child call by Lois Turner…"

"If I remember accurately, Turner's the county sheriff up there."

"She is."

"How'd we get involved?"

"When the deputy sheriff searched the property, he found no sign of anyone breaking into the house. At first, we thought a family member, possibly, the father, had killed the girl. We took him in for questioning, then we fu—screwed up. Subsequent questioning of the mother led us to a person of interest named Felicien Paradis who did odd jobs and chores around the property. Paradis and his partner, one Claudette Beaupre, fled south.

"Early Sunday Morning I got a call about a robbery/homicide at a gas station and convenience store in Sherman Station. The store's video camera showed a man fitting Paradis's description in the store around eleven that night. He had apparently robbed the store and in the process shot and killed the eighteen-year-old attendant. The video also showed the Beaupre woman and a small child, believed to be the missing child, in the store and traveling with Paradis. He has family in the Belgrade area so I followed. We have additional surveillance video showing him at a Walmart in Farmington. Now you know what I know."

Doody leaned back in her chair. "I wish I had enough resources to give you another body, but I don't. What's your game plan?"

"Wait until he surfaces again. Until then, I can help you out."

She leaned forward and said, "It just so happens that I can use you. Somewhere in the area that you think your perp is hiding is a major league chop shop. Car theft from Portland to Bangor has escalated, the Lewiston/Auburn areas have been hit especially hard. It would help me a lot if you'd keep an eye open for it. As far as I'm concerned you can work both cases simultaneously."

"I should tell you that I'm not the only one looking into this."

"Oh? Explain, please."

"There's a lawyer, Dylan Thomas, also interested in this."

"A lawyer?"

"He was formerly one of us. He was a field trooper out of Gray. He left the force and got a private investigator license while attending law school at night. His P. I. license is still current."

"What's his interest in this? Did the parents hire him?"

"He's the girl's uncle."

Doody stood up. "It sounds to me like you got yourself a real can of worms."

"Does seem that way, doesn't it?" Thibodeau stood up and asked, "You guys wouldn't have a desk and computer I can use to file some reports?"

"Sure, use the one outside my office."

Thibodeau turned to leave but stopped when Doody asked, "How much of what you told me does this lawyer slash P. I. know?"

"All of it—maybe more, he's been down here on his own all day. I don't know if he's learned anything new."

"Okay. While you're on the computer, check out a guy named Vernon Cole. I got a feeling he knows a lot about these car thefts."

"I got a job for you if you want it," Vernon Cole told Felicien.

"At this point I don't guess I got much choice," Paradis answered. "I really need some money."

Cole rounded his desk, opened the office door, and shouted loud enough to be heard over the racket of a pneumatic wrench, "Gino, get your ass in here!"

From beneath a Cadillac Escalade, a tall man in dirty oil and grease stained coveralls used his heels to pull the creeper on which he lay. He got to his feet, wiped his hands on a grimy rag, and walked toward the office. Once inside he closed the door with a loud bang and said, "You called, Vern?"

"Gino Tricroce, meet Felicien Gagnon."

Paradis was surprised when Cole used his alias. He stood giving Tricroce a quick appraisal. The chop shop man's hair was scraggly and it, as well as his beard and mustache, was in need of trimming and shampooing. His nose was a minefield of blackheads and the wrinkles around his dark eyes were embedded with grease and dirt—Felicien could only wonder what lay beneath the matted beard. Even though he'd been wiping his hands on the rag since he'd got out from under the expensive SUV, Tricroce's hands still felt oily when they shook hands.

"Felicien is gonna make the Lewiston trip with you tonight," Cole announced.

Tricroce nodded, but said nothing. He stood by the door, still wiping his hands on the rag, until Cole said, "That's all Gino, go back to work. They want that Escalade delivered tonight."

Tricroce nodded and left, closing the door so hard that the glass walls and door rattled.

"Quite the talker, ain't he?" Felicien asked.

"Gino ain't one for unnecessary talk, that's for sure. But he's solid in a tight spot. I can't think of anyone I'd rather have on my side when a shit-storm starts."

"What's in Lewiston?" Felicien asked.

"We don't chop everything we get. There's a bunch out of Boston that will buy certain cars and trucks, Caddies and Lincolns mostly.

They take them to Mexico, the country, not the town, and sell them. I guess them Mexicans can't get enough of them."

"What you want me to do?"

"You get the easy job. You ride shotgun. Gino will drive the Escalade and you'll follow in my pickup. When Gino makes contact you make sure that he gets my money and not a bullet. You own a piece?"

"I got a nine-millimeter."

"The same one you used to whack the kid?"

"Yeah."

"I'll get you another piece, one that ain't got no history if you know what I mean. You got a preference?"

"Prefer a semi over a revolver."

"Just so happens I got a Heckler and Koch USP-9." He opened the top right-hand drawer of the desk and placed the pistol and two magazines, each fully loaded with hollow point bullets, on the desk.

"I heard that 9mm bullets don't feed real good."

"In high quality guns, that ain't a problem, and the HK-USP line of handguns is top of the line," Cole answered.

"What's this job pay?" Felicien asked.

"You bring back my money from Lewiston, Gino too if you can, and I'll pay you two grand."

"And if I don't bring Gino back?"

"If you bring the money, two grand, you bring back no money and you get no money. You might say this job pays commission only."

Felicien picked up the pistol and magazines. He tucked the gun in his belt and put the magazines in his coat pocket."

Cole looked at the clock. "You got a long night ahead of you. Go home get some sleep. By the way, you won't need the generator anymore. I called the power company and got your electricity turned on." He saw the look of concern on Felicien's face. "Don't fuckin' worry, the bill will come to me." Cole stood up. "Go. Be back here at six. Oh yeah, take these." He handed Felicien two cell phones. "They're burners, no contract no bill, each one is good for one hundred-twenty minutes. The numbers are written on the tape stuck to the backs."

"Hell, Vern," Felicien handed the phones back, "you done too much already."

"Take them, I want to be able to reach you if I need you. The little woman needs one too, what if that young one gets sick again and I got you on a run? She needs to be able to get in touch with me for transportation or anything." He handed Felicien two white business cards on which only his name and a phone number was written. "I don't have to tell you to memorize that number and get rid of the card—both of them."

Felicien pocketed the cards and left.

After leaving the Chianchette house Dylan was tired. Although he was not in the habit of napping, he hadn't been getting a full night's sleep since he'd become involved with Danielle and decided to go back to his room and catch a couple of hours sleep. He parked in front of his room and walked to the lobby. He was surprised to see Danielle working the desk.

"Hey you," she said.

"Hey yourself. I thought you only worked weekends," he countered.

"I don't have classes on Wednesday, so I usually work a half-shift. It gives Uncle George a few hours off. What've you been up to?"

"You know, the same old stuff, running all over the place talking to people who don't want to be talked to."

"I get off at four, want to do something?"

He gave her a lecherous smile.

"Not that, maybe do dinner and a movie?"

"Where's the nearest movie theater?" he asked.

"Farmington is closest, but if they aren't showing something you'd like, we could go to Augusta."

"Let's do Farmington. I haven't been to a theater in so long anything will do, as long as it isn't a *chick flick*."

She laughed and said, "Not too much violence and gore, okay?"

"It's a deal. See you at what? Five?"

"I'll come to your room when I get off at four."

He looked around to see if there was anyone within hearing distance. "Is that wise? A lot of places don't like their people hanging out with the customers."

"Yes, but their uncle and aunt don't own the company."

"That could be even worse."

"Not with my aunt and uncle, I've heard stories about their visit to the Woodstock Rock Festival."

"Okay, you win, see you then."

"Be ready for some *afternoon delight.*"

"Woman you are incorrigible."

"And you love it."

He smiled. "Yeah. That I do."

Tricroce led Felicien down Lisbon Street and onto Main Street. When he exited Main at the overpass to Russell Street and the Veteran's Memorial Bridge, Felicien realized they were headed into Auburn. He glanced at the clock in the Silverado's dash, eleven at night. They crossed the bridge and the street turned into Mount Auburn Street. They left the street and turned into the entrance of the mall. Tricroce parked in the Kohl's Store's vacant parking lot.

Felicien left his truck and shivered in the frigid late-night air. He knocked on Tricroce's window. "This where we're supposed to meet these guys?"

"I didn't fuckin' stop here to buy a pair of blue jeans."

"Hey man, ain't no reason to be an asshole."

Tricroce looked out the window on the far side of the Escalade and saw a Chevrolet sedan turn into the parking lot. "Can't help it, that's the way I am. Here they are. Get back in your truck and keep an eye out."

Felicien returned to the Silverado and relished the warmth. He took the nine-millimeter pistol out of the console and placed it on the empty right-hand seat.

The Chevy slowly crossed the parking area and came to a rest slightly behind the Cadillac SUV. *Shit,* Felicien thought, *they couldn't have picked a worse location if I got to shoot at these fuckin' punks.*

A Hispanic in a leather jacket exited the Chevy and walked to the Escalade keeping it between him and the Silverado. Felicien pressed the button that lowered the passenger window and placed his hand on the pistol.

Tricroce left the motor running when he got out of the SUV. He and the man spoke briefly and the Hispanic passed a small grip across the hood. Tricroce opened it, removed a small flashlight from his pocket, and shined it into the bag. He nodded and then turned and opened the door to Felicien's truck. He saw Paradis's hand resting on the pistol and said, "It's cool."

Felicien picked the gun up and placed it on the console. Tricroce leaped into the car and closed the door. He saw that the window was open and said, "Wanna put some glass in this pneumonia hole?"

Felicien closed the window.

"Let's get the fuck out of here," Tricroce said.

Felicien drove forward, keeping one eye on the two vehicles that remained in the parking lot.

"What the fuck you looking at?" Tricroce asked. "Everything's cool. Go."

The Boston men started out of the parking lot and followed the Silverado. As he followed the same route through Lewiston, Felicien kept watching the two vehicles behind them in the mirror. "You ever have these guys try an' rip you off?" he asked.

"Not yet, but there's a first time for everything."

"They're still on our ass."

"They're probably headed for the Auburn exit to the turnpike. When we turn onto Canal Street they should go straight across the river." Tricroce noticed that Felicien still had one hand on the pistol. "Don't worry man. These guys are cool, we done business with them before. Turn here."

Felicien turned left onto Canal Street and the Cadillac and the Chevy continued straight crossing the Androscoggin River.

"See," Tricroce said, "I told you everything was cool. Let's go home."

Dylan called Thibodeau and brought him up-to-date.

"What's your plan?" Thibodeau asked.

"I haven't a clue. They're still off-grid."

"I have a description of the truck. DMV says the only vehicle registered to Paradis is a 2002 Dodge Ram, red with pinecone plates. Tag number is 2005-RD."

"Thanks. What kind of support can I expect from Augusta?"

"I'll put out a BOLO to all field troopers, toll takers, local PDs, and county sheriffs."

"Tell them that if they see them to be careful. They may be desperate enough to hurt the child."

"Okay, now let me get on this."

"Go for it," Dylan said and hung up.

Thursday: Day Six

CLAUDETTE SAT AT THE TABLE drinking coffee and smoking. She looked up when Felicien walked into the room. "How'd it go?"

He removed a roll of money from his pocket, peeled off five one-hundred-dollar bills and handed them to her. "My God damned picture is spread all over the place so you got to do the shopping. Vern lent me a truck, a new Silverado, says that my Dodge is too well known." He glanced at his watch. "It's one in the morning, I'm gonna get some sleep."

"If I go shopping in the morning are you going to babysit?"

"Fuck no, you wanted her so you take care of her. If I had my way, I'd shoot her and dump the body out in the woods."

Claudette lit a cigarette. Her eyes narrowed into slits. "You would too. Then we'd be out a lot of money. You can be one miserable son of a bitch, you know that?"

"Sounds like I got promoted. You usually call me a no-good bastard." He tossed a key to the Silverado on the table and walked to the bedroom.

She remained at the table staring at the money. *How long*, she wondered, *will it be before he becomes pissed off and kills me?* She had to admit that the kid was a problem. She contemplated waiting until he was asleep and taking off. He was a heavy sleeper and it would be easy for her to take the rest of his money and the kid and run. Once she reached Boston, she wouldn't need him, Uncle Val would take things in hand and she'd make enough so she'd never again have to allow a piece of shit like Felicien into her bed and she would be able to take care of herself.

Her thoughts turned to Vern Cole. He had completely fooled her. She should have known that he was not the nice man she had initially thought. He was worse than Felicien—if such a thing was possible. She had no doubt that if she ran, Felicien would say *good riddance*. On the other hand, Vern would most likely think that she knew too much about him and his business and send someone, possibly Felicien among them, after her. She did not know a lot about Cole's activities, but even the smallest bit of knowledge might be enough to get her killed—the child too.

Dylan sat in the lobby near the coffee urn, drinking his third cup. He picked his phone up from the table and punched in Jean-Paul Thibodeau's number. It rang three times before it was answered.

"Thibodeau."

"Good morning."

The state cop laughed, "It's morning. I don't know how good or bad it is."

"What's your agenda today?"

"Major Crimes—Central has asked me if I would look into a series of car thefts during the down time on the Paradis investigation."

"So where are you now?"

"I'm north of you in Bingham, Moscow Township to be exact, trying to locate a so-called logging operation operated by a Vernon Cole."

"He behind the thefts?" Dylan asked.

"Let's just say he's a person of interest. He's got a clean rap sheet, but for a guy who doesn't harvest a lot of timber, he seems to have quite a bit of money."

"You got enough for a search warrant?"

"No, but if I find his outfit, I may find probable cause. What're you up to today?"

"I'm going to hang out, maybe spend some time at the Farmington Walmart."

"Maybe get some lunch with Danielle Stevens?"

"How do you know about her?"

"I saw her leave your room the other morning. Not too many license plates that say *2BLUIZE*."

Dylan shook his head, but realized they should have been a bit more discrete. "You got me."

"Well, enjoy lunch. I'll touch bases later."

"Later." Dylan broke the connection and realized that he'd neglected to tell Thibodeau about his visit to the Germaine and Madeline Chainchette. *I'll catch him up later*, he thought.

Sandra stood beside the bed when Claudette woke up. She took a quick glance at the clock, seven in the morning, barely day light. "What's wrong?"

"I miss my mommy." The young girl began to cry.

Claudette rose from the bed. *Jesus Christ*, she thought, *all I need is a bawling brat*. She knew that she had to calm the girl down and grabbed Sandra up. She held the crying girl against her shoulder and wanted to get her out of the room before she woke Felicien up. Before she could get out the door, he rolled over.

"What the fuck's wrong with her now?"

"She's alright, go back to sleep."

"Like I can sleep with her caterwauling."

"I'll handle it, you go back to sleep," Claudette said. She carried the distraught child into the kitchen. She sat at the table gently rocking the three-year-old. "Don't worry, baby. I'll take you to your mommy."

Sandra inhaled deeply and looked up into the woman's face. "Can you take me now?"

"Soon, I promise." At that moment Claudette Beaupre made a life-changing decision. First chance she got she was going to take the kid and head for Boston where her Uncle would take care of the deal. "Just give me some time."

"I don't like him."

"Who?"

"Your husband."

Claudette didn't reply. How would she explain to a three-year-old that she and Felicien weren't married? She stood up, placed the little girl on the chair and said, "You sit quiet and I'll make us some pancakes. Would you like that?"

Sandra pushed her nose up and nodded.

Claudette handed her a tissue. "Here, baby, blow your nose." She turned toward the stove.

After she'd fed the child, Claudette said to Sandra, "You sit quiet while I get dressed, okay?"

Sandra nodded.

In less than five minutes, Claudette was back, dressed in jeans, a flannel shirt, and L.L.Bean rubber moccasins. She carried a canvas tote bag filled with the child's clothes. She dressed Sandra and then bundled her up in a heavy coat and ski pants. She returned to the bedroom and watched Felicien sleep for a few moments, then slowly picked up his jeans. She searched the pockets until she found the roll of money and then removed his wallet. She flipped through the stack of plastic cards until she came to a Mastercard. She took the card, replaced the wallet, and placed the trousers in the same position as she'd found them. Returning to the kitchen, she wrote a note saying she'd gone shopping, then slid the tote over her shoulder, picked up Sandra and the keys to Felicien's rusted out Dodge, and walked out the door. She hoped that since she'd not taken Cole's truck there would be no pursuit.

The cold woke Felicien up. "Fuckin' bitch let the fire die out," he moaned. He looked at his watch, it was just past noon. He struggled into his jeans and walked into the living room. The floor was cold on his bare feet. He opened the wood stove and saw that even the coals at the bottom of the burn chamber were cold. "Least she coulda done was fill it before she left."

He placed some wood shavings into the burn chamber for kindling and reached into his right front pocket for his cigarette lighter. It wasn't there; he checked his left pocket it too was empty. He suddenly realized that the lighter was not the only thing missing. Ignoring his cold feet, he stormed into the bedroom and quickly surveyed it. The canvas tote with all the kid's clothes was gone. *Sonuvawhore! The no-good bitch has taken off with the kid and all my money.* Suddenly, his freezing feet got his attention and he sat on the bed. The socks he'd worn yesterday were on the floor and he pulled them on. He thought about Cole's truck and his heart rate increased. If she took it, he'd really be up shit creek. He left the small bedroom and crossed to the living room window. He parted the curtains and saw the Silverado still in the yard, but his Dodge was gone. He went into the kitchen and rummaged through drawers until he found a box of wooden matches.

Returning to the stove, he struck three matches, breaking each one before the fourth flared up. He started the kindling burning and then placed a couple of pieces of wood into the burn chamber. When the wood caught, he adjusted the damper, and then returned to the bedroom. He found the cell phone Cole had given him and dialed the other one. When he got her on the phone, he was going to ream her a new asshole. He heard it ring—only it was ringing in the kitchen.

What was going on was evident to him. *Goddamned Claudette had taken the kid and his truck and took off.*

He broke the connection and called Cole. "We might have a problem," he said.

Claudette and Sandra left the Skowhegan Walmart and sat in the truck waiting for the heater to overtake the below freezing temperature. Sandra cuddled beside her and Claudette said, "Don't worry baby, I'm goin' to take you to your mommy and daddy." She took out the prepaid flip-phone she had bought and dialed a number that she had known for years. When the phone on the other end was answered, she said, "Uncle Val? I'm on my way with…" She glanced at the little girl snuggled against her. "…the package. I'll be there sometime tomorrow, make the arrangements."

Dylan's phone rang while he and Danielle were having lunch. He glanced at the display and said, "Excuse me, Danielle. It's my sister, I have to take it."

"Of course, I need the little girl's room anyhow."

As soon as she stood up and walked away, Dylan answered the phone. "Hey, sis, what's up."

"Dylan, we haven't heard from you in a couple days. What's happening?"

"I'm sorry, Cait. But there hasn't been anything to report."

"You could at least call and tell us that."

"You're right. I'm sorry, I'll call you every day. How're you, Oreille, and the kids doing?"

"We're doing as well as can be expected." Caitlin's voice cracked and he knew she was crying.

"Cait, have faith. We *are* going to get Sandy back. You have my word on that."

"I believe you, but when we don't hear anything from you, we… I get nervous."

"All right, Caitlin. I promise a call at least once a day."

"Alright."

"I have to go now but like I said, don't worry, we'll get Sandy back. I love you."

Danielle slid into her seat. "Get who back?"

Dylan signaled their server for their check. "My sister, she's panicking. She didn't come right out and say it, but I know she was hoping we'd have Sandy home by now."

"Sandy... like in your niece, Sandra?"

"Yes."

She glanced at her watch. "I have to run. Call me if you learn anything."

"I will." He scanned the room looking for the server. "Go," he told Danielle, "I'll get the check."

They stood and Dylan kissed her on the crown of her head. "You're terrific. I'll call and keep you filled in."

"So," Cole said, "you think she's taking the kid to Boston?"

"Certain of it."

"I tell you, man this ain't good."

"I know, that's why I'm calling you. She knows where we are and can have the cops all over us like stink on shit."

"You think she'll roll?"

"In a heartbeat. She knows that we're lookin' at a child abduction charge. If they catch her and offer her immunity, she'll sing like Dolly Parton."

Cole was silent for a long moment. "You know what you gotta do, don't you?"

"Yeah, I got to get there ahead of them. It shouldn't be a big deal. She's driving my piece of shit Dodge. If I can use the Silverado, I can catch her. She'll be usin' the interstate, even though every cop in the state will be lookin' for that truck. I can run down the turnpike and maybe cut her off before she gets to two-ninety-five."

"She gets into Portland and you'll never fuckin' find her. When you do catch them, you gotta kill 'em—her and the kid."

Felicien took Route 27 and entered Interstate 95 at exit 112 in Augusta. Once he was on the divided highway, he set his cruise control to ten miles per hour over the speed limit and felt confident that he would get ahead of Claudette and the child. He surmised she would want to stay away from the roads routinely patrolled by the state police. If he wanted to avoid police, he'd stay on either U.S. 202, which would take her all the way to New Hampshire or she could connect with U.S. 302 which would take her through Portland where she could take U.S. 1. Either would work in the winter, not so well in summer traffic along the coast.

He reduced speed as he approached the I-95 ramp to I-295 and headed toward Portland. As he raced south, he couldn't help but wonder if he was on a fool's errand. Finding Beaupre was against all odds. Crossing from Maine to New Hampshire afforded her several options: she could stay on I-95 in Kittery and cross over on the Piscataqua River Bridge or take either of the two bridges between Kittery and Portsmouth, New Hampshire. Once she was in New Hampshire there were numerous routes into Boston.

Claudette reached through her window and handed a ten-dollar bill to the young girl working at the Burger King drive through window. When the server passed over her change, a bag which held their food, and two drinks, she pulled forward and stopped to one side of the road. She sorted through the bag, handed Sandra her children's meal and drink. "There you go, honey."

Sandra bit into a French-fried potato and smiled. "Are we there yet?"

"A couple of hours. You eat, then settle back and take a nap and before you know it, we'll be there." *Provided,* she thought, *Felicien doesn't catch up with us.*

Dylan answered his cell phone on the first ring. "This is Dylan."

"Thibodeau here."

"Hey Jean-Paul."

"We got a hit. The toll booth in Gardiner reported a vehicle fitting the description of Paradis' Dodge passed through an hour ago."

"Did the license plate check out?"

"That it did, the only thing is the toll taker said that there were only two people in the truck... a woman and a little girl."

"Really? Maybe they've had a falling out and she grabbed Sandy and ran."

"What are you going to do?"

"I'm heading for Portland. It's time to run an Amber alert."

"Consider it done."

"While you're at it contact Portland PD and the Cumberland County Sheriff's Department. Have them contact their patrol cars and ask if they'd check out the hotel parking lots for the truck."

"Already done that."

Paradis pulled off route 27, parked, and walked inside the convenience store. He kept his cap's visor pulled low and avoided looking directly at the surveillance camera. He bought a twelve pack of beer, a bag of bar-b-que flavored potato chips, and two packs of cigarettes. He paid the clerk with two twenty-dollar bills, shoved his change in his pocket, and departed the store.

He turned the Silverado so that it faced the highway, opened a cold beer, and sat back. *Where would I go if I was the crazy bitch?* He finished off his beer, tossed the empty to the floor on the opposite side of the truck, and opened another. He ran the name of every relative she had through his mind, stopping when he hit on the obvious one—her mother!

Cora Cloutier lived in Boston's Mattapan neighborhood and, based upon what Claudette had told him, made Felicien and his mother look sophisticated. He'd never met her, but on more than one occasion he'd been told that the old woman lived off the State of Massachusetts for as long as Claudette could remember.

Felicien chugged the beer, tossed the empty can beside its predecessor, and drove out of the parking area. "Hang on, babe," he said, "I'm comin' for ya."

Dylan exited I-295 at exit 1 and turned into the Maine Mall. He parked and phoned Thibodeau and apprised him of his location.

Thibodeau in turn briefed Dylan on what he'd learned. "An attendant at a full-service gas station…"

"I didn't think there were any of those left," Dylan said.

"There's a few, anyhow he identified a picture of Paradis as having stopped in for gas."

"Was he able to identify the truck?"

"That's where it gets weird, he was driving a new white Silverado."

"Where did he get a new truck?"

"Beats me, none have been reported stolen. The attendant remembered the plate… said it was unusual LMBRMN 5. We're running it now. We've had aircraft flying over all the possible routes from Belgrade to Kittery. In the event she is using the turnpike we've put out a BOLO to every tollbooth from Gardiner to the New Hampshire border and every county sheriff's department in the state. In the event she ran north, we have the warden service planes patrolling from Eagle Lake south along route 11."

"Any sightings yet?"

"Not yet, Lois Turner has sent deputies from Houlton to Ashland with instructions to patrol down to the county lines. Keep in mind that from Hersey to Sherman route 11 is in Penobscot County. The two sheriffs are coordinating and working out who'll patrol what."

"You got any idea how that's gonna work?"

"If I know Lois Turner and Billy Bean; they'll work out something."

"I don't know Bean."

"He's good, doesn't worry about territory. He's all about enforcing the law, no matter whose turf it is."

"You'll probably hear something before I do, so keep me in the loop."

"Will do."

"Where are you now?"

"Just passed through Freeport, I should be near you in twenty minutes or so."

"Good. I'm going to spend the night at my house."

"I wasn't aware that you lived down this way."

"Yeah, I do. I got a small house in Gray."

"Give me the address, I'll meet you there."

Claudette drove out of the parking lot of the Maine Mall and breathed a sigh of relief. She turned left planning on entering the Maine Turnpike south. Her intention was to spend the night in Old Orchard. It was off season and she knew there would be plenty of rooms available at discounted rates.

From the corner of her eye she saw a truck pull onto the road. Her heart skipped a beat. It was a white Chevrolet Silverado. She was unable to distinguish the driver but the truck was identical to the one Vern Cole had given Felicien to drive. *Could he have possibly got ahead of me?* She did a quick calculation in her head and realized that if he drove I-95 or I-295, even at the posted speed limit it was possible. She also knew that Felicien *never* drove the speed limit; he always traveled at least ten miles faster. She looked at Sandra; the child had no idea of the danger they might be in and appeared to be napping. Claudette made a decision to stop at the first affordable hotel she encountered.

A darker truck entered the road between the white truck and hers. In her rear-view mirror, Claudette saw the white truck force the darker one to the side of the road. Seeing the white Chevy's actions, removed any doubt she had about whether or not it was Cole's

Silverado with Felicien at the wheel. Her heart raced and she panicked. She sped up, trying to take advantage of the confusion taking place behind her.

It was turning dark and even though she knew she should turn on her lights, she was too frightened to do so. She saw a pickup enter the road from her left and looking back didn't see anyone behind her. She turned left at the next intersection, drove about a hundred yards, and turned into the crowded parking lot of a Walmart store. She turned into a vacant spot in the third row from the back and shut the motor off to eliminate the possibility of Felicien seeing her exhaust, and used her mirrors to watch the road behind. Her hands shook and she was perspiring heavily and prayed that her pursuer had not seen her turn off. Suddenly the white Chevy flashed by and within seconds the darker truck raced after it.

Claudette exhaled, started the motor, and lit a cigarette.

Sandra sat up and coughed. "That smoke is yucky," she said.

Claudette spun on her and snapped, "It won't kill you. Now sit quiet while I decide what we need to do."

She reached under her seat where she knew Felicien kept his copy of DeLorme's *The Maine Atlas and Gazetteer*. She flipped it open to Map 3 and saw that she was on Payne Road in Scarborough. She drove out of the parking lot and returned to the road.

She became aware of Sandra sniffling and turned to face her. The small child was crying and rubbing her nose. Claudette opened the glove box and grabbed a napkin. "Here, baby, wipe your nose. I'm sorry for snapping at you."

Sandra took the napkin, wiped at her nose, and said, "I miss my mommy and daddy."

"It won't be too much longer, now shut up, I need to concentrate on my driving."

Felicien cursed. He couldn't believe his luck when he saw the red truck exit the Maine Mall. There was no doubt that what he'd seen was his Dodge. He peered ahead but couldn't discern much in the twilight's gloom. He came to a rise in the road and saw no tail lights ahead. He, "Son of a bitch!"

He slowed, turned at the first opportunity, and reversed his course. In a few minutes he saw the lights of a large building on his left. He spied the large Walmart sign and turned into the parking lot. He slowly cruised along the border, looking for the rusted red Dodge. He estimated there were at least five hundred cars in the lot and knew she'd lost him.

Claudette stopped on the shoulder of U. S. 1 and checked traffic in both directions. *Do I go north to Portland or south toward Biddeford?* She wished she knew exactly where Felicien was. She'd been driving south in heavy traffic for an hour. She glanced at Sandra and smiled. "Don't worry, honey," she said in a whisper so as to not wake her up, "Nobody is going to take you from me."

Dylan Thomas had just settled on his couch when Thibodeau called. "You learn anything?"

"Where are you?"

"Turning into your driveway."

Headlights flashed across the living room wall and the deep rumble of a high-performance motor announced his arrival. Dylan got up and met Thibodeau outside. "Let's go somewhere and eat," Dylan said. "My cupboard will give Mother Hubbard's a run for its money."

Dylan and Thibodeau drove to a chain restaurant and asked the greeter to put them at a remote table. When Jean-Paul showed her his badge, she said, "Of course." She consulted a seating chart and said, "Follow me, please."

Once the greeter seated them and told them their server would be with them shortly, Thibodeau asked, "You talk with your sister?"

"Not today, I'll probably call when we get back to the house."

Thibodeau didn't look happy.

"What do you know that I don't?" Dylan asked.

Thibodeau opened his brief case, removed a folder, and handed it to Dylan. "Read this."

"What is it?"

"A psych report on Beaupre—your niece may be in serious trouble."

Friday: Day Seven

WHEN CLAUDETTE WOKE UP, SANDRA sat in the hotel room's single easy chair. The child had an angry cast to her face.

Claudette rolled out of bed and grabbed the small pot from the single-cup coffee maker. She entered the bathroom, filled the pot, and returned to the small service. After she had poured the water into the coffee-maker and placed a packet of coffee into the basket, she turned to the little girl and said, "What's wrong, baby?"

"You lied."

Claudette's brow arched and her face flushed with heat. She controlled her anger and asked, "Why do you think that?"

"You said you were taking me home. This is not *my* house!"

Claudette took two steps toward Sandra, her arm poised to strike the child. She stopped in front of the ungrateful brat. When Sandra curled into a fetal ball and covered her head with her hands, Claudette paused and then lowered her hand.

"I couldn't take you there. Some bad men were waiting for us."

"Like that bad man we left?"

"Yes. He and others want to hurt us so we have to hide for a while. It won't be long. I promise."

"Are you lying?"

"No, Honey, I am not."

Sandra slid out of the chair. "I'm hungry."

Claudette poured the fresh brewed coffee into one of the disposable cups provided. "Let me finish my coffee and wash my face and we'll get something."

She gulped a mouthful of the coffee and walked into the bathroom. The long mirror along the right-hand wall showed a woman whose hair was in dire need of washing, her clothes—a flannel shirt and jeans—looked as if they'd been slept in, which they had. She turned the hot water handle and waited for the cold water to be purged from the pipes. She rested her hands on the counter top and studied her reflection. *I got to do some shopping*, she thought, *I need clothes, so does the kid.* She scooped hot water and splashed it on her face. *Shit, I don't even have a comb or toothbrush.* She walked back into the sleeping area and said, "Let's go get some food and do some shopping. How'd you like some new clothes?"

Sandra smiled and said, "Yes! Can we go to Toys 'R' Us?"

Dylan and Jean-Paul Thibodeau sat near the window of a diner near the Maine Mall. They watched a large truck turn off the turnpike.

Dylan took a drink from his coffee and said, "How unstable is Beaupre?"

"According to the report, she's not so much unstable as she is unreliable."

"What does that mean?"

"She doesn't go off rail often, but you never know when she will."

"They give any indication what sets her off?"

"From what I see and hear it's stress."

"Wonderful," Dylan said. "She's got every law enforcement officer in New England looking for her and as far as we know a pissed off psycho chasing her—how's that for stress?"

Thibodeau stared out the window where the eighteen-wheel truck swayed as it made the turn.

"What you think?" Thibodeau asked. "Is he over-weight or not?"

"Over, by a half-ton, maybe a ton," Dylan commented. "I'm surprised he didn't roll over making that tight turn."

Thibodeau returned to the subject of Claudette Beaupre. "We

haven't seen nor heard anything of her."

"I think she'll head for familiar turf. She grew up in and around Boston. She'll probably head there. She'll be looking for support of some type."

"I think you're right, if she's looking for a place where she can disappear, then the more populous the area the better."

"That's a good point."

"I'll need to talk to my lieutenant, ask if I should stay on this case or head back north to work the other one, we got going."

"Another case?"

"The Johansson murder over in Woodland."

"That the guy who was killed during a robbery at his sawmill?"

"Yup, he'd been shot and his small safe taken."

Dylan drank some coffee. "They took his safe? He keep a lot of cash on site?"

"Not really—at least that's what his wife says. Who knows though? Wouldn't be the first time a guy didn't tell his old lady how much cash he was hoarding."

"You think she was involved?"

"Truthfully," Thibodeau replied, "I don't. But I know one thing for certain, someone over there knows who did it. Woodland is the next town west of Caribou. It's not what you'd call heavily populated and everybody knows everything about everyone else. All we got to do is find that one person who'll open up."

"Good luck on that. If someone knows who did it, the killer probably knows who knows he did it. That'd be enough to scare any potential snitch into silence."

Thibodeau ate the last of his omelet and agreed. "You hit the target on that one. I think it's easier to catch a perp in a bigger city. In small towns, people keep their ears open more so than city-dwellers but they also keep their mouths shut more."

Dylan nodded in agreement. "Well. I think I'll head south. Poke around at Beaupre's family, see what I can stir up."

"Her maiden name was Cloutier. Don't forget Paradis's family. They may know something too."

"Which reminds me," Dylan said. "You find out who that Silverado was registered to?"

"You ready for this? Vernon Cole."

"Isn't that the guy you think is behind the car thefts?"

"One and the same. Maybe we'll nail him this time."

Dylan looked at the check the server had left when she brought their meal. "I got this."

"At the risk of looking as if I'm on the take, I'll let you," Thibodeau said with a broad grin. "You might want to check in with Lieutenant Pat Bigg in Augusta. He's with Major Crimes Unit—Central, if you tell him that I referred you maybe he'll be able to point you toward a detective in Major Crimes—South."

"Too bad, I'd rather work with you."

"If they allow me to stay on the case, I'll call you." Thibodeau stood up. "Dylan, I don't have to tell you to be careful with her, do I?"

"No, you don't. My niece's life may depend upon me."

"By-the-way, how'd your sister and her husband handle it when you called to tell them that their child may be taken out of state?"

"I can only describe her reaction as hysterical—he was stoic."

"Well, let's hope that we can resolve this fast."

"It's a week today, Jean. I think it's a bit late to be resolved *fast*."

"Good point."

Claudette and Sandra exited the Goodwill Store, quickly jumped into the truck, and returned to the hotel. Sandra jumped on the bed and began playing with the doll that she'd picked up.

"You play, while I take a shower and clean up."

Sandra nodded, but did not verbally answer.

Claudette picked up the plastic bag of personal hygiene products she'd bought at a local dollar store, a bathrobe, and walked into the bathroom. In minutes she stood under a stream of hot water, trying to wash away the effects of two days without a shower.

Claudette walked back into the room, wearing a terrycloth robe, and her hair wrapped in a towel. She watched the little girl playing on the bed. Sandra hadn't had a bath or shower since she'd been with Claudette and her hair was oily, along with the rest of her small body, it was in need of a thorough washing. "Put your doll away and let's get you cleaned up."

"I want to play."

Claudette's eyes narrowed and her voice was sharp and low when she said, "I told you to put the fuckin' doll away and get cleaned up. Now don't give me no goddamned lip."

Sandra picked up on the menacing tone of Claudette's voice. She placed the doll so its head rested on a pillow and said, "Okay."

Dylan was driving south on I-95 when his cell phone rang. He hoped there were no police around as he answered. "Dylan."

"We got a hit."

It was Jean-Paul Thibodeau.

"Clarify that, would you?"

"Someone booked a hotel at three o'clock this morning using a MasterCard in Paradis's name."

"Beaupre?"

"Can't think of anyone else who it might be."

"Where?"

"A hotel in Old Orchard, near the beach. It seems you were correct that she'd head for someplace where she can disappear into the crowd."

"I'm on my way. I'm coming up on the Old Orchard Beach Exit and can be there in ten-fifteen minutes at most."

Vernon Cole watched the police cruiser pull out of his yard. He heard footsteps and turned to see who it was. Seeing Gino Tricroce, he said, "We might have a *big* fucking problem."

Tricroce stood beside his boss, wiping his hands on an oily rag. "What kinda problem?"

"Fuckin' Paradis got seen by the Scarborough cops last night, driving my pickup."

"What for?"

"Don't know why exactly, but every cop in the state is lookin' for the fuckin' idiot."

"I heard you tell the cop that it was stolen during the night. You think he bought it?"

"Don't know and don't care. It's my word against that idiot piece of shit's."

"Then what's our problem?"

"The woman. She knows that Paradis was working for me and that I let him use the truck."

"And?"

"We ain't got a clue about where she is."

"You want I should go to that shack where they was stayin' and see what I can find?"

"Wouldn't hurt to take a look. C'mon, we'll do it together."

The door to the old hunting camp caved in with Tricroce's first kick. Cole preceded his henchman inside. The interior of the building was colder than the outside and their breath spiraled out of their mouths. "Check the bedroom," Cole ordered.

"Are we looking for anything special?"

"Anything that will give us a clue to where the woman may be hiding."

Tricroce nodded and walked into the small bedroom.

Cole stood in the center of the kitchen and studied its interior. The room was in the state of disarray one would expect from people who were leaving in a hurry. There was a coffee mug on the sideboard and the coffee remaining in the pot had frozen into a black ice cube. On the floor in front of the counter was a trash can and Cole walked to it. He grabbed the can and dumped its contents onto the floor. He moved the garbage around with his boot, stopping when he saw a familiar light green piece of paper. Cole removed the heavy glove from his right hand and picked up the piece of paper. As he suspected it was a piece of a check that someone had torn into pieces. More importantly it was the upper left corner with an address printed on it.

Tricroce walked in and said, "Ain't shit back there." He stood quiet until his boss raised his eyes from a piece of paper that he held. "You find something?"

"Maybe." Cole looked around the room for a second and then started for the door.

"We goin' someplace?"

"Yeah, we're going to Lewiston."

"I was just there last night."

"No shit Sherlock. You're gonna be there this afternoon too."

Most people in Maine consider Lewiston-Auburn to be a single city but they are in fact two distinctly different places. Whereas Auburn is listed as the eighth most dangerous town in Maine, neighboring Lewiston comes in at number 10. Looking at the statistics, Auburn with a population of just under 22,948 reported a crime rate of 48% while Lewiston with a larger population, 36,562, reported a 38.5% crime rate. Although the two cities are separated by the Androscoggin River, one can pass from one to the other without being aware of the change in venue.

Vernon Cole and Gino Tricroce exited the Maine Turnpike at exit 80 and followed Lisbon Street north into Lewiston. As they neared the junction of Lisbon and Maple Streets, Cole said, "Go right and then take a left on Knox."

Tricroce made the turn and Cole removed the piece of check from his shirt pocket and glanced at it. He studied the numbers on the buildings and said, "Look for number 666."

Tricroce turned onto Knox and cruised at a steady ten miles per hour until Cole said, "Here."

Tricroce pulled against the curb in front of a large three-story white house—what remained of the paint was white; the majority of the exterior was weathered clapboard. When they were standing on the sidewalk, Tricroce looked at the rest of the houses on the street. "Pretty shitty neighborhood, ain't it?"

Like his employee, Cole took in the vista. "I'll bet it was nice at one time, probably when the owners and managers who ran the mills along the canals lived here."

"Musta bin a long time ago… if this street burned down, they'd call the ruins urban renewal."

Cole didn't bother commenting on Tricroce's cynical comments. He walked about twenty feet and turned into a short walk that led to a dilapidated porch with sagging steps and roof.

Tricroce looked at the sagging and rotting steps and said, "Boss, you sure this thing's safe?"

"Fuck it, if it ain't we'll sue the shit out of the owner."

They mounted the four steps and opened the exterior door. Cole studied a bank of six mail boxes. After a second he pointed at one. "Second floor, apartment B."

Tricroce studied the small foyer.

"What the fuck are you doing?" Cole asked.

"I don't see no buzzer."

"Does this shithole strike you as the type of place to have security?"

Tricroce shrugged. "I'm just sayin'…"

"And I'm just sayin' *shut the hell up*."

Cole reached out and turned the knob on the inner entrance. The door swung inward. He turned to his companion and said, "See?"

Cole entered the building and was confronted by a stair that climbed into the dark inner reaches of the building. At the top of the first flight he saw three doors. The ones on either side had worn letters A and C in white paint. He walked down the short hall and knocked on the door marked with the broken remnants of what was a capital B.

"Go 'way, I ain't buyin' nothin'."

"Claude Cloutier?" Cole asked through the closed door.

"I said I ain't buyin' whatever it is you're fuckin' sellin'. So, beat it."

Cole stepped to one side and nodded to Tricroce, who stepped forward and kicked the door beside the knob. When the warped aged wood splintered and the door crashed open, Tricroce burst in.

Cole heard Cloutier say, "What the fuck are you crazy or some—," then a sound like someone being choked. He walked inside, pushed the broken door as closed as he could get it. He saw Tricroce holding the fattest, grungiest son of a bitch he'd ever encountered against the wall by the throat.

Cole smiled at him and said, "No we ain't crazy and we're sure as fuck not sellin' anything." He saw Cloutier's face turn from red to a very pallid shade of blue. "You better put him down, Gino. I think he's either about to suffocate or choke to death on his own puke."

When Tricroce released him, Cloutier slid down coming to a rest on his ass with his back against the wall. He placed one hand on his throat and inhaled sharply, trying to regain his breath. After several seconds of wheezing, he said, "Who are you… what do you want?"

"Who we are ain't important," Cole said. "What we want is your sister."

"What's the crazy bitch done now?" Cloutier wheezed.

Dylan took the I-195 exit to Old Orchard Beach and drove to the beach. It was evident that it was out of season, the amusement rides were all shutdown and the streets leading to the pier and water were deserted. He passed at least a dozen hotels, looking for the one where Felicien Paradis's credit card had been used. He found it a block west of the ocean.

He parked in front of the office and stood on the walk-in front of the entrance for a couple of minutes. Compared to the weather up north, the coastal area was almost spring-like. What little snow there was lay under the huge lower branches of evergreen trees where the sun didn't reach. The air, while still brisk, seemed comparatively warm—he saw a thermometer on a wooden pillar and leaned forward to read it. The red line hovered between thirty-five and forty degrees. *Won't get this warm in Aroostook County until late March or April,* he thought. He broke out of his reverie and entered the office.

A tall thin young man, wearing a name tag that said *Milford,* stood behind a half-desk. His thick black hair looked as if he had forgotten to comb it that morning. Dylan assumed it was his idea of a *slept-with* look. He sported a thick bushy mustache that resembled the type usually associated with barbershop quartets. "Can I help you?" he asked.

"I hope so. I'm trying to locate my sister's room. She and my niece called me last night but forgot to leave her room number."

"The only woman and child were in room 117—but they checked out about two hours ago."

Dylan did his best to look like a disappointed brother. "Darn it."

The clerk scanned the room and Dylan knew he was going to say something he did not want anyone else to hear.

"I think your sister might be in trouble," he said.

"What makes you think that?" Dylan asked.

"There were policemen in here asking about her too."

"Police?"

"Well, they weren't in a police car, but you know how easy they are to spot, right?"

"Really?" Dylan suppressed a smile, once again trying to appear like a brother.

"Yes, it's the way they walk, talk, and look at you."

"How do they look at you?"

Milford straightened up, reminding Dylan of a teenage know-it-all. "They make you feel as if they know more than you do and that they don't believe anything you say."

Dylan raised one eye brow and replied, "I think you're right. When I was at the Maine Police Academy, they always told us that everyone lies."

Milford's face reddened. "Are you a policeman?"

"I was but not anymore; now I'm a lawyer. You have a nice day, Milford."

Dylan turned and paused. Looking over his shoulder he said, "Did you happen to talk to my sister?"

"Only for a few minutes."

"Did she say where she was going?"

"No, but she asked if we had any maps."

"Maps—any place in particular?"

"She asked about Boston. I gave her one compliments of the hotel."

Dylan nodded, thanked the young man, and departed.

Claude Cloutier sat on his tattered and torn couch wiping at the blood that ran from his nose, across his chin, and dropped onto his yellowed white tee-shirt. "Please," he said. "Don't hit me no more."

Gino Tricroce looked at Vernon Cole.

Cole raised his hand and said, "Hold off, Gino." He turned to the pathetic slob sitting on the couch. "If she was in trouble and needed someplace to lay low for a while where might she go?"

Cloutier seemed to relax a bit. "Could I get an ice pack for my nose?"

Cole turned to Tricroce and said, "Get him an ice pack."

Tricroce looked bewildered.

"The ice is in the freezer," Claude said. "You can use the dish cloth on the counter beside the sink."

"Let's get back to our discussion," Cole said. "What's in Boston?"

"Our mother lives there… in Mattapan."

"Shittiest neighborhood there," Tricroce said. He handed Claude a dingy wash rag with several ice cubes wrapped in it.

Claude gingerly pressed the ice against his damaged nose. "Ain't that bad, North Dorchester and East Boston are worse," his voice muffled by the rag.

"Easy for you to say," Tricroce said. "You didn't grow up there. If the world was gonna get an enema, any one of those places could be where they stick the shaft."

Cole stood up and nodded his head in the direction of the door. "Claude if you're goddamned lying to us we'll be back—and this time I'll let Gino really fuck you up."

"You should soak that shirt in a pail of bleach and water," Gino said. "If you do it soon it'll get the blood out."

"I doubt if it'll make that friggin' shirt white though," Cole added. "I wouldn't use that thing to wipe oil off a dipstick."

Dylan sat in his car and spoke to Jean-Paul Thibodeau on his mobile phone. "Who you know in Boston?"

"Don't tell me she's headed to Boston."

"I would imagine she's already there. According to the desk clerk at the hotel she got a map of Boston from him and hauled ass about two hours ago."

"Son of a bitch. Let me make a couple of calls."

"Oh, Jean-Paul, we better put out another Amber Alert. We should do it for all of New England, maybe New York and Connecticut too."

"This thing is getting more and more complicated. What's your next move?"

"I'm against a wall here. Can you get some background info on Claudette? I could use the names of any living parents or siblings and if so their addresses?"

"Like I said, let me make a couple of calls. Keep your phone handy."

Claudette sat in the chair farthest from the window in her mother's apartment. Her mother shuffled in from the kitchen. Cora Cloutier was one hundred pounds over-weight, her gray hair was twisted into a bun with so many strands lose they looked like a halo, her face was so wrinkled that it made Claudette think of the bottom of a pond during a forty-year drought, all cracks and crevasses. She wore a faded cotton house dress with an equally washed-out floral pattern and on her feet was a pair of house slippers so ragged that her feet rolled over the sides. A cigarette with three-quarters of an inch of ash hanging from the end was perched between her lips. When she walked, she shuffled along, sliding along the floor's surface to keep her feet from escaping from the slippers.

Cora had lived in the same third floor apartment for over ten years. Her landlord, Bryn Patterson, thought she was the ideal tenant. She never complained about the state of the building and bothered nobody. The linoleum in the kitchen had spots worn through and the hardwood floors through the rest of the apartment were in need of sanding and varnishing. Here and there were places where the surface of the wood was so worn that the bare wood showed. The only bothersome thing about the old woman was that she was using section eight so there were annual inspections—which truthfully were a joke, about the only thing they looked at were the electrical outlets. The other tenants were another story: he believed that if they had nothing to complain about, they'd complain about that.

Cora was halfway across the floor when the ash finally gave up its uncertain grip on the cigarette and fell, bouncing off her breast and stomach. She patted the places where the ash had smeared her dress and bent over to determine whether or not there were live coals on the floor—the last thing she needed was a fire. "Whose kid is that?" she asked her daughter.

"Mine."

"I ain't believin' that for a second. She don't look nothin' like you."

"Ma leave it be."

"What you do—steal somebody else's kid?"

Claudette immediately shouted, "Did not!" She knew she sounded childish, but her mother had a way of bringing out the worst in her. She gritted her teeth and swallowed her next tirade, if her mother tossed her, she'd have no place to go and her supply of cash was dwindling fast. Most of it being spent on gas for Felicien's truck, food, and lodging.

Seeing her daughter's reaction convinced Cora that her observation was dead on. "What happened to that deadbeat you live with? He get tired of your damned drama-queen act and dump you?"

"No, he wanted to kill me so I fuckin' dumped him."

Her words shocked Cora so much that the cigarette fell from her mouth. "What?"

"He wanted to kill me and take the girl. You oughta pick up that cigarette, it's burning the floor."

Cora's brow dropped creating the aura that she had no idea of what her daughter spoke. After a second she looked at the floor and then bent down and picked up the burning stub. She studied the butt for a few seconds and shuffled to an ashtray and ground it into the surface. She picked up the pack of generic cigarettes, took one out, put it in her mouth, and lit it.

"Why'd he want to kill you? What in hell did you do to piss him off that much?"

"Weren't me, he wanted to kill the child so I took her and ran. He chased us until I lost him in Portland, Maine."

Cora dropped down into a ragged recliner, rocked back and placed one of her swollen ankles on the ottoman that sat before it. Her ankles were so swollen, pushing the veins close to the surface that the top of her feet looked purple. She placed the cigarette in the ashtray and stared at her daughter through the stream of smoke rising to the ceiling. "Why'd he want to kill the kid?"

"Who the fuck knows why he wants to kill anyone? I ran and he believes that I know enough to put him away for life."

"What's he done?"

"You mean besides killing a teenager working at a gas station, stealing this baby, and working for a car theft ring? If you do, then it's nothing."

Cora was not convinced by her daughter's story. "Why didn't you take the kid home?"

Claudette rolled her eyes and helped herself to a cigarette. "That's the first place Felicien would look."

"What's to stop him from coming here?" Cora asked.

"He don't know where you live."

"Does he know where your brother lives?"

"He might. Claude sent me a check a few weeks back... he may have seen the address on that."

"Claude sent you a check... for how much?"

Her mother's greed was obvious and Claudette said, "I asked if he could send me a few bucks—that's what the bastard did. He mailed a check for five fuckin' bucks."

"You still got it?"

"I carried it around for a week and then I got so mad that I tore it into pieces and threw it in the garbage."

"What you do that for? Five bucks is five bucks more than you had before he sent it."

Claudette glared at her mother. "Ma, you got to be the greediest person I know."

"Easy for you to say, you didn't have to put up with the miserly son of a whore who fathered you and your brother. Bastard was so tight that when he took a dollar out of his wallet, Washington blinked his eyes. Five dollars was a treat."

"I don't remember much about him."

"Ain't no loss. One time he tore the December page off the calendar hopin' you kids wouldn't know about Christmas."

"Seriously, Ma, I needed money to run and my *darling* brother sent me five bucks."

"Well, if Paradis knows where to find Claude he'll know where to find you in a matter of minutes."

"You think Claude would tell him?"

"When it comes to bein' brave, your brother has his father's backbone. If your boyfriend threatens him with violence, he'll drive him here."

"What should I do?"

"Call your Uncle Valiant."

"Do you think Uncle Val will help?"

"Of all you kids, he always favored you. If you're in trouble he knows people who'd break Paradis's arms and legs just so they'd have somethin' to do."

Dylan met Boston Police Detective Shawna O'Reilly in front of District B-3, the police district responsible for the Mattapan and North Dorchester neighborhoods. She was short, had broader shoulders than most women he knew, with black hair, cut short. When he shook her hand, the strength of her grip surprised him and he could not help but think: *I wouldn't want to take her on in close quarters.*

He looked at the traffic racing through the intersection of Blue Hill Avenue and Morton Street. "Is there someplace a bit quieter where we can talk?" he asked.

"There's a deli about a block from here."

She turned north and walked with a rapid pace that in spite of the waning daylight, the wind, and temperature in the mid-twenties had Dylan sweating in his parka. When he was beside her and keeping pace, he asked, "How do you know Jean-Paul?"

"We grew up together in the Riverton area of Portland."

"Tough part of town."

"You know Portland?"

"I live near there. Grew up in Aroostook County and moved south."

She chuckled. "Not too far south though."

Dylan liked her. Not only was she a Mainer (he usually told people from away that he was a Maine-iac) but she seemed to have a sense of humor, a quality he liked in people. "My father always thought there was no intelligent life south of Houlton."

"Mine said the same thing, only it was that hell was everything south of Kittery."

She stopped at the corner, waited until there was a break in the traffic, and then darted across. Dylan had to trot to keep up with her. She rounded a corner and said, "Here we are." She opened the door and entered.

The sudden transition from the brisk wintry dry air to the humid warm interior of the deli made Dylan feel like he had jumped into a pool of tropical water. He unzipped his winter coat and followed O'Reilly to the counter. When the counterman placed their coffees on the bar, O'Reilly said, "I'll get this."

"Then I'll carry the mugs." He picked them up and waited until she got her change and then followed her to a small table beside a window that faced the street.

Once they were settled, Dylan said, "Aren't many places like this that serve drinks in mugs."

"I get tired of take-out cups. Jean-Paul filled me in on your case. This case has run you all over the place. What makes you think this woman is in Boston?"

"Her last known location was a hotel on Old Orchard Beach. She checked out before I could get there and, on her way out, she asked for a map of Boston. Jean-Paul and I think she may have family in the area."

"What made you think she's in Mattapan?"

"To be honest, I haven't a clue. Once I learned that she had family down here, I knew I'd need someone who knew their way around so I asked Jean-Paul who he knew and he called you."

He took a drink placed the mug on the table and said, "I know you probably have a heavy case load, but I can use any help you might offer."

She laughed. "That sly frigging Frenchman knows damn well that I got a ton of vacation time on the books and my captain told me to either take two weeks off or I'd lose them." She laughed again, shook her head, and said, "I was wondering what in hell I'd do for two weeks." She reached across the table and shook his hand. "Looks like we're partners."

"It's getting' late," Dylan commented. "Can you recommend a moderately priced but decent hotel?"

"I know a couple. Today's Friday and my shift ends in an hour. You could wait here, maybe have a sandwich or something. I'll come for you and lead you to the hotels. My vacation starts Monday and I'm not on call this weekend. We can start first thing in the morning."

Saturday: Day Eight

VERNON COLE AND GINO TRICROCE cruised along the line of triple-decker buildings that lined both sides of the street. It was Saturday morning and there was not a parking spot in sight. "Don't these people ever work on Saturday?" Cole muttered.

"Shit," Tricroce answered, "most these fuckers don't even work during the week. Them that do don't move their cars from December to March. Nothin' will piss you off more than shoveling out a parking spot after a snow storm and finding someone else in it when you come home."

"That competitive is it?"

"Shit, my old man never cleared snow. He'd wait until someone finished shoveling theirs and went to work. The ol' bastard would smash out of his spot and take the clean spot before anyone else could."

"And nobody ever shot him?" Cole asked.

"Don't know. One day he left the house to buy a newspaper and never came back."

"Maybe one of the guys whose parking spot he took got him."

"It wouldn't surprise me," Tricroce said. "There's some hardcore motherfuckers livin' around here."

Cole was studying house numbers as his associate drove down the street. There was no snow on the pavement, but the gutters were frozen and smoke spiraled upward from the tailpipes of cars whose motors were running and from the chimneys of the triple-deckers.

He glanced at the address that Claude Cloutier had provided them. "Here it is," Cole said, pointing to a building in the middle of the block. The houses were butted up against each other, the only separation was narrow walks between them. "How in hell they get their garbage out to the curb?"

"Most of these neighborhoods have service roads behind the triple-deckers. Each house has a one-car garage and the garbage trucks back down the street picking up the garbage."

Cole studied the neighborhood and thought that it was claustrophobic. "Thank God I live in Maine," he commented. "Lots a fresh air and space to live. It must be a bitch backing down those narrow streets."

"It ain't all that bad," Tricroce said. "You learn to ignore a lotta stuff, like when you hear some guy whaling the shit out of his wife or kids. You quickly decide it ain't none of your business and go about your way."

"What if the guy is whaling on your niece or sister?"

"Well, that'd be a horse of a different color wouldn't it?" Tricroce said. "If that was the case, I'd sure as hell make it my business."

"Well, keep that in mind when we visit to find the Beaupre woman. If she's got family, she could have someone watchin' over her."

"Good point." Tricroce looked down the street. "I don't like parking so far away. In a place like this, too many goddamned eyes—the shorter distance between us and the truck, the better I'd like it."

Cole didn't answer. He too was studying the area.

"We could double park. Then we could run inside, grab the woman, and get out."

"We could do that," Cole commented. "We ought to wait until night to hit the place when the dark will help cover us." He nodded his head indicating that Tricroce should drive down the street. "Let's go find someplace to cool our jets until after dark."

Claudette smelled the enticing combination of coffee and cigarette smoke and sat up in bed. She looked behind her and watched Sandra sleeping. She stood put her robe on and walked into the bathroom. She heard her mother speaking with her uncle. Valiant (aka Val) LaBelle was Cora Cloutier's youngest brother and no stranger to the tough underside of Mattapan and North Dorchester. He lived in East Dorchester, a much more genteel part of Boston, but made his living selling drugs or anything else that would turn a quick profit. Occasionally he performed special jobs for several of the city's criminal elements, such as selling stolen children on The Child Exchange. It was well known that he was what the Italian mob called a *made* man; he'd made his bones by killing an informant who worked for Whitey Bulger's Winter Hill Gang.

"There she is," Val said when she walked into the kitchen. He rose from the table, hugged, and kissed his niece.

Claudette returned his embrace and walked to the counter where she filled a coffee cup and then returned to the table. "It's been too long Uncle Val."

"Yeah, it has. Now what's this I heah from your mothah?" His accent was pure Boston and the soft *R*s made her smile.

"I got some people after me…"

"That I can handle."

"They're bad people."

"What? And I ain't? Come over here, sit down, and tell me everything."

Claudette unburdened herself to her uncle. When she finished, he said, "So which of these fuck-heads is chasin' you?"

"Other than seeing a truck that I thought was his, I haven't seen neither hide nor hair of Felicien since I took off. I don't know if he's after me or not. On the other hand, he was workin' for a snake named Vernon Cole and it's him I'm most afraid of. The cops don't have a clue about his car theft ring… even if they do, they ain't got enough evidence to get him."

Val ground out his cigarette. "Now what about the kid?"

"I figure she'll bring a good price on the adoption market."

"Well, there's lots a people who'd pay a bundle for her." He saw her eyes narrow. "I ain't talkin' about no white slavery. These are good folks with enough money to pay for her to go to Hahvahd and nevah bat an eye. Takes forever to go through the agencies, kid would be eleven or twelve before someone 'dopted her. In the meantime, I'm gonna make some calls… maybe get you some protection over here."

Dylan was still toweling off the residual water from his shower. Shawna called and told him that she'd be at his hotel in a half hour. He phoned Jean-Paul Thibodeau and asked, "Paradis turn up anywhere?"

"Nothing on him. I did get you some data on the Beaupre woman though. Her mother's name is Cloutier. She moved to Mattapan from Roxbury about ten years ago. Apparently, the old woman has relatives there, a brother at least. He's a real piece of work named Valiant LaBelle. His sheet is extensive. I won't go through the entire thing, Shawna can run that for you, but there is one thing of note."

"And what's that?"

"His sheet includes everything from racketeering to murder for hire."

"A hitman?"

"I don't think so, but if the situation is such that he needs to kill someone to get his way… well, he'll do whatever it takes."

"If he's killed someone he must have been in prison."

"Never been convicted of a single crime. I believe he only kills when his bunch sics him on someone."

"And he's Claudette's uncle."

"That he is. I have no idea how close they are, but watch your ass around him."

"That's sound advice. Call me if you learn anymore."

"Don't hang up, there's one thing that I think you should know."

"I'm listening."

"You and Shawna got to move fast on this. Val LaBelle is a

known trafficker in children—especially young white girls."

Dylan's stomach lurched. "White slavery?"

"More like circumventing the adoption system. There aren't a lot of small *white* kids available, so LaBelle and his ilk will sell one to anyone who can afford to pay seven figures for one."

"You're shitting me?"

"Not about something like this. If he's got your niece you better believe his broker has a waiting list of clients. I'll be in touch."

Dylan dressed in a pair of jeans, flannel shirt, and hiking boots that were rated to keep one's feet warm to thirty below zero. He gave himself a quick once over in the full-length mirror mounted to the bathroom door and wondered if he was dressed too casually. While he was debating whether or not to change his room phone rang. When he answered, Shawna O'Reilly told him she was in the lobby. He decided to go with the attire he had on.

Upon arriving in the lobby, he breathed a sigh of relief; Shawna was dressed in jeans, running shoes, and wore a white sweater under her heavy winter coat. He waved and approached her. "Good morning," he said.

"If it wasn't so damned cold it would be a beautiful day," she replied.

They sat in a couple of over-stuffed chairs in front of a faux fireplace. He watched the electronic image for a few seconds and then turned away.

"You got any idea where we should start?" O'Reilly asked.

"I got a name from Jean-Paul—Val LaBelle. Does his name mean anything to you?"

"He lives in Dorchester. It's rumored that he's high up in the mob—he's a *made man* and needs to be handled carefully."

"Sounds as if you know him."

"There isn't a cop in Boston, Cambridge, and Somerville who hasn't run across him at one time or another." She glanced at her watch. "He's a night crawler. We may get lucky and find him at home."

Val LaBelle darted out of the bar, took three quick steps, and got into a black Buick. The driver was a swarthy man, his black hair was combed into a pompadour, and slicked back with some type of mousse that smelled like polluted harbor water. He wore a black leather jacket, white tee-shirt, faded blue jeans, and black leather motorcycle boots. He stared out at the exhaust spiraling into the frigid air from the exhaust of cars waiting for the red light to change to green.

"Ricky, you look like a refugee from a fifties teenage rebel movie."

"You call to practice your comedy routine or do you need something?" Ricky asked Val.

Val looked at him for a few seconds and then asked, "What's with the new look? You look like you're goin' to a fuckin' Halloween party dressed as Danny Zuko."

Ricky turned his head toward Val. "Who's Danny Zuko?"

"Go rent *Grease.*"

"Nobody rents grease, for Christ sake, you go to an auto parts store and buy it."

"It's a goddamn movie from the seventies."

"Never heard of it. You gonna fuckin' tell me why you called or not?"

Val sat back, savoring the heat that was blasting from the heater. "I need a favor."

"Anything you ask—you know that. Lay it on me."

"It's my niece, Claudette."

"Cora's kid, she lives in Maine, right?"

"Well, she came into town last night. She's up to her bottom lip in a pool of shit and the wave machine's about to be turned on. She got involved with some friggin' idiot up there and now she's got someone… maybe more than one someone, lookin' to put her head on a pole."

"Who are they?"

"Right now, we don't know, but she seems to think they ain't far. I need you to get a couple of boys and keep a watch on Cora's place."

"It's gonna cost. This ain't exactly weather for standin' on the corner watchin' girls walk by. We'd need three, maybe four guys, nobody can stand around outside for long in these temperatures."

"Whatever it takes, she's my only niece and she's special to me."

"Understood. What the fuck she do up there anyways?"

"She's got a kid with her that ain't hers."

"What kinda kid?"

"Not the kind you'd put to work on the streets—she's only three for Christ sake."

Ricky Deschaine smiled. "Hey get 'em young and you can train them to do things the right way."

Val's eyes narrowed. "I hope you ain't serious, Ricky, cause you're talkin' some sick shit."

Ricky leaned away from Val. He raised his hands. "Just pullin' your leg partner."

Val shook his head. "I never know when you're fuckin' around."

He got out of the car and heard Deschaine say, "Elvis." Val bent down and peered into the car.

"What?"

"Elvis made this haircut famous."

"Out-fucking-standing, man. I wouldn't sleep until I learned that." He slammed the door and watched the Buick pull away from the curb. He returned to the bar wondering if by getting Ricky and his butt-buddies involved he'd made a major mistake.

Vernon Cole and Gino Tricroce cruised past the triple-decker and, while Gino surveyed the street, Cole studied the windows. "There's a light on," Cole said.

"And a couple guys across the street. They're back in the shadow trying not to be seen," Tricroce added.

"You sure it ain't a couple of homeless bums tryin' to get out of the friggin' wind?"

"I can't be sure. But we need to check things out anyways. Last thing we need is to get our asses shot off."

"Okay, let's cruise around the block one more time, maybe we'll get a better look at them."

Tricroce lit a cigarette and cracked his window. The flow of cold air was almost refreshing; at least it cooled the interior a bit. "Okay if we take a log off the fire?" he asked Cole. "My boots are filling up with sweat."

Cole turned the heater control down to eighty. "If there's one thing I hate it's bein' cold," he said. "It's bad enough when you got no choice, but when you got a choice and you go cold, you're a fuckin' idiot."

At the end of the block, Cole made a left turn.

Val LaBelle sat in the living room, watching a Bruins game. His sister and niece sat across from him both of them giving him desperate looks.

"How much longer before the goddamned game is over?" Cora asked.

Val returned their look with one of his own, only rather than looking desperate his look was defiant. "It'll fuckin' end when it ends. If I got to babysit you two, I'll be damned if I'll watch those sitcoms and true crime shows you like." His cell phone rang and he answered on the second ring. "This is Val."

Even with her bad hearing, Cora could hear the conversation.

"What you got, Ricky?"

"A couple guys in a white GMC pickup with Maine tags just cruised by. They was goin' real slow so I think they're lookin' for something."

"Could just be a couple guys lookin' for a girlfriend's house."

"Could be, but Maine plates has me wondering."

"They make your guys?"

"Don't know. I'll have them move and split up—see if they pass by again."

"Keep me up-to-date."

Val broke the connection, turned to the women, and said, "You heard?"

"We heard," Claudette answered. "That truck sounds like Vernon Cole's."

"Who's he?" Val answered.

"He runs the car theft ring that Felicien works for. Don't underestimate him Uncle Val. He's as goddamned rotten as they come."

"Okay. Let's get ready." He handed a thirty-two-caliber pistol to Claudette. "You know how to use that?"

Claudette turned the pistol over in her hands for a few seconds; then she ejected the magazine, catching it in her hand and racked the slide back. She picked up the cartridge that flew out onto the floor, brushed it off, and placed it back in the magazine. Finally, she pushed the full magazine into the pistol's handle, and racked the slide once more. When she released it, the slide slid forward loading a bullet into the chamber.

Val had watched Claudette and said nothing until after she finished checking the weapon. "I guess you do know one end of a gun from the other." He turned to Cora. "You go in the bedroom with the kid. Me 'n Claudette are gonna deal with them." He grinned at his niece. "Ain't we girl?"

Claudette grinned and said, "Goddamn right we are."

Ricky Deschaine sat on a side street, the motor in his Buick running and the heater blasting. It was the coldest night of the winter thus far; he glanced at the digital display on his dash; the thermometer showed the outside temperature at minus one. He redeployed the two men he had watching Cora Cloutier's apartment, ended the conversation, and tossed his cell into the passenger seat. He sighed, not looking forward to what he was about to do.

He shut off the motor and got out of the car. He pulled his coat collar up and held it tight against his neck. *Fuckin' Val is goin' to owe me big time,* he thought. He walked around the corner and crossed the street. In front of the steps leading into the foyer of the triple-decker he checked both ways for any sign of his two men. He couldn't see them, but knew they were in place. Ricky trotted up the four stone steps and into the warmth of the apartment house's foyer. He took a revolver from his pocket and used the butt end of the handle to break the low wattage bulb that illuminated the vestibule. He settled back into the shadow to await what was inevitably coming.

Cole and Tricroce made another circuit. While they passed the building again, Cole asked, "You see anything?"

"Nope, there's nothing where I seen them guys. They must a been homeless like you thought."

"If they were, they sure as hell took off fast. You'd think that we'd spot them on the street."

Tricroce shrugged. "Street people have plenty of holes they can crawl in to keep warm. They could be any friggin' place."

"I guess you're right," Cole answered. "Now all we got to do is find a parking place close by. I don't want to be walkin' very far in this weather."

Tricroce pointed to his right. "We may have another problem."

"What?"

"When we passed last time there was a light on in the entrance to the building—it's dark now."

"That is worrisome."

A quarter of a block ahead of them a car's exhaust drifted up through the cold air. Cole slowed, creeping up on the vehicle. When the car pulled away, Cole deftly parked in the vacated spot.

Dylan and Shawna were just finishing dinner and neither of them were looking forward to walking out of the warmth and cozy atmosphere of The Irish Setter Pub. The server placed their check on the table and asked, "Can I get you anything else?"

Dylan looked at his companion. "I'm all set, how about you, Shawna?"

"I'm fine."

The server, a petite and attractive twenty-something, said, "I'll take that when you're ready." She turned and approached another table.

Dylan watched her walk away and heard Shawna remark, "She's quite attractive, isn't she?"

Dylan smiled an embarrassed smile. "And way too young for me."

"Age is a relative thing."

"How so?"

"It's all a state of mind. If you think that you're old, then you're old. But if you think young... Well you get the idea." She picked up her coffee, took a sip and asked, "So, are you married?"

"Divorced."

"Too bad."

Dylan maintained eye contact with her, not quite sure where she was headed. "Not really," he said. "Moira hated my being a cop. She just got tired of waiting for that phone call telling her I'd been shot in the line of duty. I couldn't... or wouldn't, give it up, so we split."

"Where's she now?"

"Still living in Portland. We've been able to maintain a friendship and we see each other a couple of times a month."

"So, there's a chance that you can get back together—you aren't on *the job* any longer."

"That's out of the question."

"Why?"

"She remarried and has a couple of young kids now. She's happy."

"But you still see each other."

"Yeah, we do." He replied.

"What's her husband think about that?"

"Douglas is okay with it."

"You're sure of that?"

"He and I are friends, we've known each other since we were kids. He's an M.D. now. What about you? No husband or significant other?"

"I'm between relationships right now."

Dylan picked up the plastic folder, opened it, and studied the bill.

"What's my share?" Shawna asked.

"I got this."

"Really, I don't mind."

"You can buy next time."

"Okay." She checked her watch. "It's just past eight, now what?"

"I haven't a clue. Do you think LaBelle may be home now?"

"I doubt it. Guys like him are nocturnal. There is one thing we could do."

"What's that?"

"He has a sister in Mattapan. We could check that out."

The server returned and Dylan slid his Amex card into the small pouch designed for it and handed the bill folder to her. She took it, smiled at each of them in turn, and said, "I'll be right back."

Cole and Tricroce walked into the foyer and saw someone standing against the left-hand wall. Due to the lack of light in the vestibule, Cole used a cigarette lighter to read the bank of mailboxes, seeking the one marked Cloutier. Tricroce watched the man closely until he heard Cole say, "Got it—3rd floor."

Tricroce wondered what the guy was doing hanging out in the entrance of an apartment house. The man said nothing and was dressed way too nice to be a homeless bum squatting in the foyer to get in out of the cold. When he heard Cole open the inner entrance door, he backed toward it. The man reached inside his coat and Tricroce tensed. The man took his hand out of his pocket and Tricroce reached for the revolver he wore under his open coat. When Tricroce saw that the man was holding a cell phone he relaxed and moved his hand away from the handle of his gun.

"Waiting for my wife to bring the car around," Deschaine said. "She should be here by now."

"Your wife is bringing the car around? How long it take you to train her?" Cole asked.

Deschaine grinned. "Twenty-five years."

"C'mon Gino," Cole said and Tricroce turned to follow him inside.

Once Cole and Tricroce were inside, Deschaine hit a speed dial, waited a second, and said, "They're coming up—two, both carrying." He hung up and dialed another number. "You and Maguire get over here. It's about to go down."

By the time he reached the third-floor landing, Cole was breathing hard. "He held up his hand and said, "Gimme a fuckin' minute—okay?" He drew in a deep breath and bent forward resting his hands on his knees.

"You should give up them cigars, boss."

The downstairs door opened and the stairs creaked as someone began climbing. Cole raised his head and in the artificial light, his face shined with sweat. "Go check it out, while I get my breath." He inhaled deeply. "Last thing we need is company."

Tricroce walked down the stairs. When he reached the second landing he almost bumped into the stranger from the foyer. "I thought you was waitin' for your wife." He realized that something wasn't right—then he saw the pistol in the stranger's right hand. Tricroce reached for his revolver but was not fast enough. The first bullet hit him in the chest and, as he tumbled forward, he fell into the path of the second, which tore his throat out and severed his spinal cord.

"Gino! You okay?" Cole called. Getting no response, he drew his weapon and looked around in panic. He saw the door to 3-A opening and fired a shot. The bullet hit the wall on the left side of the door, blowing out a chunk of wallboard. He knew he'd lost the element of surprise and looked around. He saw a rear fire exit and ran to it. He yanked the door open and ran inside, almost tumbling down the stairs. Cole ran down the stairwell, jumping three steps at a time to the bottom. He ripped open another door and felt the sudden blast of freezing air. He leaped out, doing a roll on the hard-frozen lawn, and came up onto one knee. A bullet snapped by his head and he saw a shadowy figure in the narrow opening between the apartment houses. He fired at it. He was rewarded by the dull thud of a bullet hitting home and the sudden cry of pain that followed.

Cole ran to the gap, jumping over the body of the man he'd just shot. The walk between the buildings was so narrow that at first, he thought he'd have to turn sideways; as it was, he held his hands at his sides as he raced to the street. He prayed that no one would appear in the exit from the passage. He'd never get his hand around to shoot—and he'd be the proverbial fish in a barrel.

Val turned the knob and a bullet slammed into the wall across from the door. He told Claudette, "You stay here while I check things out." He met Ricky Deschaine at the top of the stairs. "What happened?"

"They must a heard me come inside," Deschaine answered. "When I reached the landing for the second floor one of them was coming down. I shot him twice." He looked around. "You get the other one?"

They heard a shot from the backyard. "You take the back, I'll go to the front," Val said. He sprang down, jumping multiple stairs.

Cole felt like it was hours before he reached the front exit. When he ran out of the constricted opening, he stumbled over a small hedge, and landed on his face, slamming into the frozen ground. He scrambled to his feet and burst out into the street. He paused to get orientated and then ran for his truck, digging in his pocket for his keys as he ran. Finding the remote starter, Cole pressed the button and the motor turned over and came to life as he reached the door and, in a few seconds, he was in the truck. He placed the key into the ignition and drove out, sideswiping the car in front of him.

As they settled into her car, Shawna's phone rang. "This is O'Reilly." She listened for a few seconds and then said, "Thanks, Ed."

"What's up?"

"Shooting in Mattapan—at Cora Cloutier's building."

Dylan stared at her and he thought of little Sandy. It would devastate Caitlin and David if anything were to happen to her. "Let's get over there," he said.

"You read my mind."

Claudette dashed into the bedroom, grabbed her backpack, and Sandra. "What in hell happened?" her mother asked.

"I don't know—what I do know is that the cops will be here in minutes and I got to be gone when they do."

Cora didn't hesitate. She knew that her daughter was right. For her to be caught with a stolen child would get her life in Framingham. She gathered Sandra's clothes and began stuffing them into another backpack, ran into the living room, and almost ran over her Uncle Val. "I gotta get the fuck outta here," she said.

"We all do." He looked at Cora. "You gonna be alright?"

"I ain't done nothin'. I'll be fine, you two get the hell out of here."

"Where did I put my car keys?" Claudette asked.

"Fuck 'em, we ain't got time. Besides every cop in New England is lookin' for that truck."

Val led the way down the stairs and across the street to where his car was parked. He unlocked the door and urged his niece and the kid to get in. They pulled out and turned left at the end of the street. In his rear-view mirror Val saw the night light up with the flashing lights of the first cop car to swing onto the street they'd just left.

Dylan and Shawna arrived at the scene of the shootings twenty minutes after the fact. The building had been cordoned with yellow crime scene tape and a uniformed officer prevented them from entering until Shawna presented her badge. The officer stepped to the side and raised the tape.

There were several plainclothes officers standing at the entrance to the stairs that led to the upper floors. One of them looked up when they approached. "I thought you were on vacation, O'Reilly," he said.

"Hey, Brad, I'm helping a friend find his missing niece," she answered.

The officer she called Brad looked at Dylan and said, "Just be careful not to contaminate the crime scene."

Dylan offered his hand. When Brad gripped it, he said, "Not to worry. I used to be on the job. I know my way around a crime scene."

"Now that the introductions are over, what you got?" Shawna said.

"Two down, one on the second-floor landing and another in the back yard. No I. D. on the one inside, but the one out back was Michael Maguire. He's well known in Southie and his rap sheet reads like the script of a *Boondock Saints* movie."

"You have any idea what happened?" Dylan asked.

"We're still putting the pieces together, but Maguire hung with Ricky Deschaine's mob and Deschaine is…" He held up two fingers, which he'd crossed. "…this close to Val LaBelle—whose sister just happens to live on the third floor. Now ain't that a coincidence?"

"Can we see the John Doe?" Dylan asked.

"If the M. E.'s people are finished."

"There was a witness of sorts," Brad announced. "Guy was walking his dog. He said that a guy jumped into a white GMC pickup with Maine plates. He couldn't make out the number, said it was coated with mud and snow. Then he said about five minutes later a man and woman ran out of the building, got in a car and took off. From the description it was LaBelle."

"Did the witness say if the woman had a child with her?"

"Don't recall, but that's him over there talking to that uniform—go ask him yourselves."

Shawna thanked him and led Dylan to the witness. When they were close, she showed her badge to the officer and said, "We need to speak with this gentleman."

The officer stepped back, "By all means." He nodded to her and walked toward a police car that was idling by the curb.

"How are you, sir? I'm Detective O'Reilly and this Mr. Thomas. We'd like to ask you a few questions, if you don't mind."

"I don't know what I can tell you that I haven't already told the other officers."

"We're primarily interested in one thing… Mr.?" Dylan said.

"Bangs, Eddie Bangs. Okay, ask what you will."

"The man and woman who left in the car, did they by chance have a child with them?" Dylan asked.

Bangs seemed to be lost in thought for a few seconds. "Now that you bring it up, she was cradling something in her arms—it could have been a child." Suddenly Bangs shivered. "It's awfully cold out here, can I go home?"

"Unfortunately, that's up to the detective in charge, which I'm not," Shawna said.

Bangs nodded; his disappointment evident.

"I'll send him over," Shawna said. "Thank you for your help."

Bangs asked, "I'm not gonna have to go to court, am I? I don't want no trouble."

"That will be up to the district attorney. If you'll excuse us, we have to inspect the crime scene."

They left the cold witness, scaled the concrete steps, and reentered the foyer. The transition from outside to inside made Dylan realize just how cold it was. He pulled off his gloves, placed his curled fingers against his lips, and blew on them. "That is brutal out there."

Shawna didn't respond, instead she forged ahead stopping at the threshold of the stairs. Above her she saw the representative from the medical examiner's office. She held her badge up and called to them. "Excuse me. Can we see the vic before you bag him?"

One of the EMTs waved her up. "The crime scene techs are finished with him and so are we. Come on up. It's getting late and we'd like to put this guy in the chiller and go home."

"Won't take but a minute." She motioned for Dylan to follow her up.

Reaching the landing Dylan looked at the body. He didn't know the man's name but he'd seen him someplace before. On a hunch he took out his cell phone and took a close-up picture of the body's face.

"Hey, who're you?" the ambulance medic asked. He turned to Shawna, "He ain't supposed to be taking pictures… for all I know he's a reporter for the friggin' *GLOBE*."

"He's a detective too."

The EMT paused and then said, "Okay, you guys about done here?"

"Take him away," Shawna said.

"As they climbed the stairs Dylan said, "Shawna, don't go putting your job in jeopardy here."

"I'm not worried. I learned a long time ago that you got to treat those guys like children: answer their question and don't offer anything more. If they want more let them ask another question."

Dylan couldn't hold back a short laugh. "Do you have any idea how long it takes to teach a client that lesson? Many of them never learn and when they are cross-examined on the stand a good lawyer will blow them out of the water."

Brad stood at the top of the stairs. "What you got up here?" Shawna asked.

"One shot fired into the wall over there."

Dylan saw the hole in the wallboard beside the door to apartment 3-A. "Who lives there?" he asked.

"Cora Cloutier, Val LaBelle's older sister. She looks dumber than a rock, but is as sly and cunning as a wounded fox."

"How do you think it went down?" Shawna asked.

"Looks as if one of our perps shot at someone coming out of the Cloutier apartment..."

"Val?"

"Most likely."

"Any I. D. on the vic on the landing yet?" Shawna inquired.

"Nada, not even a driver license."

"Give me a few minutes," Dylan said, "and I may be able to put some light on that." He stepped away and accessed his contacts and sent a text: *Know this guy?* to Jean-Paul Thibodeau adding the picture of the dead man.

He heard Shawna say, "You think the second perp took the back exit?"

"Most likely. Whoever killed *John Doe*—"

"Your John Doe has a name and a rap sheet in Maine," Dylan said. "Gino Tricroce. He has a couple wants and warrants out for grand theft auto."

"What in hell is he doing in a gunfight in Mattapan?" Brad queried.

"Getting killed," Dylan answered, "among other things."

Val turned off Sullivan Boulevard onto Dorchester Avenue. The cold weather had driven most of the night people indoors and the streets were deserted with the possible exception of one or two hardy people taking their dogs out for the final time that day.

"We going to your place?" Claudette asked.

"That'll be the first place the police will look."

"Then where *are* we going?"

"Charlestown, I got some people there who'll put us up until it's safe to surface again."

Claudette lit a cigarette and cracked her window to allow the smoke to exit. "How long you figure that might be?"

"Depends on how soon I can learn who it is that wants you so bad."

"You might start looking at Vern Cole."

"That's twice you've mentioned this guy. Who's *Vern Cole*?"

As Claudette spoke, she stared out the window at the closed stores and open bars that lined the avenue. "Cole runs an auto theft business up in Maine. Felicien was working for him when I took off. I would imagine that Cole thinks I know too much about his business for him to allow me to run loose."

"Do you?"

"No, all I know is that Felicien and some guy named Gino took a stolen car to Lewiston and turned it over to some people who bought it from Cole. I've never been to Cole's place or met any of his people." She finished the cigarette and pushed it out of the window. "He's probably toast anyway. If the police get their hands on Felicien he'll roll over the first time they threaten him with jail."

"Not too reliable, is he?"

"Felicien and reliable don't belong in the same sentence."

"So, either way this guy Cole is fucked?"

"He ain't got anything to worry about from me."

They drove in silence until Val passed City Square. "You thought about how you're gonna deal with her?" Val nodded at Sandra who was nestled against Claudette and sound asleep.

"I'm workin' on that, I need money, and I need it fast."

"Well, if you're planning on moving her you better do it soon… as long as you got her the cops will never stop looking."

Sunday: Day Nine

THE MORNING SUN WAS BRIGHT and the temperature in the mid-twenties. Since before dawn, Dylan and Shawna had been sitting down the block watching Val LaBelle's Dorchester home, a relatively new duplex. The streets were deserted with the exception of a large Roman Catholic Church which apparently held mass every hour of the morning.

Dylan took a bite from the doughnut he was eating and then a sip from the take-out cup of coffee. "Good coffee," he said. "I always preferred Dunkin' Donuts over Starbucks."

"It's the unofficial state restaurant. The first one was opened just a few miles from here, in Quincy."

"Hmm, I didn't know that."

"It was originally called the Open Kettle opened in 1948. In 1950, the owner, William Rosenberg, changed the name to Dunkin' Donuts and the rest is history."

"You know a lot about it."

"There are three industrial giants in and around Boston, Rosenberg, Ken Olsen, one of the founders of DEC, and An Wang, founder of Wang Laboratories."

"Deck?"

"It's what we commonly called Digital Equipment Corporation. What's truly amazing is of the three only D and D is still around."

"Well, more people drink coffee than own computers."

"I don't know about that. What it did prove is that if you don't change with the times you'll die. Wang and DEC didn't get into the PC market fast enough. Wang disappeared and DEC was bought by COMPAQ, a PC company that was later bought by Hewlett-Packard."

Dylan absorbed the history lesson on the demise of the big computer giants of the 1970s and 1980s for a few seconds. He nodded toward LaBelle's house and asked, "You think he's in there?"

"If he is, he's a fool. He should know this will be the first place we'll look for him. It wouldn't surprise me if Brad or one of the other detectives on the case was here within two hours of the crime."

"So, why are we sitting here, burning gas, and drinking coffee?"

"Because you never know," Shawna said. "It's been my experience that career criminals aren't all that smart. However, like doctors, they don't hesitate to bury their mistakes."

"You think Val was burying his mistakes last night?"

"No. I think Val was at his sister's place when this Tricroce guy and his accomplice came calling. Someone else killed the two punks. I think Ricky Deschaine took out Tricroce and Tricroce's partner took off down the back stairs and Maguire got in his way, so he shot him."

"Then Val grabbed his niece and took off."

"That's about it. Now it looks like Val and the girl have gone underground and we'll play hell trying to find them."

Val walked into the living room where Claudette was watching a morning news show and the kid was playing with a doll. He watched the girl for a few seconds and then nodded for Claudette to join him in the kitchen.

"You made up your mind yet?"

"I been thinkin' over what you said last night—about the cops not giving up while I got her… I guess I got to get her off my hands as soon as possible." She had been looking at the floor while she spoke to her uncle, suddenly her head came up. "But I don't want to sell her so quick that I got no bargaining power."

"The thought of reducing the price never crossed my mind. I got a lawyer friend who handles stuff like this. He has a list of rich clients looking to adopt kids—nice little *white* kids. Going through the system takes time and money. These people got lots of cash so that ain't an issue. But the time and the fact that there ain't many like her available through the system are an issue."

"You wouldn't shit me about this would you, Val?"

"No. You'll get a pretty nice paycheck out of this no matter how fast we make the deal."

"Okay, call him."

Vern Cole sat on the edge of the bed in his hotel room. The TV was tuned to the New England News Network and the commentator was doing an editorial rant on the increase in Boston crime. He ran down the facts of the fuck-up in Mattapan and shook his head when they identified Gino as one of the two men shot to death. "Shit," he muttered to himself, "how in hell did they learn who he was so friggin' fast?" He debated his next step. Should he keep hunting for the woman and kid or just cut and run home?

He realized that if he was going to continue hunting, he needed help. He picked his cell phone off the end table and dialed a Portland number.

Val LaBelle sat on the couch across from Wilson Pettigrew. The lawyer wasn't happy. "You know I don't like you coming to my home, Val."

"Tough shit, Wilson. I got a business proposition for you… one that couldn't wait for tomorrow."

Pettigrew leaned back in his expensive leather easy chair. "What sort of business?"

"Female, cute little thing, three years old, smart as a whip, and available right now." He accessed his mobile phone and showed Pettigrew a photo he'd taken of Sandra that morning. "That's the merchandise."

Pettigrew looked at the photo, liked what he saw, and quickly ran some numbers through his head. Each time he did a mental calculation the sums came up large, very large. He didn't let on to Val what an expensive commodity the child was so he tried his best to look nonchalant and only slightly interested when he said, "You got my interest."

"There's a hitch."

"There always is. What is it?"

"The kid's hot. They're looking for her from Maine to who knows where."

"I may have a client—one who's from out of state—a long way out of state."

"She's gonna cost you more than the usual—a lot more. The party who has her will need to go underground for a long time… and we both know how much that costs."

Cole walked into the gigantic mall at the junction of routes 3 and I-95 (or 128 as the locals still referred to it). He glanced around the tables in the food court and saw Greg Frost and Tim Sanger sitting in front of a pizza place. He walked over and sat beside Sanger and across from Frost. "You boys made good time," Cole said.

"Not really," Sanger commented, "Portland to Boston ain't that far. So, what's this job you got for us?"

"I need you to find someone."

"You gonna be a little more specific? Boston ain't Jackman you know."

"I'm looking for a woman and a kid."

"A kid?" Frost said. "I ain't poppin' no kid."

"I could give a shit less what happens to the kid, it's the broad that can put me in Warren for twenty-five to life."

"Okay, you got some place for us to start?"

"Cora Cloutier…" He gave them the address in Mattapan.

"Why ain't you usin' Gino for this? He grew up near here and knows his way around better than either of us." Sanger asked.

"Gino's gone."

"Gone? What kind of *gone*—he quit you or get whacked or something?" Frost inquired.

"He was killed last night."

Sanger looked at his partner and then said, "Vern, I got this funny fucking feeling that you ain't told us everything."

"The Cloutier woman, Cora, she has this brother…"

Val entered the apartment. "Where's the kid?"

Claudette sat on the couch, thumbing through a magazine, and ignoring the talk show on the TV. "Sleeping—I put her down for a nap."

Val walked into the kitchen, opened the refrigerator, and took out a beer. He walked back to the living room and stood at the threshold. He popped the beer can open and said, "It's all arranged."

Claudette tossed the magazine aside and asked, "How much you get?"

Val saw the same look of avarice he was used to seeing on Cora's face and was surprised. Never before had he seen this side of Claudette. On the spur of the moment he came to a decision on the question he'd been chewing on since leaving Pettigrew's office—*should he give her the full seventy-five grand he'd negotiated or only a portion?* He sat across from her and kicked up the recliner's foot-rest. "I got him to agree to twenty-five grand."

"That's all?"

"Hey it's sort of like robbing a bank. Say your share of the take was ten grand—a fence will only give you pennies on a dollar. If you're lucky you'd get three or four grand. This deal is like that. My contact is taking all the risk. He's paying you up front and taking it on faith that his customer will make it worth his while."

"I understand all that, but twenty-five won't go far."

"Claudette, you either take it or you leave it and risk getting caught with her. This guy will make her disappear and that'll be the end of it."

"I suppose. When do we get our money and give her to him?"

"I'll call him and tell him it's a deal and make the arrangements."

Cora Cloutier answered her door, thinking it was the repairman the landlord had hired to fix the hole in the wall. When she opened the door instead of a repairman, she was confronted by two men. One was over six feet tall, sandy haired, sported a mustache, and had the square jaw some women found attractive. He was dressed in a heavy black leather jacket, tan Dockers, and a pair of the low-cut boots L.L.Bean sold; the black jacket accented his pale blue eyes.

The other man was five or six inches shorter than his companion, clean shaven, and his black hair curling from under a dirty Red Sox cap. He dressed like one of the poachers depicted in *Northwoods Law*. He wore a padded vest over a plaid flannel shirt, blue jeans, and work boots.

Cora remembered that it was Sunday and it would have been almost impossible to find a repairman willing to work on the Sabbath.

"Mrs. Cloutier?" the good looking one asked.

"Yes."

"We're trying to locate your brother and wondered if you could help us out."

The red neck was looking around the hall and seemed to be checking to ensure there were no witnesses about. "I ain't heard from him…"

When she tried to close the door, the good-looker placed his foot against it. “Maybe,” he said in a low, sinister voice, “we could come in?” He forced the door inward driving Cora back into the room.

Once inside good looking said, “Tim, check out the place. Mrs. Cloutier and I are going to have a talk.”

“We’ve been here six hours now with no sign of life,” Dylan said. “What’s next?”

“We check out some of his haunts.”

“You know where he hangs out?”

“We’ve had our eyes on LaBelle and his sister for a long time. Over the years we’ve learned a lot about Valiant, aka Val, LaBelle including where and who he likes to hang out with.”

“Okay, you’re the driver,” Dylan said.

“First stop, Somerville.”

“What’s in Somerville?”

“Winter Hill, home of the now defunct Winter Hill Gang.”

“Bulger’s bunch.”

“At the end, yes.”

Shawna took Broadway to Mystic Avenue and followed it until it passed under I-93. She parked in front of a neighborhood tavern.

“What’s this place?” Dylan asked.

“One of Val’s favorite watering holes.” She opened the car door and when Dylan reached for the handle on his, she said, “Do me a favor and sit this one out. I got a snitch that hangs here.”

“Sure, just leave the heater running, this damp cold sinks into your bones.”

Shawna disappeared and Dylan absentmindedly watched traffic racing out of Boston like the interstate was a NASCAR track. He wondered: *Why in hell do they even bother with speed limits around here?* His reverie was interrupted when Shawna jumped into the car.

"You're right," she said, "it's colder than a well-digger's ass."

"Any luck?"

"Val hasn't been in for a while. Rumor is that he's holed up over in Charlestown."

She put the car into drive and made a U-turn on Mystic. She followed Broadway until she reached Sullivan Square and then entered Charlestown on Rutherford Avenue. "There's another place near Bunker Hill where Val hangs. If he's gone to ground over here, we may never find him."

"Why's that?"

"You hang around Boston long enough you'll learn that the life expectancy of a cop in Charlestown isn't very long. The Townies, the real ones, not the affluent ones who live on this side of town, would rather die than be seen talking to a cop."

"What's on the other side of town?"

"The Mystic Piers, between here and there is where most of the thugs who were responsible for the epidemic of armored car robberies from 1990 to 1996 live. During those years, Boston averaged sixteen armored car heists per year and one in five of them took place here in Charlestown. It was so bad the FBI brought in a special team to investigate them."

"Interesting. What finally brought an end to it?"

"Beginning in 1991, the DEA targeted the community and spent at least $2 million in just one case to provide thieves and drug dealers immunity from prosecution and new identities with the witness protection program. As a result, the Code of Silence that protected them crumbled and by 1997, the number of armored car robberies had dwindled to two."

Shawna left the wide boulevard and entered a series of streets so narrow that Dylan braced himself for the inevitable sideswipe. "Right now," he said, "I'm damned glad you're driving."

Shawna laughed and stopped beside a small tavern. "Here we are." She got out and leaned her head inside the car. "You coming?"

"Sure." Dylan squeezed out of the door thankful that he wasn't an inch thicker. He looked up and down the street. Her car made it impossible for anyone else to pass through. "You going to leave it here?"

"If we tried to find a parking spot on a Sunday, we'd be driving for hours and still wouldn't find one. Once the Townies have a spot they don't move until they have to go to work on Monday morning. Even then they take the *T* if they can."

She slammed her door and walked into the bar. It was just past noon and the place was already packed. As soon as the door closed behind them all conversation ceased. A voice from the back called out *"Five-oh is here!"* Shawna ignored the air of hostility that permeated the bar and walked to an open stool at one end of the bar. She slid onto the seat and Dylan stood at her side.

The barman ignored them for several long moments. After few minutes, he realized that the cold shoulder treatment was not going to drive them away and slowly made his way in their direction, checking with each customer between him and them. On three occasions he served refills; then he was in front of Shawna.

"What you havin'?"

"I'll have a Sam," Shawna said.

"Same for me," Dylan said when the bartender looked at him.

"Bottle or tap?"

"Tap," Shawna and Dylan said in unison.

In minutes the bartender was back and scooped the ten-dollar bill Shawna had placed on the bar. "Val been in?" she asked.

"Who?"

"Val LaBelle, I was told he comes in here a lot."

The bartender flexed his mouth, shrugged his shoulders, and said, "Never heard of the guy." He turned and shouted over the crowd and hollered, "Anyone know a Val LaBelle?"

No response. The bartender turned back to Shawna and Dylan. "Whoever told you this *Val* fellow hangs out here was blowing smoke up your ass." He walked to the register, rang up their beers, and returned with two dollars change. He placed the money on the bar and left them.

Shawna took a sip from her beer, then slid off the stool. "I'm finished, how about you?"

Dylan was surprised and his face showed it. Never before in his life had he walked out of a bar leaving a four-dollar beer on the bar. He took a swallow and said, "Sure."

Once back in the car, Dylan asked, "What did we learn in there?"

"Nothing much... yet. Hey, you ever seen the U.S.S. *Constitution*? It's just down at the bottom of the hill."

She drove down the steep hill and into a parking lot along the waterfront.

Dylan looked at all of the empty spots and said, "You would think the *Townies* as you call them would use these."

"The cold is keeping the tourists away today. The ship may even be closed, I don't think they heat it. During the summer if you leave a car here for more than a couple of hours, they'll tow it."

There was a knock on the window behind Dylan and he started with surprise.

Shawna acted as if she had been expecting the intruder. She unlocked the door and a skinny man who smelled of cigarette smoke slid in. "Damn," he said, "it's cold enough to freeze the balls off a brass monkey."

Shawna opened her purse and took out two twenty-dollar bills which she handed over her shoulder. In seconds they were in the pocket of the snitch. "What you got for me, Louie?"

"I seen Val LaBelle last night."

"Where?" she asked.

"He was picking up take-out pizza at a joint down near Main Street and Austin."

"You got any idea where he's staying?" she queried.

"No, but I'd bet it ain't too far from the pizza joint. He was walkin' an' this weather ain't exactly spring-like."

"Okay, keep your ear to the ground. If you find out where he's staying there'll be something in it for you."

Dylan felt a blast of cold air when the back door opened and then slammed. He looked back and Louie was shuffling across the street.

"Well," Shawna said, "we got it narrowed down a bit."

Dylan looked out the rear window and saw houses crammed beside one another as far as he could see but no sign of the snitch. "We do?"

Cora Cloutier was slumped in a kitchen chair, her hands secured to the wooden arm with plastic tie-wraps, and her hair hanging down, obscuring her face. Blood dripped from her broken nose onto her lap. Greg Frost sat across from her smoking a cigarette. "Tell me where to find your brother and daughter and this will end," he said in a controlled voice. "I don't know why you're holding out because sooner or later, everyone talks." He ground out the cigarette in an overflowing ashtray and then reached out and hooked Cora's chin with the side of his crooked index finger and lifted her face so that it was even with his.

She opened her eyes and peered through the left (the right was swollen closed). Her lips were split open and she spit blood at him. He slapped her and bolted from his chair. Frost walked into the living room where Sanger was watching a cable news channel. "You getting anywhere with the old bitch?" Sanger asked when he saw Frost.

"I don't think she knows shit."

"Well, work on her for a while longer. Who knows? She may know more than even she knows she knows. Like you told her *everyone talks*."

Frost turned toward the kitchen, took a couple steps, and stopped when there was a knock on the door. Frost peered through the spy hole and saw a pizza delivery man standing in front of the door. "It's a fuckin' pizza delivery."

Sanger shrugged. "I didn't order it. Take the fucking thing, so long as it ain't one of those goddamned pineapple and ham things, I'm hungry, but not that hungry."

Frost opened the door. The fool stood there holding the pizza in one hand and the other behind his back. "Who the fuck are you?" he asked.

"I'm the pizza deliveryman." He shoved the pizza box into Frost's chest and when he exposed the hand that was behind his back it held a nine-millimeter H&K VP-9 with a sound suppressor. He pulled the trigger twice. There were two muffled pops and Frost staggered back.

The deliveryman pushed his way through the door and Frost fell on his back.

Sanger jumped to his feet and said, "What the fuck…" The VP-9 popped two more times, one bullet hitting him in the right shoulder, making it impossible for him to reach his gun, and the second smashing his right kneecap. He dropped to the floor, grabbed his shattered knee, and cried out, "Sonuvawhore…"

The deliveryman squatted over him and said, "I'm Val LaBelle. I'm told you boys are looking for me." He shot Sanger in the other knee and then removed the handgun from his pocket. Val studied the gun for a few seconds and then said, "Nice piece, I think I'll keep it."

Sanger moaned in pain, ground his teeth, and rocked from side-to-side. Val smiled at him. "I believe I just heard you say: 'Everyone talks'? Well, you just remember that. I got to check on my sister, I won't be long. Then we'll talk."

Val closed the apartment door and walked to the kitchen saw Cora strapped to a kitchen chair. He took a pair of shears from the counter and cut the tie-wraps. She tumbled forward and he caught her. "I got you, sis." He eased her back in the chair and then walked into the bathroom. In a couple of minutes, he returned with a moist washcloth and began gently dabbing at her wounds.

"How'd you know to come?" Cora asked.

"Lisa across the hall called said she saw two men force their way into your apartment."

"Lisa? She has your number?"

"Of course, someone has to be able to reach me if you have a problem." He handed her the cold compress and said, "Here, take this. I got some cleaning up to do."

Val returned to the living room. He stood over the first hood and stepped on his chest. A low moan came out of the man's mouth, but no intake of breath. "Must be dead." He turned to the second thug and pointed to the body beside him. "You agree with me—he's fuckin' dead?" The wounded man didn't reply. "I guess you do."

He squatted beside the wounded man looked at his wounds and said, "You won't die from those wounds. Still you ain't gonna run no marathons ever again." He used the butt of the pistol to tap the thug on one of his shattered knees. When the man screamed, Val smiled. "You know this little talk will go a lot better if I knew your name."

Val rolled the wounded hoodlum over and took out his wallet. He flipped through until he found the guy's driver license. He held it up and read it: "Timothy Sanger… that your name? That's one big mouthful, I think I'll call you Tim."

He hit Sanger on a knee again. "Who sent you after me and my family, Tim?"

No response from Sanger.

Val put his hand on Tim's damaged shoulder and pushed on it. "C'mon Tim be smart, you and I both know that you'll talk eventually."

Val stood up. "You know Tim if there's one fucking thing I hate, it's bullies who pick on women and kids." He bent over and ripped Sanger's vest and shirt open. He looked at the shoulder wound. "Man, that looks bad. I'll bet there's all sorts of damage to tendons, bones, and shit like that." He rose to his feet, reached over to an end table, took a cigarette from the pack that was always there, and lit it. "I'd better cauterize that so it won't get infected."

When Val touched the cigarette to the open wound, Sanger yelled out, "Vern Cole… Vern Cole sent us."

"Now we're making progress. *Why* did this Vern send you after my sister?"

"He didn't."

Once again, Val touched the cigarette to the bullet hole.

"Wasn't your sister… your niece. He wanted us to whack her. For Christ's sake, man that's all I know."

"Everything? How about tellin' me where I can find this asshole."

"I don't know. All we had is his phone number. He met us at a mall. That's all I know... I swear."

Val stood up. "For some reason I think you're telling me the truth." He shot Sanger through the heart. He put the pistol away and called Ricky Deschaine. "I need some help man. I need someone to clean my sister's apartment and dispose of a couple pieces of garbage."

"We're on it, anything else?"

"You know a doctor who'll see Cora today and not ask a bunch of questions?"

"I know one or two. You want I should set something up?"

"Yeah, man, call me on my cell."

Val took time to search the two hit men; he removed all of their identification, as well as their mobile phones. He checked the contacts on Sanger's phone and hit pay-dirt. Listed under the *C*s was one Vernon Cole.

Cole paced back and forth in his hotel room. It was past the time when he had expected Frost and Sanger to update him on what they'd accomplished. He walked into the bathroom and took a cold beer out of the ice with which he'd filled the small sink. He popped the top and took a drink.

The phone rang and, in his haste, to answer it, Cole almost dropped the beer. He glanced at the smartphone's display and saw Frost's name. "It's about time. What the fuck's going on?"

"Hey, Vern, cool it..."

The voice was unfamiliar. "Who is this?"

"Val LaBelle. I want to talk to you about the way you and your people been treating my sister and her daughter."

"How'd you get Frost's phone?"

"Right now, that's the least of your troubles, besides he ain't gonna need it again—ever. On the other hand, *you* do have a problem."

Cole felt sweat beading on his forehead and grabbed a towel off the rack and wiped at it. He tried to sound like the call had no effect on him. "What might my problem be?"

"C'mon, Vern, you been chasing my niece across three states and your goons have assaulted my sister, what the fuck you think your problem is?"

"Give me a clue."

"You'll get a clue when I cram a nine-millimeter up your ass. I'm coming for you. You won't be able to run far enough or fast enough to get away from me. I'll be in touch."

The phone went dead and Vernon Cole's legs lost their strength. He sank down until he was seated on the toilet. He stared at the screen of the iPhone and inhaled deeply. He got off the commode, staggered into the sleeping area, and started cramming his belongings into his luggage. If he was going to go head-to-head with a psycho, he was going to do it on his own turf.

Dylan pressed the disconnect icon on his smart-phone and looked across the table at Shawna. "Sorry about that," he said.

"Problems?"

"My sister, Caitlin, she and her husband are going crazy with worry."

"That's understandable."

Dylan stared out at the East Dorchester neighborhood. The street lights illuminated the inside of Shawna's car like slow, low-intensity strobe lights. "This part of Dorchester seems more upscale than the other side."

"East Dorchester has started to make a revival of late. On the other hand, North Dorchester is still one of the more depressed neighborhoods in Boston."

"Ironic, isn't it?"

"What?"

"As soon as criminals steal or embezzle enough money, they move out of the neighborhood on which they prey. It's good enough for someone else's kids, but not theirs."

"Isn't that the American dream? To move up and do better than your parents."

Dylan turned away from the window and looked at her. "That doesn't sound like the answer I'd expect from a member of a big city police department."

"Dylan, you've been there, people will go to drastic ends to escape a bad childhood."

"You may be right. There are, however, ways other than crime to do it."

"Agreed. You and I know that, but a bunch of others don't and if you try to tell them they can use legitimate methods to leave shithole backgrounds, they won't believe you. It's not a paradigm they've grown up with. It'd be easier to convince them they have a one hundred percent chance of owning the only ticket on a one-billion-dollar lottery pool."

"I will agree that it isn't easy, nevertheless didn't you say that you and Jean-Paul grew up in the Riverton area of Portland?"

"I did."

"That's the toughest area of Portland—you guys got out."

"We did. I moved in with my aunt and uncle in Webster, Massachusetts and Jean-Paul joined the army. My uncle was a cop and he got me interested in law enforcement and then got me enrolled in a C. J. undergrad curriculum at Worcester State University.

"The army made Jean-Paul a military policeman, later CID."

"Still," Dylan countered, "you did it anyone can."

He noticed that her attitude changed and she was becoming angry. "The last thing I'm going to say is this: Yes, Jean-Paul and I did. We did it because we lucked out, I had a strong uncle and aunt who took me in and mentored me, told me that I could do it. Believe me it took many late-night talks with my uncle before I became convinced.

"In the army, Jean-Paul learned that he was capable of doing anything he set his mind to. Many inner-city kids don't have that advantage. By the time most of them are sixteen they've dropped out of school or already have a rap sheet—either of which eliminates them from joining the military."

They drove in silence for several minutes; each was lost in their own thoughts. Shawna finally broke the silence. "Did your sister happen to say whether or not anyone has contacted her about ransom?"

"No."

"What about the feds, anyone contacted them?"

"I'm certain that if the local authorities haven't then Jean-Paul has by now."

"Has the FBI contacted you?"

"No. They haven't. I've been so busy chasing these people that I didn't even think about that."

"Dylan, we have to get them involved. The absence of a ransom request is disturbing. It has me wondering..."

He knew where she was headed. He'd had similar thoughts, but didn't want to accept the inevitability. "Are you talking white slavery?"

"Well, a form of it. If she was fourteen and not three, I'd really be concerned."

"What other form of it is there?"

"There's a thriving black market for white kids."

"Are you saying that Sandra might be sold?"

"I am."

"Who'd buy a kid? Hell, she's not much older than a toddler."

"It can take years to get a white child through an adoption agency. There are places where one can be ordered. There is a bright side to it."

Dylan stared at her. He was incredulous. "I don't believe you said that."

"The going rate for a child like your niece is mid-six to low seven figures. No one will lay out that kind of cash and then abuse the child."

"You're one hundred percent sure of that?"

She didn't answer, but the look on her face told him that she was not one hundred percent sure.

Val sat on the opposite end of the couch from Claudette. "I'll call Pettigrew in the morning. It'll take him a few days to get everything set up."

"You tell him that I want cash money, no checks unless he wants to wait until it clears to get the kid."

Val noticed that she had started talking about the child as if all she represented was the biggest payday she'd ever had—come to think of it he'd never had one this large either. Claudette was starting to wear on him; all he wanted was to put this behind him and get rid of her. He'd told her that her mother had been roughed up, but he'd got there in time and got her into the emergency room in time to save her. Claudette shrugged and had not asked about her. Val's attitude had changed from her being his favorite niece to one of *fuck her*.

He stood up and gave her a disapproving look that she didn't see; her attention was locked onto some stupid goddamned sitcom. He held back the derogatory comment he wanted to make about the intellectual level of anyone who'd watch such total bullshit.

He looked at the clock and said, "I'm gonna call it a night."

Claudette raised a hand, her eyes never leaving the television screen.

"Don't be smoking in here. My friend who owns this place don't smoke. You need to step outside."

She dismissed him with a flapping wave of her hand.

Vern Cole crossed the Mystic River on the Tobin Bridge and followed route U. S. 1 toward Wakefield. The traffic was light at this time of the night and it was an easy run to I-95 north. He crossed into New Hampshire and shortly after midnight he passed over the Piscataqua River Bridge and entered Maine.

When he passed exit 1, he sighed it was two hours at most to home. He had an epiphany as he approached the toll booth in York.

If the cops had Paradis in custody, he'd probably been exposed; if for no other reason than the fact that if Paradis had been arrested it had happened while he was driving one Cole's trucks. He punched the steering wheel with the side of his right fist. *Fifteen years I've operated my business without the cops having so much as a hint—then I got involved with two fuckin' child stealers. What was wrong with my fuckin' head?*

Monday: Day Ten

FELICIEN PARADIS PARKED THE WHITE Silverado in the Government Center Parking Garage. He turned off the motor, left the key in the ignition, and tossed the parking ticket on the dashboard, secure in the knowledge that the truck would probably be gone within the hour. He walked away, looking for a car to boost. He sought a particular type of car… one he would buy to use for hunting deer out of season, an old piece of shit that would be no loss if he totaled it hitting a deer crossing a road. For a few moments, he considered getting the Chevy's keys and leaving them for whoever owned the car he stole. He realized there was no way they would ever get them because the parking spot he left would not be vacant for long.

One level below he found exactly what he sought; a rusted out fifteen-year-old Oldsmobile. In no time he jimmied the lock and had the motor running. He departed the garage busting through the barrier and racing away. Now all he had to do was find out where the bitch's mother lived.

Claudette walked out of the apartment building, holding Sandra's hand. Sandra was crying and pleading, "I want to go home."

Claudette stopped, released the child's hand, crouched down, and pointed a menacing finger in the child's face. "I told you that I can't take you there. There are bad men looking for us and if they find us, they'll hurt us."

"I don't care. I want my Mommy." Sandra's cheeks were red from the freezing air and her tears shined as they flowed down them.

"Stop bawling. You'll be safe if you go with the nice people Uncle Val found."

Sandra's eyes narrowed and her face twisted into a defiant look when she said, "I don't like Uncle Val."

Claudette inhaled with exasperation. "Stop asking so many questions—and stop your goddamned crying. Do you want the nice people to think you don't want to go with them?"

Sandra clenched her hands into tiny fists and stamped her feet when she said, "I don't want to go with them… I *want* to go home."

"One more word out of your mouth and you'll regret it."

Claudette stood up, grabbed Sandra's hand, and dragged the recalcitrant girl to Val's car. She opened the back door, picked the child up, threw her into the back seat, and slammed the door shut.

When she was settled in the front seat, Val gave her a hard look. "The kid gonna cause problems?"

Claudette looked over her shoulder at the small girl, who sat still, staring at her feet, which barely passed the edge of her seat. "She won't be no trouble." She looked at Sandra and added, "Ain't that right?"

Sandra sniffed and wiped her nose with her right hand. She looked hopeless and scared when she looked at Claudette. "I'll be good."

Claudette turned around and said, "I told Felicien that she was too goddamned old. We should have waited and found one under one."

"Well," Val said, "she's what we got, so we'll make the best of it."

"I suppose but if she fucks this up for us, I'm gonna kill her."

Val knew that she didn't mean it figuratively and shrugged. "Well, we ain't got time to fuck around. Pettigrew is expecting us at ten and it's past eight now."

Shawna and Dylan parked in the public parking lot adjacent to North Market Building. Dylan looked at the foot traffic in and around Faneuil Hall Square. "How we gonna find this guy here?"

"He'll find us. All we got to do is grab some coffee and find a place to sit."

They left the cold and entered Quincy Market. Dylan was immediately assaulted by the scent of brewed coffee and the cornucopia of food stands that made up the market. He saw vendors selling everything from fresh bread and pastries to pizza and seafood. They bought two coffees and Shawna led him to the center of the building to an area of tables and stools. There were no empty spots so they stood in the main corridor, sipping on their hot drinks while they waited for a table to become available. After five minutes a couple of businessmen vacated one and Dylan and Shawna swooped in like two gulls diving for fish.

Once they were settled Shawna said, "Now we wait."

"How's this guy supposed to help us?"

"He's undercover, working the white slavery rackets."

"Now there's a shitty job if I ever heard of one. I thought drug dealers were scum, but white slavers—they ought to be shot on sight."

Shawna waved at someone and then said, "Here's our guy."

A man wearing an expensive suit approached. He was a little over six feet tall with dark hair that he combed straight back, clean shaven, and his shoes were shined to a gloss high enough to use as mirrors. He looked like anything but an undercover cop, a financial broker came to mind.

"He looks like a frigging bank executive," Dylan commented.

"We're talking about people who deal with some high rollers True white-collar types—not all white slaves are sold into the sex trades."

The undercover operative waved back and walked to their table. Shawna stood and shook his hand. "I'm glad you could make it, Alex."

Alex shook her hand and appeared to be suspicious when he

looked at Dylan. Shawna picked up on his reluctance to join them. "Alex," she said, "this is Dylan Thomas. He's a lawyer and investigator from Maine. He's the guy I told you about."

Alex seemed to relax and slid onto the empty stool beside Shawna. He held his hand out toward Dylan and said, "Dylan Thomas... like the poet?"

"My mother was an English teacher and a big fan of his." Dylan grabbed the offered hand and shook it.

"Alex Gold, glad to meet you."

"That your cover name or your real one?"

"Cover."

Dylan nodded his head and said, "Alex will do for me."

Shawna took over the meet. "Now that social hour is over, let's get down to business."

"That's why we're here," Gold said, "and the sooner we conclude it, the better."

"Dylan is looking for his niece. She was snatched in Maine ten days ago."

"Hell, she could be working a club in Tijuana by now."

"I think not," Dylan said, "she's only three years old."

Gold stared at Dylan. "Don't be so damned sure. These people worship one thing—money. They'll do some pretty fucked up things to get it, too. What makes you think she's in Boston?"

"She was last seen with a woman known as Claudette Beaupre," Dylan said. "I've tracked her here."

Alex looked at Shawna, but said nothing.

"We do know that Claudette Beaupre is connected to Val LaBelle, possibly related to him."

"I'd like to get my hands on that one," Gold said. "We know that he's into the business of selling kids and that he's as dangerous as a cornered cobra."

"We've seen proof of the dangerous part," Dylan said. "I'll defer to Shawna."

Gold looked at her. "Let me guess, the shootings in Mattapan?"

"Yes, Val's sister lives in the building."

"If LaBelle is involved then he'll be working through a broker." He turned to Dylan. "Do you have a picture of the child?"

Dylan took out his wallet, removed a photo, and handed it to Gold.

Gold studied the picture for a few seconds. "She's three you said?"

Dylan nodded and took the picture when Gold offered it back.

"A white girl with blond hair will attract a lot of money."

"She's sandy brown, not blond," Dylan said.

"She's close enough. I'm thinking Wilson Pettigrew."

Shawna said, "Shit."

Dylan looked at each of them in turn. "Shit? You know who this guy is?"

"I've been trying to get a link to him and white slavery for two years." Shawna said. "I know the bastard is a big, big broker, but proving it is impossible."

"Why's that?" Dylan asked.

"Connections, for one thing," Shawna replied. "He's covered his ass three ways to Sunday. Rarely, if ever, does he deal directly with the kidnappers. We know he's got people in both the city and state governments. What we don't know is who they are."

"If Pettigrew's in this," Gold said, "you better move fast, because you better believe that he will."

Shawna and Dylan entered the lobby of the building which contained the law offices of Wilson Pettigrew. They walked to the bank of elevators and Shawna said, "Someone's been having some big paydays."

"How so?" Dylan asked.

"This elevator is dedicated to a single floor—which just happens to be the floor completely occupied by Pettigrew's offices."

"Good point. Your own personal elevator must cost a lot of bucks."

Shawna pressed the button to summon the lift and stepped back.

She looked up at the digital indicator and saw that it was coming down.

The bell sounded and the door opened. A man dressed in a Georgio Armani suit that Dylan believed had to cost $2,000.00 stood in the lift. He had an equally expensive overcoat draped over his right arm and carried a beautiful leather briefcase in his left hand. When he walked out of the door, Dylan stepped forward, but Shawna held him back.

"Mr. Pettigrew?" she said to the dapper man.

"Yes."

"Could we have a few minutes of your time?"

"I'm on my way to an important meeting, if you call my secretary, she'll gladly set up an appointment."

Shawna reached inside her coat and brought out her badge. She held it in front of the lawyer and said, "This is too important to wait. I'm sure whoever you're meeting with will understand."

Pettigrew sighed and glanced at his Rolex. "I can spare ten minutes, no more."

"It might be best if we could talk someplace a bit less public," she said.

Pettigrew said, "Follow me," his body language and voice advertised his exasperation. He walked to the front desk where an elderly security guard sat behind a desk. "Is the conference room available?"

The guard took a ledger-style book from the drawer at his left and opened it. He flipped through the pages until he came to the page he sought. "Yes, sir."

"I'd like to use it for ten minutes."

"That shouldn't be a problem, Mr. Pettigrew." He pressed a button and the sound of an electronic lock opening came from the door behind his desk. The security officer smiled and said, "How you been Shawna?"

"Terrific, Roger, how's your wife and grandchildren?"

"Doing great."

Pettigrew cleared his throat, a definite sign that he didn't appreciate the small talk. He circled the desk, opened the door and walked inside without waiting for his visitors.

When Shawna and Dylan walked in, he said, "I wondered how you got past security. How do you two know one another?"

"When I was a rookie patrol officer," Shawna said, "Roger was my training officer."

Pettigrew nodded once and dropped into the chair nearest him and Dylan and Shawna seated themselves across from him.

"How can I help you, officers?"

"Detective," Shawna corrected him.

"Okay, how can I help you, Detectives?"

Shawna took the lead. "Do you know Valiant LaBelle?"

Dylan studied Pettigrew closely; if he was taken by surprise, he was good. He gave not a single indication that Shawna had thrown him a high and tight fastball.

Pettigrew gave a stellar performance as a man searching his memory. His lips puckered and protruded; after several seconds he seemed to reach a conclusion and said, "I don't think so."

Pettigrew's eyes moved up and to the left. A reflex that often indicates the person was lying.

"Is it possible you may know him better by his nickname—Val?" Shawna asked.

Again, the dramatic play at trying to recall if he'd ever heard of anyone named Val. Once again, his lips protruded and he shook his head. "Nope, I've never heard of anyone by that name. What's this about?"

"Child abduction," Shawna said.

That got a reaction. "What is this?" Pettigrew asked, his tone turning indignant.

"You tell him," Shawna said to Dylan.

"Ten days ago, two people, Felicien Paradis and Claudette Beaupre, snatched a three-year-old girl from her parents' home in Eagle Lake, Maine."

"I've never heard of those names either."

"To cut to the chase," Dylan said, "We were closing in on Paradis in Maine, but Beaupre took the girl and fled. I have traced them to Boston. Claudette Beaupre is the niece of a Boston hood—one Val LaBelle."

Pettigrew sat back and said, "What are you doing… grilling me?"

Shawna took over the interview. "Sources have told us that you know quite a bit about the adoption racket."

"What do you mean *adoption racket*?"

"You're a baby broker," Dylan said, his voice rising with ire. "You help people circumvent the time-consuming adoption system—for a fee—a very lucrative fee."

Pettigrew stood up so sudden that he almost over-turned his chair. "This discussion is over. I would like both of your names and what organization you represent. You can't walk in here and throw these absurd accusations at *me*."

Shawna said, "I'll gladly give you my vitae, but if I do, you better believe me that I'll be looking into your activities—I'm going to be all over you like a cheap prom dress."

"I'm not local," Dylan said. "However, I'm sure that when I tell the authorities in Maine why you're calling about me, they won't give a shit. I'm not a cop."

"Then what right do you have to be interrogating me?"

"I haven't started yet," Dylan said. "Like you, I'm a lawyer, who's also a licensed private investigator. But more importantly, that child is my sister's daughter."

Pettigrew's mouth dropped.

"That's right you overpaid piece of shit, I'm her *uncle*."

Rather than go to his *meeting*, as soon as Pettigrew left the conference room he walked straight to the elevator and returned to his office.

When he stormed into the reception area, his staff took one look at his face and looked away, afraid to say the wrong thing and suffer the full power of his wrath. He paced across the room, entered his office, and slammed the door.

He threw his overcoat and briefcase onto the couch that faced his expensive desk and dropped into his desk chair with enough force that it rolled back. He ignored his office's panoramic view of Boston Harbor and Logan International Airport and took out his cell phone. In seconds his party was on the line.

"Where are you?" Val LaBelle asked. "We've been waiting for you to pick up the package."

"Keep your goddamned package. The deal is off."

"What do you mean the deal is off?"

"I just got fucking interrogated by a Boston cop and *the package's* uncle! They know about you, they know about your stupid bitch of a niece, and they have suspicions about me."

"Now hold on," Val protested.

"Lose my phone number. If I ever hear from you again, I'll have you turned into fish chum." Pettigrew broke the connection.

Val threw his cell phone out of the car window. It hit the pavement and burst into pieces. "Son of a bitch is welching on us."

"What do you mean by *welching*?"

Val looked at Sandra who was cowering in the back seat.

"Pettigrew backed out. He got a visit from the cops and the kid's uncle. I don't know what they said to him, but he's running like a meth-cook escaping a lab explosion."

"So, what do we do now?" Claudette asked.

"Make a couple of calls to see if I can work a deal someplace else."

"And if you can't?"

Val glanced at Sandra again. "We'll deal with that if and when the time comes."

Felicien hated cities; the masses of people made him feel small and insignificant. Then there was the uncomfortable feeling of being lost; he did not like not knowing his way around.

He stood in line at the counter of the Dunkin' Donuts that was across the street from the flophouse hotel where he had stayed over the weekend shuffling his feet. Never one known for his patience, he was especially irritable after a night listening to the carnal groans and thumping beds coming from the rooms adjacent to his. When the idiot in front of him ordered a goddamned croissant sandwich, Felicien wanted to kick him in the ass. He longed for the days when the D&D menu was restricted to coffee and donuts. *If you want a friggin' sandwich go to a deli,* he thought.

When he finally made it to the counter, a pimply-faced kid, wearing his hat with the visor turned to the rear, took his order—not that it was all that complicated, black coffee and two old fashioned donuts. He paid the kid, took his food, and surveyed the room. He saw an empty table and walked toward it. A young couple entered the building and the woman veered off and took the table before he reached it. Felicien glared at her even though she did not look in his direction. He changed course and sat on a stool at the counter that ran along the window over-looking the street. He ate one of the donuts and stared at the steady stream of traffic on Blue Hill Avenue. He glanced at the newspaper dispensers that lined the entrance and the headline caught his eye: *MATTAPAN SHOOTOUT LEAVES TWO DEAD!* His curiosity peaked. For the first time in recent memory, Felicien Paradis bought a newspaper. He stood in front of the displays and compared prices. The *Boston Globe* sold for two dollars and the *Herald* for a dollar-fifty. He walked to the counter, handed the kid two dollars and asked for change in quarters. The kid took the money and handed him eight coins. "Cost of a newspaper is ridiculous, ain't it?" he commented.

Felicien stared at the kid as if he had a lot of nerve to address him. He said, "Yeah," and walked to the paper dispenser and bought a copy of the *Herald*. Its tabloid format with lots of pictures appealed to him more than the literary appearance of the *Globe*.

Back on the stool, he sipped from his coffee and scanned the article about the Mattapan gunfight. When he saw the name, Gino Tricroce, listed as one of the two men killed, he began reading the story in detail. *If Gino was here*, he thought, *Vern was too*. He ate his second donut, cramming it into his mouth, and carried the coffee and newspaper across the street to his hotel.

Once in his room he placed his coffee on the table beside the bed, sat down, and read the entire article. He paid close attention to the names listed. One of which jumped out at him: Cora Cloutier. *That was Claudette's mother's name.* He opened the drawer of the small desk and found a phone book. He found Cloutier's name, jotted the Mattapan address listed there on a sheet of stationery with the hotel's name at the top, and drained his coffee. He grabbed his cell phone and called Vern Cole.

Cole answered on the second ring and did not sound pleased to hear from him, "Where in hell are you and where's my goddamned truck?"

"I'm in Boston. I see that you were too."

"That," Cole said, "turned into a real shit sandwich…"

"Well, your troubles may be just starting," Felicien said.

"How so?"

"Gino's fuckin' name is in all the Boston papers. It won't take the cops long to connect him to you."

"Fuck. The papers say anything else?"

"Just his name… has he ever done time?"

"He did a stretch in Warren."

"Then," Felicien said, "they know he's from Maine and they'll be contacting the Maine State Police—"

"I get your drift. You still driving my Silverado?"

"No, I left it where it has probably already been stolen. The paper said that someone left the Mattapan scene in a white truck with Maine plates. Last thing I need is to be pulled over in a truck registered to you."

"Okay," Cole said, "I'll report it as being stolen."

"What about Gino's stuff, what if they didn't find any keys on him?"

"I'll just say that he must have had a partner."

"Okay."

"Felicien."

"Yeah?"

"Your woman was there. Some asshole was with her and they took the kid and ran."

"That means my truck must be somewhere around there," Paradis said.

"Not sure you should go within five miles of it. The cops up here may have put out the word about it."

"Good point. I'll figure something out."

"What you got planned?" Cole asked.

"I'm gonna find that bitch and put her in the ground."

"If I was you, I'd start with the old woman."

"She'll shit when I show up on her doorstep."

"Why?"

"She came up to Maine once, I'm certain she'll remember me... the old bitch hates me."

"Well, good luck and keep in touch."

Val hung up the phone and lit a cigarette.

"Well?" Claudette asked.

"Pettigrew must have put the word out that the kid is hot. None of my usual people are willing to touch her."

Claudette rose from the table and paced around the kitchen. She picked up a pack of cigarettes and lit one. She stared out the window at Dorchester Ave. "So, what are our options?"

"Way I see it, you got three: First, you hang on to the kid until things settle down."

"Ain't that risky?"

"Then there's number two: I don't think I need say what that is."

"I don't want anything to happen to her."

"That takes us to number three: we drop her off in front of a local precinct or something."

"But," Claudette said, "she knows our names."

"There is that problem."

Dylan and Shawna hit a dead end. They had checked out all of Val LaBelle's usual haunts and there was no sign of him. They had asked any number of people who knew him if they knew where he might be. It was no surprise when all of them professed to have no knowledge of him.

They stood in front of a neighborhood bar in South Boston, huddled against the freezing wind blowing off the harbor. "You sure we're in Boston and not northern Maine?" Dylan quipped.

Shawna pulled her coat tight and replied, "What do you expect? It is early March and the last time I checked Boston was still in New England."

"You got any idea what we should do next?"

"Not a one. We've checked every place that I know he hangs out. He's been walking on the dark side so damned long he may have more holes to hide in than there are in a fish net."

They got into her car and savored the heat that gushed from the vents in the dash. "There is one other avenue," Dylan said.

"What's that?"

"Claudette had a boyfriend and real bag of puke named Felicien Paradis. He's got a murder warrant pending in Maine—"

"Who's he supposed to have murdered?" she interrupted him.

"Kid working the late shift at a twenty-four/seven convenience store. We have surveillance video of the crime."

"How does this help us?"

Dylan pulled his heavy gloves from his hands. "We believe that he's involved in a local car theft ring up there. The state police believe they know who the ringleader is and that maybe if some pressure was to be applied, he may give Paradis up."

"The boyfriend helps us, how?"

"Claudette and he took my niece together. If they had any plans on auctioning the child off, Paradis will not want to be cut out of the deal. We know he is looking for her too."

Shawna put the car in gear. "He may also know that her mother lives in Mattapan. That would be a logical place for us to start looking for him."

"This is your town, go for it."

The sun was setting when Val entered the smoke-filled private room in the back of the Claddagh Pub, a popular Southie watering hole owned by Jimmy O'Leary, a local mobster, better known as Jimmy O. He nodded to the five men sitting around a hexagonal table playing table-stakes poker. "Talk to you for a moment, Herb."

A stocky man with a gray mustache and goatee looked up from his cards. "I'm kinda busy right now, Val."

"It's important, but not all that urgent. I'll wait in the bar until you got a minute."

Without taking his eyes from his cards, Herb said, "You do that." He threw two cards into the middle of the table. "I'll take two."

Val took a seat at the bar and when the bartender approached, he said, "I'll have a Guinness and a shot of Jameson."

"You turning Irish, Val?"

"No, just in training for Saint Patty's Day."

The bartender grinned. "That ain't a bad idea. You want stout or blonde?"

"The blonde that new stuff they've started making?"

"Yeah, they call it American beer. Wanna try it?"

"Sure, why not."

Val downed the shot in a single drink and chased it with a swallow of the Guinness Blonde.

A man slid onto the stool beside him. "What's so fuckin' important that you'd interrupt a man during his weekly poker game?" Herb Daly asked.

Val chugged down the beer. "Let's take this outside."

"You got any idea how fuckin' cold it is?"

"Don't give me no shit, Herb. I got my reasons, okay?"

"Sure, but you better make it fast."

They walked through the crowded bar and out the door. After the super-heated interior of the Claddagh Pub, the cold was like a wall of ice. "All right," Daly said, "we're outside—although I can't think of a single goddamned reason why."

"I got a proposition for you and knowin' how Jimmy O feels about kids... well I thought it wasn't too smart—or good for our future health to talk inside."

"Alright, already. Talk to me."

"I got some merchandise to move."

"What sort of *merchandise*?"

"Blonde, three-years-old."

"I gather you ain't talkin' about beer."

"No."

Herb lit a cigarette and checked the street looking both ways. "Why me? You usually deal through Wilson Pettigrew."

"I had it all set up with him, then at the last minute he backed out."

Herb exhaled smoke. The cold air pushed down on it so it hung around his head like a cloud. "This merchandise hot?"

"No hotter than usual."

"I'll see what I can do. What are you asking?"

"All I can get. The more there is, the higher your... let's call it a commission... will be."

"Call me tomorrow, about this time."

"Thanks, Herb. Sorry I interrupted your game."

"No big deal I, was tryin' to fill an inside straight anyways and we both know how that usually works out."

"Yeah." Val nodded. "Get out of the cold. I'll call you tomorrow."

As soon as Vern Cole turned off route 27 and headed for his place, the blue lights came on behind him.

"Goddamnit." He pulled off the road on the right side. In the side mirror, he watched the cop approach and he leaned across the truck to get his registration out of the glove box.

When the cop tapped on his window, Vern opened it. He saw a female state trooper with the rank insignia of a sergeant. "Was I speeding, officer?" He saw a name tag on her coat. "Officer Doody."

"You failed to signal when you turned off twenty-seven. Could I have your license and registration please?"

Cole handed her the requested documents and breathed a sigh of relief. A minor traffic ticket was no problem. As a matter of fact, if Paradis found the woman and took care of her it may come in handy as an alibi should Paradis be caught and implicate him.

"I'll be right back," Doody said.

Cole closed the window and sat quietly, drumming his fingers on the steering wheel as he waited for her return. Although it was dark and he was virtually blinded by the harsh brilliance of her blue hazard lights, Cole knew she was checking for wants and warrants. He had a brief moment of concern while trying to recall if he had anything outstanding.

She returned and he opened the window again. She handed him his license and registration and said, "I'm issuing you a warning. In the future please ensure you signal when turning." She passed a rectangular piece of paper through the window. "You have a nice evening, Mr. Cole. Drive safely."

Cole shoved the license, registration, and warning into his shirt pocket and pulled out. As he drove toward his property, he watched her in his rear-view mirror. She was still sitting on the side of the road with her emergency lights strobing through the night.

Sergeant Arlene Doody watched Cole's tail lights grow smaller as he drove away. She used her personal phone to call Jean-Paul Thibodeau.

When he came on the line she said, "Hey, I just made contact with one Vernon Cole."

"And?"

"You're right, he's as slimy as a freshly caught trout. He will definitely bear watching."

"Well, caution whoever you assign to watch him to be careful. It wouldn't surprise me to find out that he's been into stuff a lot worse than grand theft auto."

Dylan was anything but impressed by Cora Cloutier. She looked as if she had one foot in her grave and the other in the express lane during rush hour. Her clothes were rumpled and needed laundering. If asked to describe her dress he'd say: "She looked like an unmade bed full of dirty linen."

"You haven't seen your daughter in two years?" Shawna asked, trying to keep from letting her dislike of the older woman show.

"She ain't exactly a model daughter," Cloutier replied.

"If that's the case," Dylan asked in a much harsher tone than Shawna's, "on the night of the shootings who were the man and woman seen running out of here carrying a child?"

"Ain't got a single clue. I ain't the only renter in this building."

"No, you aren't," Dylan pressed her. "But you are the only one who has a bullet hole in the wall."

Shawna studied her face. "What happened to your face, Cora?"

"I fell."

"And landed on your face? Have you seen a doctor?"

"No."

"Why not? Don't you have insurance?"

"Yeah. But thanks to that 'Bama-care my deductible's so goddamned high I may as well have none."

"Cora, the black bruises under your eyes are a sign of a broken nose. Tell us the truth," Shawna begged. "Who did this to you? Was it your brother?"

"I told you, I fell, tripped over the goddamned carpet." Cloutier stood up and shuffled across the room. Her swollen feet ran over her deformed slippers and she walked on the sides. "I want you to leave now."

While walking down the stairs, Shawna said, "She's lying like a rug."

"About what?" Dylan asked; he had a very good idea what her answer would be.

"Everything. There's no damned carpet anywhere in that apartment."

Felicien hunched back into the shadows of the entrance to a triple-decker across the street from Cora Cloutier's. Earlier he had approached her building when he saw the man and woman enter. The man looked familiar, he was certain that he'd seen him someplace, but couldn't recall where. The woman was new, but she had cop written all over her. He watched them get into a car and then waited a full five minutes to give them time to get out of the area before he crossed the street. Cora was going to give him the answers he needed, whether she wanted to or not.

He scaled the stairs two at a time, not worrying about how noisy he was. When he reached the third floor, he turned a sharp left and stopped in front of Cloutier's door. He rapped on it and stood just to the side of the spyhole. He heard the woman's plodding gait approach door and could picture her ugly fucking gouty feet sliding across the filthy floor. When the door opened a crack, he forced his way in.

Tuesday: Day Eleven

CLAUDETTE PACED AROUND THE SMALL kitchen, smoking a cigarette, and pausing to look out the window at the street on every pass. Val LaBelle sat at the table, watching her, a tabloid newspaper open in his lap. "For Christ's sake, woman, will you sit down someplace? Your friggin' pacing back and forth is getting' on my nerves."

Claudette took a final drag on her cigarette and then ground it out in the ashtray on the table. "I hate this damned waiting. When will we hear from this guy?"

"Herb won't know nothin' yet. The people he needs to talk to work nights and most likely ain't up yet." He shook a cigarette out of the pack that lay beside the ashtray and lit it. "Where's the kid?"

"In the living room, she's watching *Sesame Street* or some other shit."

"*Sesame Street* ain't shit... now that one about the friggin' sponge, watchya call it?"

"*Sponge Bob, Square Pants.*"

"Yeah, now that's shit."

"It'll be two weeks tomorrow since Felicien snatched the kid. I got a feelin' he ain't far away," Claudette said. "I ain't heard from him in days and that ain't like him—not when there's money involved."

"How you gonna hear from him? He's got no idea where you are."

"He knows Ma lives in Mattapan. Sooner or later he's gonna show up."

Val stood up and reached for the wall-phone. "If it'll make you settle the fuck down, I'll call your mother."

"We never should have left her in that apartment."

"You think we could get her to walk down three flights of stairs? Hell, she even has the supermarket take her order by phone and send it in a cab."

"You should have made her leave after those two assholes roughed her up."

"I know, I know. Now shut up so I can call." He punched the number using the keypad and held the phone to his ear. After several minutes he placed the handset in its cradle. "She ain't answering. I'll run over there and see what's up."

"I'll get the kid dressed and we'll go with you."

"No. We're too close to finishing this deal and it ain't smart to be seen running all over the city with her. You stay here and relax."

"How in hell can I relax when I got every cop in New England looking for me? Then there's Felicien…"

"All the more reason you should stay here. I won't be long—a couple hours at most."

"Alright, but you call if anything ain't right."

"Not to worry, I got this covered."

Val got off the MBTA at the Mattapan station and walked into the harsh daylight. He hunched his shoulders and turned his collar up against the cold and turned onto the street where Cora lived. He stopped short when he saw a crowd gathered in front of her building as well as an ambulance and police car. Not wanting to standout so that he would draw attention, he sidled up to the outer fringe of the bunch of gawking spectators. He asked a young woman wearing a knit cap, winter coat, leggings, and boots that came to just below her knees, "What's going on?"

"I heard that an old woman fell down the stairs and hurt herself real bad."

"That's awful. When did it happen?"

"I was told sometime last night; another tenant found her when he was going to work this morning. I heard she may not make it. They're taking her to the hospital."

"MCHC?" he asked using an acronym for Mattapan Community Health Center?"

"I haven't heard, but if she's as bad off as I heard, I'd take her to Boston Medical Center or even Mass General."

Val wished her a good day and walked away. He had no doubts that the woman was Cora. He worked his way through the gathered crowd until he stood near the ambulance. The medical people appeared at the door, guiding a gurney down the steps, taking great care not to drop it. They reached the sidewalk without incident and rolled past Val. He saw Cora, her face was covered in dried blood. The covers hid the rest of her from his view so he had no idea how extensive her injuries were, but it was obvious that she was unconscious.

Val turned and walked from the scene without asking where they were taking her; that would draw attention to him. He'd call around to find out where they were taking her. As he walked, he thought about what the young woman had said. *No way in hell Cora fell down those stairs… her feet were not strong enough to allow her bulk to scale the stairs. No,* Val thought, *someone fuckin' pushed my sister down that flight of stairs. If I catch the sonuvabitch, I'll throw him down an elevator shaft.*

Felicien wiped down the piece of shit Oldsmobile, using bleach and wearing latex gloves. In the event anyone had seen him driving away from Cloutier's building, he wanted nothing left, neither fingerprints nor DNA, that might lead to him.

He touched his left cheek and winced as he inadvertently touched the scratches there with bleach covered fingers. The last thing he had expected was for the old bitch to fight as hard as she did. It took all of his strength to force her out the door to the top of the stairs. The look of surprise on her face when he sent her flying down the stairs was small consolation given the fact that she hadn't told him one goddamned thing that would help him find Claudette, that backstabbing bitch.

The subsequent search had been fruitful though. During a thorough search of the apartment he discovered a shoe box in her closet and inside it was a bunch of old Christmas and birthday cards. Among them were several signed by her brother, Val LaBelle, and there was a Dorchester address on the envelope.

He was chuckling to himself as he finished sterilizing the car. Of one thing he was certain, he was closing in on that double-crossing bitch and the brat.

Dylan walked into the lobby of his hotel and saw Shawna sitting on a couch with two steaming cups of coffee on the table before her. He sat beside her and picked up the cup that had no lipstick on the rim. He took a sip, savored the flavor, and said, "Thanks."

"Someone tried to kill Cora Cloutier last night. Either threw or pushed her down the stairs in her apartment building."

"How bad was she hurt?"

"Still in the I. C. U. at Mattapan Community Health Center."

"What's the overall prognosis?"

"The doctors say it's touch and go, but they said the next twenty-four hours should tell whether or not she'll recover."

Dylan stared out the window at the exhaust rising from cars as they passed. "Looks cold," he said in an absentminded fugue.

"It's all of that and then some."

"I thought that it started warming up about now."

"It'll be late April before we can safely say that winter's over."

"Hell, it sounds like Maine."

"That it does." Shawna stood up.

"Where we off to?" Dylan asked.

"There's one guy with whom I want to talk. He's a former partner of Val LaBelle. He may know where he might be."

The city of Quincy rests across the Neponset River on Boston's southern border. It is densely populated and solidly middle to upper-middle class. Shawna wove through the narrow neighborhood streets and then turned onto a causeway.

"This doesn't look like the sort of neighborhood where buddies of a hood like Val LaBelle would live."

"Why not? If it has a choice, a dog won't shit where it lives."

"I never thought about it that way. Most of the criminals I deal with in Maine come from places so bad if you brought a dog there, it would bite your arm off."

"Well, even in the neighborhood where I grew up, the hoods and muggers worked other neighborhoods. If you lived in Riverton neighborhood it was the safest part of Portland."

"And if you didn't live there but was just passing through?"

"That would be a horse of a different color. You'd better not stop for a red light or stop sign."

It seemed to Dylan that every square inch of Squantum was developed. As in any city environment the houses were crammed as close as they could get without touching. "The developers must have wanted to squeeze every penny they could out of this peninsula."

"Island."

"Oh?"

"Squantum is an island; its only connections are causeways between the mainland and Moon Island. You probably thought it was a peninsula because of all the vegetation alongside of the causeway—it's wetland."

She followed the road around the perimeter of Squantum and stopped at a gatehouse that was occupied by two uniformed police officers. One stepped out of the small booth and approached the car. Shawna rolled down her window and passed her BPD credentials to him.

The officer scanned her identification and said, "What's the purpose of your visit, Detective?"

"We are going to do an interview at the Tobin Building on Long Island."

"Are you expected?"

"Yes, I called them earlier."

The gatekeeper handed her credentials back, stepped away from the car, and signaled the other officer.

The barrier raised and they passed through onto another causeway. "This will take us to Moon Island. No one lives on Moon Island, it's the site of the Boston Fire Academy and the BPD has its firing range here. We're headed for Long Island."

Dylan looked to the left and detected the Boston skyline. "Are we over Boston Harbor?"

"Actually, Quincy Bay."

"Shawna where is it we're going?"

"Long Island, like Moon Island, is closed to the general public." She spoke without taking her eyes off the narrow two-lane bridge. "Although a part of Quincy, the islands belong to the city of Boston. It's the site of social service programs operated by the Boston Public Health Commission. The Long Island Health Campus has facilities in nineteen buildings. One of these is the Tobin Building, which houses the Long Island Shelter for the homeless. There are also a number of substance abuse rehabilitation centers on the island."

They left the causeway, once again they circumvented a small island and then entered a longer causeway.

"Who are we here to see?"

"Cyril O'Bannon. At one time he was a member of Whitey Bulger's Winter Hill Gang. He was facing enough charges to ensure he'd never see the outside of a maximum-security prison again. He cut a deal."

"They'd let someone like that cut a deal?"

"They'd do anything to get Whitey behind bars for the rest of his natural life. O'Bannon settled for a ten-year stretch, got out six months ago and has been living at the homeless shelter since. As part of his deal he's going through rehab for an opioid addiction."

"And this guy can help us… how?"

"After Bulger went on the lam, he and Val LaBelle became partners."

The causeway gave way to solid ground and Dylan let out an involuntary sigh of relief.

"You okay?" Shawna asked.

"Yeah, I got this thing about bridges—an innate fear that one will fall into the water while I'm on it."

The road intersected with a street that looped to the left and right. Shawna followed the road left until she came to a brick building with parking spaces in front of it. She pulled in to the visitor spot and slipped her handgun and holster off her belt. She looked at Dylan for a second and then asked, "I should have asked this before, are you carrying?"

"No. Even in Maine, where a permit is not required to carry concealed, I seldom carry."

"Good enough." She opened the glove box placed her weapon inside and locked it. "Let's go see O'Bannon."

If Cyril O'Bannon were given a nickname it would most likely have been Shipwreck. He shuffled when he walked and his nose was so swollen from alcohol abuse that it was bulbous. His hair was so thin that his scalp showed.

Rather than sit in the chair across the table from Dylan and Shawna, he seemed to collapse into it. He took a pack of unfiltered generic cigarettes from his breast pocket and when he tried to take one out his hands shook so violently that he broke it.

Dylan took the pack, looked at Shawna, and asked, "Do they allow smoking in here?"

She nodded. "They figure kicking booze and drugs is hard enough without dealing with nicotine withdrawal as well."

Dylan took a cigarette out of O'Bannon's pack and gave it to him. It took the addict three tries before he was able to line it up with his mouth. He fumbled for his lighter and Dylan picked it up. "Let me do that for you."

O'Bannon sucked in the smoke and sat back in the chair. He placed his hands on the table and they seemed to beat a Bongo drum solo on it. He looked at Shawna and said, "You, I know, who's he?"

"My name is Dylan Thomas."

"Like the poet?"

Dylan couldn't suppress the surprise he felt learning that a project thug from South Boston was familiar with the Welsh poet.

O'Bannon laughed and it turned into a period of phlegmy coughing. After several long moments he inhaled so deeply that a loud wheeze came from his mouth. "You don't think a mick from Southie would know about a Celtic poet? You scratch a Welshman and you'll find Irish blood... scratch an Irishman and you get Welsh blood."

Dylan acknowledged O'Bannon saying, "I apologize. Yes, I was named after the poet."

"You write verse?"

"Legal briefs, I'm an attorney."

"Hmmmph. Where was you when I needed you?"

"Cyril," Shawna interrupted. "We need to locate Val LaBelle."

"An' people with migraine need relief. Ain't neither one gonna get what you want." He started to laugh at his witticism but it quickly evolved into another fit of coughing and wheezing. He reached into his pocket and took out a handkerchief that was spotted with yellow stains. He turned his head, placed it over his mouth, and coughed so loud and hard that Dylan thought he would spit blood. When O'Bannon stopped coughing, he opened the bandana and inspected the yellow glob. He crammed it in his right back pocket and then turned back to face his visitors and said, "Either of you got any idea what coughing up black shit means?"

"Cyril," Shawna said, ignoring his gross behavior. "If Val wanted to stay low, where might he go?"

O'Bannon inhaled another deep draft of smoke. "What's the asshole done now?"

"We have reason to believe," Dylan said, "that his niece, Claudette Beaupre, has a young girl and that she and Val are trying to sell her."

"How young?"

"Three years," Dylan answered.

O'Bannon leaned forward. "That don't sound like the Val I knew. You sure about this?"

"Very," Dylan replied. "The girl is *my* niece."

"That sonuvabitch. Even Whitey wouldn't stoop that low." O'Bannon looked at each of them in turn. "D'chester."

"We've already staked out his home, he hasn't been there," Shawna said.

"I didn't say his home. I said *D'chester*. He's like one of them prairie dogs, he has more dens than you got fingers and toes. He wants to he can go three weeks or more and never sleep in the same place twice." As he spoke, O'Bannon ground out his cigarette accenting his words with a grinding motion. When he finished the butt had been reduced to torn paper and bits of tobacco. He slid the pack across the table, looked at Dylan, and said, "Give a hand would ya?"

Dylan placed another cigarette between his lips and lit it. He looked into O'Bannon's rheumy eyes. "Could you be more specific?"

"I ain't seen Val in over five years and I got not a single goddamned clue about where he might be."

Dylan sat back and looked at Shawna. "Well, I guess that seals it—another damned dead end."

"Hold on just one goddamned minute," O'Bannon said. "I may not know, but I'd bet your life that I know who would."

Dylan and Shawna leaned forward. "Tell us," Shawna said.

"His sister, Cora."

"Someone threw her down a flight of stairs yesterday. She may not make it."

"When Val hears about that some fool is gonna end up on the wrong end of a thrashing machine—he always had a soft spot for her. If she's out of the picture Herb Daly is your guy."

Dylan looked at Shawna. He arched his brows and she picked up on his silent question. "Daly is one of several heirs to Bulger in Southie."

They both looked at O'Bannon.

"If Val ain't seen him yet, he will. You find Daly and follow him and you'll find Val, his niece," he looked at Dylan, "and yours."

"Where might we find Daly?" Shawna asked.

"He used to hangout in The Claddagh Pub, a joint on West Broadway."

"Jimmy O's place," Shawna said, "back in the day that was one of Bulger's haunts."

Felicien stood about 100 feet north and across the street from a single-family home on Rosseter Street, a short street off Geneva. He'd been watching the house for twenty minutes with no sign of inhabitants. All the stakeout had given him was frozen feet and a runny nose. He had to give this character credit. There were multiple exits from the street and it would be impossible for him to watch them all.

He opened the contacts on the old woman's mobile phone and scrolled to the name she'd given him for her piece of shit brother. *What kind of shithead would have a name of Val?* The only Val he knew of was a nickname for a broad named Valerie, who he'd dated once. He couldn't help smiling the tune of a song about some guy whose old man had named him Sue. He believed the name Val would have the same effect on a kid as being named Sue, he'd have to learn to fight at young age or he'd die. He continued scrolling through the numbers going from *A* to *V*. He stopped when he came to a number for a bar, The Claddagh Pub—whatever the hell a Claddagh was. *Why would that old woman have the number of a bar in her phone?* He opened the browser and did a search for the joint. It took him to a web page that showed the pub as being on West Broadway in South Boston. He wondered if it was a backup number for Val. He called the number and when it was answered he asked if Val was there. He was told that he hadn't been in yet today. When he was asked if he wanted to leave a message. He said, "No, I'll call back later."

He shut down the phone, debating whether or not he should throw it down the next sewer grate he came across. After all, some of these damned things had a built-in GPS. He walked to the Four Corners/Geneva MBTA station and studied the route map; in a few minutes he had a route to South Boston figured out.

Shawna and Dylan arrived in Southie in mid-afternoon. She threw a sign identifying the car as a police vehicle and double-parked in front of the Claddagh. When they walked in it was as if a neon sign reading Five-Oh lit up. The bar was half-full and most of the customers swiveled around on their bar stools and stared at them through narrowed eyes.

"Something tells me we're not exactly welcome here."

She smiled. "This is a warm welcome. You should have been here before gentrification came to Southie."

She walked to an empty spot on the bar, smiled at the bartender who was wiping glasses, and said, "Is Herb around."

He nodded toward a door at the rear. "I'd knock before entering if I was you."

"Do me a favor, I know you got some sort of buzzer under the bar, hit whatever code you use to call Herb out."

He placed the towel on the bar and then reached under it. "He should be out shortly. You want anything?"

"Just to talk to Herb." She turned and beckoned for Dylan to join her in a booth along the wall across from the bar.

"Well?"

"He'll be out… once he makes us wait a bit."

The bartender called to them, "You sure you don't want anything—it's on the house."

"You want something?" Shawna asked.

"I could use a cup of coffee about now."

She turned sideways and said, "Two coffees and we'll pay for them." She turned back to Dylan, "We wouldn't want anyone to think we were on the dole, would we?"

They were finishing their coffee when the back door opened. Dylan got a quick look at several men sitting around a poker table. "Looks like we interrupted their game," he said.

A stocky man with gray hair and mustache stopped beside their table. "You lookin' for me?"

Shawna looked up at him. "Your name Herb Daly?"

"Yeah."

"Then I'm looking for you."

Daly looked at Shawna and said, "I know you, you're five-oh. Who's this guy."

"Sit," Shawna said, "and we'll tell you."

Daly turned to the bartender and said, "Bring me a Guinness and a shot of Bushmills and bring them a refill."

Daly sat and Dylan slid over to make room for him. "You own this place?" he asked.

"No, I manage it, but I've probably spent enough money in here to own it."

The bartender placed a pint of Guinness and a shot in front of Daly and then walked away, returning in less than a minute with a pot of coffee and refilled their cups. "Anything else?"

"That'll do it for now," Daly said. He turned back to Shawna and asked, "So what does Boston's finest want with me?"

"Val LaBelle."

"Haven't seen him in a couple of weeks. The last time we talked he was thinkin' of goin' south, spend the last couple of months of winter in Florida... maybe catch a couple of Sox spring training games."

"Well," Shawna answered, "he didn't go and he may be up to his chin in shit and sinking."

"What's he done?"

"Besides kidnapping?"

"Whoa! What's this kidnapping shit?"

"His niece, Claudette Beaupre, has a three-year-old girl," Dylan said.

Daly said, "You still ain't told me who in hell you are."

"I'm the kidnapped girl's uncle."

"Now that," Daly said, "is some heavy shit."

"Heavy shit," Dylan said, "is the fact that Val and his niece are looking to sell my niece. Anyone who gets involved in this is looking at a federal beef. The child was abducted in Maine and then taken across state lines. That makes it an FBI case."

"Well, I ain't seen him, but if I do, I'll tell him you stopped by."

"Rather than that," Shawna slid a business card across the table, "call us."

Daly downed the shot of whiskey picked up the pint of stout and stood up. "I just might do that," he said. "Now I have a game to get back to."

"We're serious, Daly," Shawna said. "You don't need to be an accessory to this. It'll get you hard time for life."

"I'll remember that." Daly walked to the back of the room and disappeared through the door.

When they were back on the street, Shawna spun around and cursed. "Fuck. I'm getting tired of these scumbags thinking I'm a fool."

"Yeah," Dylan agreed. "It's been a long time since I've had this much bullshit thrown at me."

Felicien departed the subway at the Broadway Station. He walked east and soon found The Claddagh Pub. He entered, sat at the bar, and ordered a draft. When the drink arrived, he asked, "Val been in?"

"Nope. Haven't seen him in a couple of weeks." The bartender reached beneath the bar and pressed the buzzer.

Felicien finished the draft and signaled for another. A man slid onto the stool beside him and said, "What you need?"

"I'm looking for Val."

Daly looked at the bar tender. "Val's got to be the most popular guy in Boston."

"Somebody else lookin' for him?"

"Maybe. Why you lookin' for him?"

"Not lookin' for him so much as his niece. She took something of mine."

"What might that be?"

"I don't see where it's any of your business. Who the fuck are you?"

"I'm the guy who can make you take a dive in the harbor wearing cement overshoes if you piss him off."

Felicien stared at the man and knew he was in way over his head. "Maybe we got off on the wrong foot." He offered his right hand. "Felicien Paradis."

The man gripped his hand and applied a crushing pressure. "Herb Daly. There, now we're old fuckin' friends so answer my question."

"Me an' the woman had an arrangement. We got some merchandise up in Maine that we was gonna sell here. She ran out on me and took the merchandise with her. I just want what's mine."

"Well, Val ain't been around in a couple of weeks. I think he went to Florida or Arizona, one of them places where it's warm. But if I hear from him, I'll be sure to tell him you stopped by." Daly motioned to the bartender. "Give this man one on me."

Daly entered the backroom and walked past the poker game. When the other players protested, he gave them a scathing look and said, "I got urgent business. I won't be long."

Daly entered the stockroom and closed the door behind him. He walked to an antique roll-top desk and dropped into the wooden office chair. He picked up a land line and punched in Val's number. When the phone was answered he said, "Val what in fuck have you got me into?"

"What's wrong?"

"I'll tell you what's wrong. For over a year now I've stayed below the horizon, since you showed up here yesterday I've had a cop, along with your package's fuckin' uncle in here and now some goddamned hick from the Maine woods is sitting at my bar and tells me he's your niece's boyfriend for Christ's sake."

"Calm down Herb. The cops got nothin'. Did you make those calls?"

"No and I ain't goin' to either. Right now, your merchandise is way too fucking hot. You're goin' to have to go to New York if you want to find someplace to off-load it." He placed the phone in its cradle.

Val stared at the phone for a second and then placed it on the table. He looked at Claudette and said, "What the fuck did you get me into?"

"What are you talking about?"

"That was Herb and he just read me the goddamned riot act. What is that kid, the governor of Maine's daughter or somethin'?"

"She was the daughter of some guy that Felicien did odd jobs for—"

"That's another thing," Val said, "your dumb shit boyfriend is askin' around about you. He was in The Claddagh today askin' about me and you in particular."

"How did he find out about that place?" Claudette asked.

"I got my suspicions," Val's voice rose in volume. "If I find out that he's the bastard that tossed your mother down the stairs I'm gonna strangle him with his own asshole."

Claudette lit a cigarette and walked to the doorway between the kitchen and the living room where Sandra sat engrossed in yet another of the endless cartoon programs that seemed to mesmerize her. "So, what do we do with her?"

Val opened the refrigerator, grabbed a beer, and popped the top.

"That's your call. I will say this though. I've done some bad shit in my day, but I never killed no kid—and that's something I want to be able to keep sayin'."

Claudette turned away from the door and looked at her uncle. "I suppose we could drop her off at one of the police stations…"

"I think we're beyond that, Claudette. Even if you give the kid back, we're staring a kidnapping beef square in the eye."

"I need to think on this," she said.

"You do that." Val downed the last of the beer, dialed a number into his cell phone, and grabbed his coat.

"Where you going?"

"Herb said your boyfriend was still at the bar. I think it's time I had a talk with him." He turned toward the door and spoke into his phone, "Herb, is that fuckin' guy still at the bar?"

He listened for a second. "I'm on my way. Here's what I'd like you to do…"

Dylan and Shawna stood outside the ICU staring through the small window in the door. A man in green scrubs approached and asked, "Detective O'Reilly?"

They turned and faced him.

"Yes," Shawna said.

He offered his hand and said, "I'm Doctor Flynn. You inquired about Mrs. Cloutier?"

"What's her prognosis?" Dylan asked.

"And you are?" Flynn asked.

"Dylan Thomas."

"Like the poet?"

Dylan sighed. "I must get asked that fifteen times a day. Yes, like the poet and no, I do not write poetry. I'm a lawyer, and Detective O'Reilly and I are working together."

Flynn nodded. "She seems to be coming around, but she's not in the clear yet. She was concussed and until the swelling in her brain goes down, we won't know whether or not she has long-term damage."

"Has anyone else been here to see her or called to inquire about her?"

"You'd have to ask at the nurse's station. Even then, I doubt they'd recall. From time-to-time, things get kind of crazy around here."

Shawna gave him one of her cards and said, "Could you leave this at the desk along with a request that they keep a log of all callers?"

Flynn gave her a quizzical look.

"It's possible that whoever did this to her may inquire about her."

Flynn's expression changed to one of understanding. "Sort of like the criminal returning to the scene of the crime?"

"You never know," Shawna said. "But I think it's more like wanting to know if she'll regain consciousness enough to identify him—or her."

Val sat beside the only person in The Claddagh Pub wearing a heavy wool, plaid shirt, faded blue jeans, and those boots that L.L.Bean sold—the ones with the rubber bottoms and leather uppers. He looked past the man and saw Herb sitting in a booth near the back of the bar. He gave a slight nod toward the stranger and Herb in turn nodded.

Val ordered a beer and, when it arrived, he raised the glass and drank a quarter of it in a single drink. "I hear you been askin' about Val," he said in a normal tone of voice.

The stranger turned toward him and asked, "You a friend of his?"

"You might say that. What's your business with him?"

"He's got something of mine."

Val downed another quarter of the beer. "That don't sound like the Val I know."

"Then, maybe it's a different Val."

Val held the beer before his mouth and replied, "I don't think so. There's only one Val that I know. What's this thing of yours that he has?"

The man slowly turned his head. "What you doing? Writing a book or something?"

"Maybe."

"Then kiss my ass and make chapter three a love story."

"You know," Val commented, "what one of the problems with society today is?"

"I can think of a few, but I suppose you're gonna tell me which one eats at you the most."

"Yeah, I am. What lights a three-foot-high fire under my ass is when every goddamned hick in the world thinks he's a fuckin' comedian."

Val finished his beer and stood up. "You want some advice, mister?"

"Do I got a choice?"

"No, but you can take it or leave it. This is a tough neighborhood. People here don't take kindly to strangers with a wise-ass attitude. You should try and be a bit more sociable—otherwise someone is gonna hand you your head in a basket."

Val returned the wise guy's glare.

"I can handle myself."

"Just so you know, people 'round here cut their teeth on guys like Whitey Bulger. As far as they're concerned, you ain't shit. Have nice evening."

Val knew without a doubt that he had just met Felicien Paradis. Having met his niece's boyfriend, he was certain he'd also met the asshole who'd tossed Cora down that flight of stairs. He could feel the man's glare as he walked out of the bar.

Val jogged across the street and hid in the shadows of the entrance to a tenement building. He zipped his coat up to his chin, jammed his hands into his pockets, and hoped that Paradis had not planned on spending the night in the bar. He had barely settled in when his quarry burst through the bar's door. He stood on the street looking in both directions and then trotted toward the MBTA station. A minute later a couple of Herb's guys walked out, spotted Paradis, and followed after him.

Val gave them a few seconds and then returned to the bar. He walked to the back of the room and sat down across from Herb. "I owe you for this, man."

"How certain are you that he's the bastard that fucked Cora up?"

"About ninety percent, the only way he could have learned about this place is from her."

"You think she told him?"

"No, but I know she had this phone number as a backup number for me."

Herb motioned to the bartender. "Seamus, c'mere would ya?"

The bartender walked the booth. "Yeah, Herb, what can I do for yuh?"

"Anyone call here this afternoon askin' for Val?"

"Yeah, some guy called. He wouldn't leave no message though."

"Bring me the phone."

"Sure."

Val watched Seamus walk away. "How's the phone gonna help?"

"Caller I. D."

When the phone arrived, Herb showed Val how to access the caller listing and handed it to him. After several seconds Val said, "The chances of him being the one fucked Cora up just went to one hundred percent." He slid the phone across the table. "That's her cell number."

Herb looked at Seamus. "That call," he referred to the display, "it come in around two?"

"That'd be about right."

Herb handed him the phone. "Thanks."

Seamus nodded at them and retreated to his perch behind the bar.

Herb turned his attention to Val. "You want some advice?"

Val grinned. "Sure, why not?"

"Get rid of your niece and the kid. Sooner or later she's going down and if you ain't clear, you'll get buried in the carnage. Take it from me, man. Time served in a max or super-max is hard time and you don't want no part of that."

"You got a point. As soon as I deal with Claudette's boyfriend *Shithead*, I tell her she's got to go it alone. I'll give her some cash and a couple train tickets and send her south."

"It's your ass. My guys will follow him to whatever hole he's crawling in and out of. Once I hear, I'll be in touch."

Val stood and said, "Did I tell you that I owe you?"

"Yeah, you owe me—big time. Now get scarce."

Val got the call two hours later.

"He made my guys and ditched them."

"Damnit," Val said.

"I got word out around town, if he shows his redneck ass, I'll know about it."

Felicien entered the MBTA Train Station just as the doors closed on a red line train and pulled away. He saw a recessed doorway and quickly slipped into it. He watched the two men who had been tailing him pass through the turnstile and stop. One of them walked to the edge of the platform and looked down the track.

"We lost him," he called to his partner.

"What you mean we lost him?"

"He must have caught the train that just left."

They stood still for several moments and then the second man said, "We should check this place out. He could be hiding someplace."

"Fuck it. It's colder than my third wife in here. Let's go back to The Claddagh."

They climbed the exit stairs and Felicien remained in hiding until their voices faded away. He walked to the platform's edge and looked to the left. In the black abyss of the tunnel he detected the shaft of light that presaged the arrival of a train.

The Red Line train stopped and the doors opened. Felicien walked to the last car which was unoccupied. He dropped into the first seat and in less than a minute the doors closed and the train began moving. He thought about the men who'd followed him and could only come up with one reason why they had. Val LaBelle had been somewhere in that bar. *Tomorrow,* he thought, *I'll have my hands around that double-crossing bitch's throat.*

Wednesday: Day Twelve

"HERE'S TO HOPING THAT WE find Claudette today," Shawna said. She held up her glass of orange juice and clicked it against Dylan's.

"I can't help but wonder what Sandy's mental state is. Today makes twelve days since she was taken."

"Well, she does have one thing in her favor."

"Really? What might that be?"

"Kids bounce back fast. The most important decision your sister and her husband will have is whether or not to get her some counseling."

"Seems to me that's a given," Dylan said. He grew pensive and moved scrambled eggs around his plate with his fork.

"I believe there's a couple of ways to look at it. First, she's young enough that she may forget all about this in time. Second, if she doesn't, she's going to need a professional to guide her through recovery."

"You bring up some good points. Caitlin will probably opt for counseling. I'm not so sure about Oreille. I don't know how he'll react to it. He may think it's an admission that she's mentally ill."

"Are you serious?"

"People up north in the Saint John Valley are raised with a different outlook from that of many other places. They come from tough, stubborn Acadian stock and have a serious aversion to having someone else do anything they think they can do themselves."

Shawna asked, "Are you saying they're the type that will say: *Get a grip on yourself*?"

"Yup."

"I hope that you'll try and talk some sense into your brother-in-law."

"Easier said than done. So, what's on the agenda for today? I hope causeways aren't included."

"Truthfully? I've exhausted everything I can think of. Can you come up with anything?"

"Well, we can start by calling the hospital, maybe Cora Cloutier has regained consciousness."

"Sounds as good as anything I can come up with."

Val walked into the kitchen and said, "We need to move today. There's a place in Somerville where we can stay for a few days."

"Why?"

"It ain't smart to stay in one location for more than a couple of days."

"Does this decision have anything to do with why you were out late last night?"

Val poured a cup of coffee and leaned against the counter. He blew across the surface of the beverage in a completely useless attempt to cool it. "I was out late seeing some people."

"What people?"

"Your boyfriend for one."

Claudette's face paled. "You met with Felicien?"

"Yup, he doesn't know it though. He thinks I was just some nosy ass who bothered him in a bar."

"What if he followed you here?"

"He left before me. Herb had him followed, but his guys lost the shithead when he got on the T before they could catch up to him."

Claudette's hands shook when she lit a cigarette. "Val, don't screw with him—he may be from Maine, but he's as crafty and sly as a fox."

"Don't worry. I put things in motion to find him and take care of him."

"I don't know who you have helping you, but tell them not to underestimate him. He has no conscience and has killed one person that I know of."

Val thought of his sister laying in the I. C. U. and thought: *Maybe two...*

Vern Cole threw two pieces of firewood into the furnace and then looked around his shop. He heard the outside door open and then slam shut and turned toward the sound. Two state cops walked across the shop floor on a collision course with him. The female he knew, she was the one who'd stopped him for not signaling a left-hand turn; the male he had never seen before. He walked forward to intercept them. "Officers, to what do I owe this visit?"

The woman took the lead, "Good morning, Mr. Cole."

"I remember you. You gave me a warning the other night."

"This is my superior officer, Lieutenant Nykriem."

Cole nodded. "What can I do for you?"

"Mr. Cole," Sergeant Doody said, "we were notified by the Boston Police that a pickup truck that is registered to you was found in a vacant lot in Roxbury, Massachusetts yesterday."

"What?"

"A white Chevrolet Silverado, it was stripped and probably totaled."

Cole turned his head and yelled, "Lloyd, where is the Silverado?"

"You let the Gino use it last week."

"Where's he now?"

"You got me, Boss. Ain't seen hide nor hair of him since."

Cole turned back to the cops. "You can't get good help anymore. He must have taken off with it."

"What's the name of this employee?" Nykriem asked.

"Tricroce, Gino Tricroce."

"And you haven't heard from him since—when?"

"Friday," Cole said.

"Are you in the habit of giving company vehicles to employees and then losing track of them and the vehicle?"

"Not usually, but Tricroce seemed reliable and needed transportation. Looks like I misjudged him."

"Maybe," Doody commented. "On the other hand, if I had stolen my company truck, I probably wouldn't bother showing up for work either."

Nykriem took out a notebook. "You insured?"

"That," Cole said, "is what really sucks. It cost me so much for insurance that I'm self-insured… which is a fancy way of saying I'm out over $40,000.00."

Doody took a sheet of paper from her back pocket, unfolded it, and offered it to Cole. "Well, here's the name and number of the officer in Boston who has the information."

Cole took it and said, "Thanks for dropping by. A phone call would have been just as good and would have saved you time and gas."

Doody nodded. "Probably, but I've heard a lot about your operation and I wanted to see it first-hand."

Cole realized that her statement could be taken several ways and kept a straight face. "Well, feel free to drop by anytime."

The officers turned and walked out of the shop. When the exterior door closed behind them, Cole stared out through the shop window until the blue state police cars departed his property. He walked inside his office and called Felicien.

"The cops just left here. Did you report the Silverado stolen?"

"Yeah, I went back a couple of hours after I parked it and then called the cops and reported it."

"Fuck."

"I screw up?"

"No, but I may have I told the cops that Gino had the truck."

"Well, we'll have to deal with that as we come to it."

"Well, stay out of here for a while. They think that when it was stolen Gino panicked and hasn't been to work since."

"Not a problem."

"Any news on your other situation?"

"Slowly but surely, I'm making progress."

"Well, I don't have to tell you what you gotta do, do I?"

"Course not. I could use some help though. You got anymore contacts here?"

"Yeah, although after what happened to Gino, I don't know how willing they'll be to help us."

"Well, give it a try, would'ya?"

"I'll make some calls."

Thursday: Day Thirteen

VAL OPENED THE DOOR AND then stepped aside to let Claudette and the kid enter the tenement. Claudette stopped in the threshold and saw the worn linoleum flooring in the kitchen and the threadbare yellow-green shag carpet in the living room.

"Uncle Val, every time we move to another of your safe houses things get worse. I hope we don't have to move again—I'm not sure the place would pass a section-eight housing inspection."

"Val looked around the interior of the apartment. "I know it ain't the Ritz-Carlton or the Four Seasons, but it has its good points."

Claudette was not so easily placated. "I hope by *good points* you ain't talkin' about that old shag rug—same color as piss."

"I'm basically talking about neighbors who have been trained by the three monkeys."

"How in hell can anyone be trained by a monkey?"

"You know, *see no evil, hear no evil,* and more importantly, *speak no evil.* These people know how to ignore what ain't their business."

"How much longer is this going to go on, Uncle Val?"

"Today, tomorrow at most, I'm going to see some people today. But you need to be flexible, Claudette. As hot as that kid is, you may have to come down in your asking price. We ain't gonna get the half million you been asking for. We may have to cut the price considerably."

Claudette pushed Sandra before her as she walked deeper into the apartment. "I don't want her sold to some pimp who'll raise her to be one of his stable of whores."

"No matter what the price, no pimp is gonna pay anything for her. Hell, it'll be nine or ten years before she'll be an earner."

"How do you know the people we sell her to won't be the type who like to *play* with little girls—like my piece of shit father."

Val concluded that Claudette was not going to give up and walked into the living room. He flopped on the shabby couch and felt the cushions sag on its broken springs. He understood where she was coming from. After all, he was the one who took Raul Cloutier for the last ride of his useless life. He recalled the night Cora had discovered that her husband had been forcing six years-old Claudette to perform oral sex on him. He and Raul visited an abandoned quarry on the south shore. Only Val returned. He wondered what the bastard must look like after thirty years in that murky black water.

"I'll do everything I can," he told his niece, "But I can't control what happens after the turn-over."

Claudette turned the television on and tuned in WGBH so Sandra could watch *Sesame Street*. She removed the child's coat and threw it and her coat into a chair. "Let's talk in the kitchen," she said. "I hope there's coffee in the cupboard."

Felicien walked into the diner and saw two men sitting in the booth Vern had told him to look for. He could not recall the last time he'd been in one of these old-style railroad car diners, but the decor gave him a déjà vu feeling. He stopped beside the booth and stood there for a couple of seconds—neither of the men said anything. They stared at him and Felicien began to wonder if he'd made a mistake and these were not the men he'd come to meet.

The two mobsters looked like opposite ends of the criminal spectrum. The one sitting on Felicien's left looked to be in his fifties and if the one on the right was more than twenty-five, he would be surprised. The older man's face was hidden by a full beard and his long hair was pulled back into a gray ponytail. Felicien thought that since the top of his head was completely free of hair, the man looked stupid—like an old man trying to appear young. He sported a full mustache, with twisted ends that he'd used mustache wax on to shape into two upward curved spikes resembling the tusks of the wild pigs Felicien had seen on one of the animal shows he was addicted to—still he thought he looked like the evil villain in a silent movie.

The younger tough had a shaved head and a swastika tattoo was visible on his left wrist. He wore a black tee shirt beneath a black leather vest. His piercing blue eyes seemed to cut through Felicien, who was startled when he said: "You Paradis?" that he almost jumped.

"Yeah."

The skinhead offered his hand, gave Felicien a single shake, and then slid over to make room beside him. "Vern called us."

Once Felicien was settled, the old man offered him a menu and said, "You eatin'? This place is probably the best breakfast place in the city."

Felicien took the menu and looked at it. "What would you recommend?"

The old man said, "Can't go wrong with the pancakes. My name is Wayne Cloutier."

"Cloutier, I know that name."

"You should—my brother was Claudette's father, Raul."

"If you know about her then you must also know why I want her and her uncle."

"Valiant LaBelle is why I jumped at the chance to be in on this. These days I usually let my men, like Dolph beside you, do my wet work."

"You sound like you have a personal issue with this Val."

"You might say that—I believe he killed my brother Raul."

Felicien nodded and then said, "I want the woman and the kid, you can deal with Val for killin' your brother any way you want."

"There's no proof of it… Raul's never been seen since he went for a ride with LaBelle. Needless to say, I been looking for a reason to have a *talk* with Val for a long, long time."

"There is one thing that strikes me as bein' kinda fucked up 'bout this."

"What's that?"

"If Claudette's father was your brother, then that makes you her uncle, just like LaBelle. It don't bother you that I'm gonna break her fuckin' neck?"

"Naw. Like her bitch mother, she ain't had nothing to do with us." Cloutier leaned back in his seat. "You the one that threw the old bitch down that flight of stairs?"

Felicien stared at the older man for a couple of seconds, trying to decide whether this entire meeting had been a set up. He decided that Cloutier was on the level and said, "Yeah that was me. She's a tough old bitch, she still wouldn't give up either her brother or her daughter."

"Well, last I heard she was still alive," Cloutier said. "Which means she can identify you and if you don't get your business here finished, you're gonna be in deep shit."

Val LaBelle stomped his feet in a futile attempt to keep the blood flowing in them. He blew into his freezing hands as he rubbed them together. A white Lincoln MKT limo turned the corner and stopped. The back door opened and Val scrambled in. The opulence of the interior caused Val to pause with his butt over the seat.

"Please, sit Valiant."

Val dropped down and turned his undivided attention on his host. Arkady Izmailov looked like the *before* photograph in a weight-loss commercial. He sat on the long bench seat close to the window that separated the passenger compartment from the driver.

"Good morning, Mr. Izmailov. Thank you for seeing me."

"I was intrigued by your call, Valiant."

Val did not try and correct the Russian mobster who always addressed people in their given name rather than their nickname or moniker. He was very careful how he addressed Izmailov. He was the *pakhan* of the Boston Bratva of the Russian Mafiya, the equivalent of the godfather of an Italian mafia family. The Bratva controlled a large piece of the drug action in the area and had its tentacles deep into the prostitution, protection, and illegal gambling rackets. At one time, Val looked into the infrastructure of the Russian organization and came to believe that it was a system based on paranoia. Immediately below the pakhan were several under-bosses called Brigadiers as well as one or more spies. Spies were responsible for ensuring that no one, down to the lowest levels of the Bratva (a Russian word interpreted to mean *roof* and the equivalent of an Italian familia, or family) gave into temptation and *ripped off* the pakhan. In spite of the Russian's huge midriff, bloated face, and pudgy fingers, he was not a person to take lightly—he was also a stone-cold assassin. Everyone in Boston's criminal subculture knew that Izmailov had killed so many people in Russia that the higher-ups became afraid of him and had him sent to the United States. His short temper and thin skin were also well known by the criminal element throughout Boston. All Val had to do was say the wrong thing and he would not leave the stretch limo alive—in fact, he couldn't help but wonder how many people had spent the last minutes of their lives in the spot upon which he sat.

"So, tell me Valiant, what is this *merchandise* you are looking to sell?"

"A three-year-old, blond hair, the prettiest blue eyes you ever saw."

"And what would I do with this… little package?"

"I would not be so arrogant as to tell a person of your importance what to do with anything."

Izmailov chuckled and it set his double chins and massive stomach bouncing like a bowl of stew during an earthquake. The obese gangster leaned forward and rapped on the window separating them from the driver. "Nickolai, drive along the Charles please—take Storrow Drive. Valiant and I have things to discuss."

Val heard the chauffer say, "*Dah*."

The Russian once again turned toward Val, only this time he was not chuckling. Val's stomach rolled and he knew if he were to try standing his legs would fold under him.

"Now, Valiant, are you trying to take advantage of me—or even worse set me up?"

"I would never do that."

Izmailov said, "Why do you come to me when it is common knowledge that there is a great deal of interest in this child. I am told there is so much that Wilson Pettigrew has severed his business relationship with you. Then you approached Herb Daly, who also refused to get involved."

Val felt sweat trickling down his neck and scrambled to repair any damage he may have done. "Yes, Pakhan, you are correct there has been some… interest in this."

"*Some* interest? I am told there is a cop looking into this along with the child's uncle. There is also a group from Maine led by your niece's boyfriend, a psychopath who dresses like your country's legendary woodsman—what is his name?"

"Paul Bunyan is the legend, Felicien Paradis is the boyfriend."

"This Felicien, a strange name is it not? I am told he is looking all over the city for your niece and it is not for an evening of make-up sex."

Val saw the Charles River with a thin coat of ice on it pass by the window and wondered if he would be floating in it at the end of this meeting. Val relaxed, but only a bit. He caught a brief glimpse of Kenmore Square and Fenway Park. He wondered if there were any Red Sox games in his future—or had he seen his last one.

Izmailov rapped on the window and the limo exited Storrow Drive, passed by the Boston Conservatory of Music, and turned on to Boylston Street. He turned back to Val. "I suggest that if you want to get anything for your *merchandise,* you should take it somewhere other than Boston—New York or even Chicago… if not further to the west."

There was a small refrigerator built into the bench seat across from Izmailov; he opened it and took out a pastry. Val thought that it looked like a marshmallow sandwiched between a cookie and a thin layer of chocolate. Izmailov saw him staring and said, "*Ptichie*

Moloko, birds' milk cake, it is very good. A favorite pastry in my country, would you like some?"

Val shook his head no. If he was about to die, he didn't want his last meal to be the Russian equivalent of a s'more. "No thank you. Unfortunately, I'm diabetic."

The Russian looked at him and seemed to be empathetic. "I understand now why I never see you drinking alcohol."

Val remained quiet. He was nowhere close to being diabetic and did drink alcoholic beverages, only not when he was around a member of the mob. He did not want insult anyone while drunk—so he abstained.

The limo turned off Boylston and onto Arlington Street and headed toward Herald Square. "Do you have a vehicle?" Izmailov asked.

"No, parking around here is a real pain in the ass so I took the T."

"Where would you like to be dropped?"

Val wanted to say, *anywhere but in the marshes*; however, he kept his mouth shut. "Anywhere along here will be fine."

Izmailov rapped on the window again and the driver stopped alongside a line of parked cars, causing a minor traffic jam behind them. "I wish you a good day, Valiant. Be careful, there are people around the city who are quite put out with you."

Val nodded and exited the limo, closing the door behind him. He passed between two parked cars to the sidewalk and watched the white limo turn onto Stuart Street and disappear from his line of sight. He suddenly felt chilled and realized he had sweat so much that his shirt was stuck to his body. He crossed the street and entered the T station.

Dylan answered his phone on the second ring. "Hello."

"Dylan?"

"Hey little sister, what's up?"

"I need you to pick me up."

"Where are you?"

"Logan Airport. You haven't been so good at keeping me informed, so I decided to join you."

"Alone?"

"Of course, someone had to stay with the kids. Since you and my husband don't get on very well, I decided that it was I who had to come."

"Which terminal?"

"Terminal B, look for either Pen Air or Alaskan Airlines."

Dylan couldn't help but smile. He was aware that Peninsula Airlines was headquartered in Anchorage and had a sharing agreement with the larger airline. Caitlin was like most rural people in that she believed that no one knew about life in her area, let alone cared. It was an area that generated low self-esteem. "Okay," he said, glancing at the clock, it was 11:45 in the morning, "give me a half hour depending on traffic in the tunnel."

"What's up?" Shawna asked.

"A complication, hopefully it won't be a major one. My sister Caitlin is at Logan. Obviously, my communication habits don't come up to her standards."

Shawna smiled. "I can empathize with her. When her children are in danger a mother will always want to know what is happening at any moment in time."

"I guess."

"Look at it this way," she said, "when we find Sandra—and we will—having her mother close by could be a major plus, for us as well as them."

"You think?"

"I think. You ever have to deal with a hysterical child who's scared out of her wits?"

Dylan's lips twisted and his brow furrowed while he pondered her question. "Can't say I ever have."

"Take it from me, it isn't fun."

"What's the fastest way to the airport?"

"From where we are, the Callahan Tunnel is quickest." She gave a turn signal and pulled out into the downtown traffic.

Dylan spotted Caitlin the instant he walked through the door between arrivals and baggage claim. He stepped forward and, when he hugged her, felt her tenseness. He stepped aside and said, "Caitlin, this is Detective Shawna O'Reilly, she's been helping me search for Sandy."

Caitlin's body language telegraphed her unhappiness with the way things had worked out thus far. She turned to her brother and said, "I hope that you have something positive to report… it will be two weeks tomorrow since she was taken from us."

Dylan couldn't hold back his anger at her cold attitude. "Yes," he said in a sharp, unforgiving tone, "and, if you'd contacted me on that first day who knows what may have happened."

"Mrs. Dufore," Shawna said, "I know how frustrating these things can be and I want you to know that Dylan has done everything in his power to find your daughter."

Caitlin sighed and her shoulders dropped. She looked at her brother and said, "Unfortunately, my brother is not very good at keeping my husband and me up-to-date on your progress."

Dylan grabbed the handle of the super-sized case and pulled it toward the exit. "We're in the parking garage," he said.

As they entered the Sumner Tunnel, Dylan and Shawna briefed Caitlin on the current status of the case. She listened quietly, allowing her brother and his partner to finish talking, before asking, "So where does this leave us?"

"Unfortunately," Shawna replied, "not one hell of a lot better off than we were a week ago."

Caitlin sat in the back seat directly behind Dylan. When he turned to face her, she looked at him and then at Shawna, sat back, and said, "I know I shouldn't ask this, but I have to know. What are the chances that we'll find my baby alive?"

The silence from the front was all the answer she needed. Her face twisted and Dylan saw tears streaming down her cheeks and said, "Sis, we *will* find Sandy before anything happens to her..."

Caitlin's voice trembled when she said, "I-if th-they haven't already hurt her."

The sudden silence was deafening.

It was after dark when Val entered the bottom apartment of the three-family wooden row house in Dorchester and almost bumped into Claudette. She leaned against the kitchen counter with a cigarette in one hand and what appeared to be a glass of whiskey in the other. "You learn anything?" she asked.

"Only that your crazy fuckin' boyfriend has been lookin' everywhere for you and the kid."

Claudette stood upright, ground the cigarette into a glass ashtray, and took a drink. "Only way we're gonna stop him is to kill him. Because if we don't, he's sure as hell going to kill me and if that happens, he'll sell that kid in there to the first perv who makes him a half-way decent offer." She nodded her head toward the door to the next room.

Val closed the door and took a cigarette from her pack. A high-pitched laugh came from the living room. He walked to the door and looked inside as he lit his smoke. The kid sat on the floor with her legs crossed. She was no more than ten feet from the television and her face was illuminated in the screen's glare. She was completely engrossed in the cartoon program she was watching and her face was lit up with delight and her mouth agape at what was happening on the screen.

He watched her for several moments and for the first time he felt like a rotten bastard. In a way he envied the kid, he'd give anything if he could escape into her head for even a few seconds. To be free of his life, the violence, and misery it seemed to attract. He sensed more than heard Claudette walk up behind him and he turned and walked back into the kitchen.

"What are you thinking?" she asked.

"Do you know how to reach her uncle?"

"Hell no, I've only heard street talk about him."

"Maybe we ought to just drop the kid off at a police station. Put her on the sidewalk and point her to the door."

"And what? Turn my back on the money I need to survive?"

"This job has been nothin but a pain in my ass," he snarled more than said. "You fuckin' near got your mother killed. There are who knows how many assholes looking for you. You've probably put the screws to every workin' relationship I got. Have you considered that every day her value goes down? No one is gonna pay shit for a kid that every goddamned cop in five states is lookin' for."

Claudette's face was red with anger. "You don't think I haven't thought about all that? That kid..." She pointed toward the inner door, "...is all I got! I give her up without getting paid for her and I might as well go steal a grocery cart, cause that's what I'll be livin' out of."

Val saw a bottle of bourbon on the counter and picked it up. He opened the cupboard and found a cocktail glass. He poured three fingers and took a sip. He placed the bottle back on the counter and sat at the table. "All right, I'll give you one more day—two at most. Then you either get rid of the kid or you're on your own."

"I'll accept that."

Val slapped the table and said, "You fuckin' better, 'cause I'm serious about this. You got two goddamned days."

In the living room, Sandra laughed again.

Caitlin checked into the same hotel as Dylan. While she took her bag to her room, they waited in the lobby. "What's our game plan?" Shawna asked.

"Until we locate Sandy, she's going to be a liability. I think I should take her for something to eat and then once she's settled in her room, you and I should see if we can get a line on some of Val LaBelle's home boys."

A bell sounded and the elevator door opened. When Caitlin walked off the lift, Dylan asked Shawna, "You want to join us for dinner?"

"I'd love to."

Wayne Cloutier cruised along the Dorchester backstreet, keeping a close eye on the buildings on his left. He saw a figure standing in a doorway out of the frigid wind and stopped. The figure dashed across the sidewalk and slid into the back seat, shutting the door to seal it from the sub-freezing air.

Felicien sat in the front passenger seat, turned his head until he was looking over his left shoulder, and asked, "You found him?"

"Yeah," Dolph answered. "You were right, rather than drive he took the *T.* I rode the Red Line all afternoon. About six o'clock he got on at Park Street Station and rode to Ashmont. I gave him a couple minutes and followed him here."

"Good job. Which house?" Cloutier asked.

"Fourth on the right, he entered the bottom apartment."

Cloutier slowly cruised his car toward the house Dolph had indicated. They drove up and down the narrow street until they found a vacant parking spot across the street from the line of brick row houses. Cloutier parked and they settled in, listening to a Bruins game on the radio, while enjoying the heat.

"You got a plan?" Dolph asked.

"We listen to the game and wait for them to go to bed. Then we make our move."

After an Italian meal at a restaurant on Prince Street in Boston's North End, Shawna dropped Dylan and Caitlin at the hotel. "You up for a nightcap?" Dylan asked his sister.

"If you don't mind, I'll take a pass. It's been a long day and I'm exhausted."

"Understandable," Dylan replied. "Come on, I'll walk you to the elevator."

"You aren't coming up?"

"I'm still wired from all the coffee I drank today. I'll take a walk around the block before turning in."

"Dylan, don't lie to me. It's freezing out there and you are *not* going to take a late evening walk."

He felt his face flush. His little sister was not as gullible as he believed. "The truth is that Shawna and I have a couple of things we want to check out. These people are creatures of the night—like vampires, they prowl until the wee hours of the morning and then sleep until after noon."

"I understand. Just don't try to snowball me, okay? If you have something to do and think that I'll be in the way, just say so. I don't want to do anything that will jeopardize getting my baby back." She held out her hand. "Do we have a deal?"

He grasped her hand and then pulled her into a hug. "Deal."

He watched the elevator door close behind her and then turned and walked to Shawna's car. "How'd she handle being left here?" she asked.

"No problem," he replied, "she doesn't want to do anything that may keep us from finding Sandy."

Shawna held his eyes with hers. "Are you sure that she's serious and not just paying you lip-service?"

"I believe her. Caitlin is a small-town girl. She'd no sooner venture into Boston alone than a priest would hold a service in an ISIS compound."

"Okay, I just don't want to see anything happen to either Caitlin or her daughter."

Dylan appreciated her concern and said so, adding, "Where are we off to?"

"Val seems to like hanging out in Southie. There are a couple of pubs near the Old Colony projects where I'm told he hangs out."

Wayne Cloutier looked at Felicien and then at Dolph, then back to the brick triple family row house. "I think it's time to get into action," he said.

"How we gonna do this?" Felicien asked.

"There's only one way to do it. One of us has to circle around this line of row houses and take position in the alley so they can't run out that way. The others will hit the front door." He turned and rested his arm on the back of the car seat. "Dolph, you know your way around here best. I want you to take the alley." Cloutier reached across Felicien and opened the glove box from which he took out three handguns, two pistols and a revolver. He looked at Felicien and asked, "You got a preference?"

Paradis took one of the pistols and said, "This works for me."

Cloutier nodded at Felicien and then passed the other pistol back to Dolph. "We'll give you five minutes to circle around to the alley, then we'll hit the front door. This has to happen fast you guys. We got to do our thing and then get the fuck outta Dodge… ready?"

When Felicien and Dolph nodded, Cloutier said, "Let's do this."

Val LaBelle had been sitting in the dark, watching the street for the better part of an hour. He paid particular attention to a car that had cruised the block several times and then parked. Above all else, there was one thing that had caught his attention. No one had exited the car since he had first seen it.

"Claudette," he called.

She appeared in the door leading to the bedroom that she and Sandra shared. "Yes?"

"I got a nasty fuckin' feeling. I think you and the kid need to be ready if we gotta leave here real quick."

She crossed the room and stood beside her uncle. "I wondered what you bin watchin' so hard."

"See that car, across the street and four to the left?"

"Yes."

"It parked there over three quarters of an hour ago."

"And?"

"And nobody got out."

"Could be a couple of kids makin' out."

"I don't think so… look."

Claudette saw three men exit the car and immediately recognized one of them when he stepped into the bright circle created by a streetlight. "Shit," she muttered.

"What? You know them?"

"The one under the streetlight is Felicien."

Another man became visible and it was Val's turn to curse. "Sonuvabitch, if it ain't your Uncle Wayne."

"My father's brother?"

"One and the same." Val picked up his pistol from its resting place on the small table beneath the window. "You got your piece?"

"Yes."

"Get it—this is a family reunion you ain't gonna enjoy. Get that kid ready too. You two may have to run for it."

Felicien followed Cloutier across the street. He raised his collar to obscure his face from anyone who might be watching and scrambled down the steps to the front of the building. "What's the plan?"

Cloutier glanced at him. "I'm gonna fuckin' waste LaBelle… you do whatever you want to the woman and kid."

Felicien paused for a second. "She's your niece…"

"So what? I ain't seen neither her nor her useless mother since my goddamned brother disappeared twenty years ago."

"Still—"

"I hope you ain't gonna give me none of that blood's thicker than water shit. As far as I'm concerned, she's like any other strange woman to me. Besides, you bin shackin' up with her for how long?"

"Couple of years."

"And you're lookin' to either beat the living shit out of her, kill her, or both. Now, are we gonna do this or what?"

Felicien nodded, "Yeah, let's do it."

Val saw the three men split up; two started across the street and the other headed toward the corner of Dorchester Avenue. He nodded to himself and thought, *Apparently, Wayne has learned some lessons, he's sending one of his punk bastards to cover the rear.*

Claudette walked into the room, carrying Sandra, who was draped over her shoulder and sleeping. "What's happening?" she asked.

"Your boyfriend and Wayne are coming across the street. The other guy walked toward Dorchester Ave., probably to watch the alley behind these houses."

"What do you want to do?"

"I want to get you and the kid out of here. Do you remember how to get to the garage where I parked my car?"

"Of course, but it's in the alley. You just said they were watching it."

Val reached into his right hip pocket and pulled out a key ring. "Here's the car keys. If you go now, you can get to the car before the guy can get close enough to stop you from getting away." He held the keys toward his niece.

Claudette's complexion was pasty with fear when she took the keys. "What about you?"

"I ain't your worry…"

"Nor am I yours."

Val gave her a hard look. "I can make a better stand if I ain't got to worry about you." He took his wallet out, removed a plastic card from it, and handed it to her. "If I get side-tracked and you gotta run you'll need to find a place, use this credit card to pay for whatever you need—now go."

Claudette turned to the door and looked over her shoulder at Val when he said, "Carry your pistol in your free hand and don't hesitate to use it if you see him coming at you."

She nodded her head and disappeared through the rear door.

Once she was in the unlit hall, Claudette wasted no time exiting the building. She hunched over and pulled Sandra close against her chest while running toward the alley and the line of garages. She recalled that Val's Mercury Grand Marquis was in the single car shelter located just to the right of the gate that offered access to the alley.

She paused, not happy at the way a street light with a high-wattage mercury lamp lit up the alley like Fenway Park during a night game. She glanced both ways and then darted across the narrow lane to the garage where Val's car was parked. Pausing before the door, she checked both ways again and then grasped the handle to open the door. When she twisted the T-shaped handle it refused to turn. She twisted it both ways hoping to free it, but it remained fast. It was then that she realized that the door was locked. She stood Sandra on her feet and the child rubbed her eyes and seemed dazed by the brilliant light. Claudette placed a finger across her lips and hushed the little girl before she could speak. While fumbling with the key ring, hoping to identify a key that looked like it would fit the T-handle's lock, she looked like an animal seeking a means of escaping from a larger predator and hoped that she would find the key before the third thug entered the alley and saw her.

She tried a couple of keys to no avail and glanced in each direction again. A shadowy figure appeared at the mouth of the alley and she tried a third key. She was close to tears when the key turned and the door started up, almost pulling the keys out of her grasp. She grabbed the handle and whispered to Sandra, "Quick inside."

The child slipped past her and Claudette wrestled the key ring free and bent below the door to follow. Inside, she pulled the door down and fumbled with the latch until she found the release that would lock it. Once the door was secure the inside of the garage was as black as obsidian and she whispered, "Sandra, come here." She almost fell when the child collided with her and wrapped her arms around her waist. Claudette dropped to her knees and held the small head snug against her chest. She moved her mouth until her lips touched the girl's ear and whispered, "Be very, very quiet, now."

Her eyes slowly adjusted to the dark and the outside light illuminated the borders of the garage door like a brilliant picture frame. She tightened her grasp on Sandra and started when someone tried to turn the door's handle. The person on the outside tried turning the T-handle several times and then she heard footsteps moving away.

There were three gunshots and Claudette jumped back.

Val stood beside the door that led from the hall into the apartment's living room, holding a nine-millimeter with its muzzle pointed at the ceiling. He heard someone speaking in a low voice and knew that the two intruders were separating so that one of them was at each door. He waited for several seconds and when he saw the door knob turn he fired three shots: one through the center of the door and one through the wall on both sides of the portal. He was gratified to hear a grunt and then a thud as someone fell.

Val heard the back door crash open and turned toward it. He saw a man crash through the door and into the kitchen. He fired two shots and when the intruder scrambled to get out of the line of fire, used the interlude to open the living room door and race into the hall. He saw another a familiar figure and shot at it, before running for the rear stairs.

Val vaulted up the short flight of stairs that led to the outside door, leaping over all three, and almost lost his balance when a bullet passed his ear and slammed into the wall with a loud, angry SNAP. As he ran, he thought: *They're right, you only hear the ones that miss, not the one that hits you.*

Reaching the landing at the top of the stairs, Val ripped the door open and immediately saw the black figure of a man standing in the middle of the yard. He fired at him and the figure seemed to melt as it dropped into the snowy grass. He ran across the backyard and vaulted the low fence that separated it from the alley beyond.

Claudette heard the sound of someone running past the garage and stood up. She picked Sandra up and felt her way along the car until she located the door handle. She silently prayed that the car doors were unlocked because she wasn't sure she could locate the door key on the keyring. She pulled on the handle and the interior light came on and blinded her with its sudden brightness. Returning to the Mercury, she placed the child on the front seat. "You sit there and don't move," she whispered.

Sandra said nothing. But the wide-eyed look communicated her terror and fear at what was happening.

"I'm just going to open the door so we can get away from these bad men. I won't be a minute."

Holding her gun in one hand, Claudette quickly located the locking mechanism on the garage door and unlocked it. She slowly raised the door, keeping a watch on the alley in the event that any of the attackers were still in the alley. When she felt it was safe, she scrambled back to the car and got in. Her hand shook like someone in the late stages of Parkinson's as she flipped through the keys. Time seemed to race by while she searched for the ignition key. She found it and on the third try was able to push it into the key slot on the side of the steering column. She prayed that the car would start as she twisted the key. She almost sobbed when the engine turned and caught. She yanked the gear selector into drive and the tires chirped as the car leapt forward. A man stood in the center of the drive and she recognized Val in the headlights. Swerving to the right, Claudette barely avoided hitting him. She jammed her foot on the brake pedal and stopped beside him. Val ran around the car and opened the door. He grabbed the child and saw Wayne Cloutier and the man from the kitchen burst out of the apartment house. He fired his pistol until the two men dove to the ground, and the slide on his pistol locked back indicating an empty magazine. Val slid into the car, placed the kid on his lap, and shouted, "GO, GO, GO!"

Claudette rammed her right foot on the accelerator causing the rear end to fishtail. Approaching the end of the thin lane, she asked, "Which way?"

"Right…" Val turned in his seat, dropped the child into the back seat, and when he was once again facing forward, removed a full magazine from his pocket. He ejected the empty one and pushed the full one into the pistol's handle. In her haste to exit the narrow drive, she cut the wheel too sharp, and the passenger side scraped the curb. Once on the street, she pushed the accelerator pedal to the floor and tore down the boulevard. She braked at the end and glanced in the rear-view mirror where she saw her uncle and Felicien Paradis step out of the alley. As she turned the corner and sped away, she saw Felicien raise his hand and knew he was shooting at her.

Tearing along Dorchester Avenue, Claudette released an explosive burst of air and she realized that she'd been holding her breath. She inhaled deeply and said, "Where are we going?" to Val.

"Get onto the interstate and head for Quincy. I know a place where we can stay."

Felicien and Cloutier stood on the sidewalk watching the tail lights of the car disappear. "What now?" Felicien asked.

"I imagine every goddamned cop in Boston is headed here. We should check on Dolph and get the hell away."

They returned to the apartment house and Felicien asked, "Where is everyone? You'd think they'd want to see what was goin' on."

Cloutier laughed. "Ain't no motherfucker stupid enough to stick their head out during a gunfight."

They found Dolph struggling to get to his feet, the snow around him covered in blood. "You hit bad?" Cloutier asked.

"Not so fuckin' bad that I can't get out of here." Dolph grimaced and asked, "What about Val?"

"Motherfucker must go to church reg'lar," Felicien said. "I had him dead to rights and he almost got me before running out of the apartment." He noticed blood dripping from Cloutier's left wrist. "You hit?"

"It's nothin'. We got to get a move on."

Dolph nodded his head and grunted. "Help me up."

They were navigating one of the narrow streets in Southie when Shawna's cell phone rang. She answered it and spoke while expertly threading their way between the cars parked along both sides of the street.

She said, "Thanks, we're on our way."

Dylan looked at her and she must have felt his eyes boring into her. "That was one of the detectives I work with. There was a gunfight in Dorchester tonight."

"And?"

"Looks like at least one someone got shot."

"We're going there, why?"

"The scene was an apartment known to be frequented by Val LaBelle."

Friday: Day Fourteen

DYLAN AND SHAWNA ARRIVED AT the scene of the Dorchester shootings about 1:00 a.m. Shawna flashed her identification and they were allowed past the crime scene tape. A detective who was a tall, balding man with Roy Orbison glasses met them in the foyer of the apartment house. "Hey, O'Reilly," he greeted her, "looks like we found Val LaBelle's lair for you."

"Chip Gage, meet Dylan Thomas… Dylan this is Chip Gage, we were partners in a past life."

Gage reached his hand out. "Dylan Thomas, like the poet?"

Dylan sighed. "You have no idea how many times a day I get asked that. I've even considered changing my name to Mort Fartquartz, anything." He grasped Gage's hand.

"Dylan used to be on the job," Shawna added.

Gage nodded. "Why the interest in a piece of shit like Valiant LaBelle?"

"Two weeks ago, my niece was abducted up in Maine. We believe that LaBelle's niece Claudette Beaupre and her boyfriend, a dirt-bag by the name of Felicien Paradis, took her. We traced them to Boston," Dylan answered.

"We have information that LaBelle was helping her," Shawna added.

Gage nodded. "That adds a piece to the puzzle. We found a child's clothes and a teddy bear in the apartment. How old was the child?"

"Three years old," Dylan said.

Gage nodded again, Dylan thought if he didn't succeed as a detective, Gage could get a job as a bobble-head doll. "That," Gage said, "fits."

"Anyone get hit?" Dylan asked.

"We got blood splatter on the hall wall and more blood in the backyard—no bodies though." He turned to Shawna. "You got any ideas as to where we might find LaBelle?"

"He has a sister, Cora Cloutier," she said.

"Gage took a notebook out of his back pocket and a pen from his shirt pocket. As he wrote he asked, "You got an address?"

"Mattapan Community Health Center—in the I. C. U."

Gage peered at Shawna over the top of his glasses. "What's goin' on, Shawna?"

"We believe the child was abducted to be sold…"

"Sold? A three-year-old kid?"

"We can't be sure but there's evidence that the child, Sandra, may have been taken in an adoption for cash deal. A three-year-old girl would have a high value."

Gage's eyes narrowed and his voice took on an ominous tone. "I got you, the goddamned Child Exchange." He motioned to the open apartment door. "You want to look around?"

"Sure," she answered.

"If LaBelle was helping her peddle the kid, why try to kill him?"

"Because," Dylan interjected, "Claudette Beaupre's boyfriend, Paradis, has all the motive he needs—he wants his cut of the money they'd get for selling Sandra…"

"And Sandra is?" Gage asked.

"The child… my niece."

Gage nodded. "I'm starting to get the picture. Beaupre took off with the kid and this Paradis is chasing her."

"If the uncle, Val, wouldn't give her up, Paradis is unstable enough to shoot him."

"That explains the professional-style attack."

"Witnesses?" Shawna asked.

"People upstairs heard the shooting and called 9-1-1. They also reported hearing a car tear out of the alley in the back."

"They see anyone? Possibly get a license plate?" Dylan inquired.

"You kiddin'? Not in this neighborhood. We were lucky they called us—no way in hell were they about to stick their heads out a door or window."

Shawna scanned the dimly lit hallway. "Is that the blood you mentioned?" She pointed at the wall."

"LaBelle wasn't about to go down quiet. Looks like he got off three shots—one through the door and one on each side—and hit someone. They must have taken off with their wounded."

"Perps?" Dylan asked.

"Probably three, two who were wounded and another. Here's how we think it went down. There were probably three, possibly more, hitters. One tried to go through this door and LaBelle nailed him. At the same time, another kicked open the back door and it appears that some way or another, LaBelle got past him."

"What was the third perp doing while all this was going on?" Dylan said.

"Probably watching the alley in case someone tried to get out through the back… it didn't work, though most of the blood in the snow out back is possibly his. We found a garage with its door open. The people upstairs said it belonged to this apartment—that was probably where the car they heard had been parked." Gage turned and led them inside the apartment. "Watch your step. I don't think C. S. I. is done processing the scene."

"Where did you find the clothes and teddy bear?" he asked.

"They were in the bedroom, over there." Gage pointed to a door on the right side of the living room.

Dylan walked to the doorway and peered into the small bedroom. There were children's clothes scattered on the floor and the bed was in disarray as if someone had been asleep. It was obvious that whoever was staying here had left in a hurry. *Now,* he thought, *all we got to do is figure out where they are now.*

Claudette was exhausted. She had driven onto I-93 as Val directed and was weaving around parked cars on the narrow streets of Quincy. Along with fatigue she was scared and had no idea when this was going to be over. Weariness made her head feel as if it weighed a hundred pounds and she wanted nothing more than to find some place safe and get some sleep. "How much further, Val?"

"Not far, a couple of miles at most."

A quick glance at the instrument panel showed that her gas tank was close to empty and they would need to find an open gas station soon. Her head dropped forward and Val yelled at her. She snapped up and rubbed her eyes.

"You want me to drive?" Val asked.

"It might be best," she answered.

A Seven-Eleven Store appeared and he said, "Pull in here."

"We need gas."

"Then pull up to the pumps."

Claudette turned off the road and slowly approached the gas pumps. When she was parallel to the island, she stopped, turned off the motor, and gave Val the keys. She got out of the car and stretched, trying to alleviate her stiff muscles. "I could sleep through a tornado," she commented.

"You want a cup of coffee?" Val asked as he inserted the nozzle into the gas fill.

"I want a bed."

Val chuckled and said, "It won't be long."

"Thank God."

Claudette rounded the car and dropped into the passenger seat. She glanced at Sandra and saw that the child was in a deep sleep. She knew that Boston was notorious for its lack of signage. There were small street signs labeling cross streets, but nothing to tell you the name of the street on which you were driving. She remembered commenting on that to Val, to which he replied: *"If you don't know where you are then you don't belong here."* More than at any time in her life, Claudette was well aware that she was in fact in a place where she did not belong.

A loud SNAP told her that the car was completely refueled. She leaned her head back and was asleep before Val got in the car.

She was abruptly wakened when her cell phone rang. She answered—then Felicien spoke, "Hey Babe, where you at?" She knew that he was never going to leave her alone, stifled a sob, and disconnected the call.

When Val said, "We're here," she sighed. A quick glance at her cell phone told Claudette that it was 2:45 a.m.

"End of the line," he announced.

It took fifteen minutes for them to check into two rooms. Ten minutes later, Claudette was in a deep sleep.

Wayne Cloutier exited the O'Neil Tunnel and Paradis took a cell from his coat pocket, punched in a number, and said, "Hey Babe, where you at?" He chuckled and put the phone back in his pocket.

"Who was that?" Wayne asked.

"Our girlfriend."

"She stupid enough to tell you where she is?"

"She ain't the sharpest crayon in the box, but she ain't that dumb."

Dolph was in the back. He groaned and slid down until his back was on the seat, his legs bent at the knee and his feet on the floor. "I need a doctor," he said, his voice strained. You want to drop me at the first emergency room we pass?" His voice was strained and it was evident that he was in a great deal of pain.

"Fuck no," Wayne said, "the instant they see you been fuckin' shot they'll be callin' the cops. I know a guy."

"I hurt bad, Wayne."

"That'll teach you to get your dumb ass shot."

Claudette jumped up when the room phone's brassy, loud ring startled her awake. The last thing she wanted was to speak with anyone, but the goddamned bells made her head feel like an evil gnome was driving spikes into it. She snatched the handset from its cradle. "Yeah?"

"I may have us a buyer."

"Val, this better not be one of your pervert buddies who will sell the kid to some pedophile."

"Hell, no, this family is so goddamned rich they can't count all their money."

"Val... if you're blowin' smoke up my ass..."

"No way kid, this is on the up-and-up."

"How much are they offering?"

"Two-hundred-fifty-grand... cash."

All vestiges of sleep left Claudette. "You're shitting me..."

"I shit you not, kid. However, they want to see the merchandise at ten o'clock."

"What time is it now?" Claudette looked over Sandra's sleeping form at the clock—two hours until the rendezvous. "These people will treat the kid okay—you're sure of that."

"Positive."

"Okay, let's do it."

Shawna O'Reilly and Dylan Thomas were on their second cup of coffee when Caitlin Dufore walked into the dining room where the hotel served its complimentary continental breakfast. She joined them at the small table near the coffee urn that the hotel staff kept filled twenty-four-seven.

"What's on today's agenda?" Caitlin asked."

"About all we can do is wait and see where Val LaBelle or Claudette Beaupre surface," Dylan said.

Caitlin turned to Shawna, "Your people have no idea where he may be?"

"No."

Shawna's cell phone rang, she glanced at the display, and said,

"Excuse me, I need to take this call." She got up from the able and answered the call while walking toward the lobby.

"Have they called the FBI yet?" Caitlin asked her brother.

"No," Dylan said.

"Why not?"

"Possibly because once they learn that they took Sandy and crossed state lines, the FBI will ask why we didn't contact them right away." Dylan turned to his sister, "They didn't give you a time frame—just *later*?"

"Just *later*."

Shawna returned from the lobby and said, "We may have gotten a break. We've been monitoring the phones of a couple who an informant said were looking to adopt a child without having to go through the long process of adoption. They seem to have made a contact and are meeting with them at Copley Square at ten…"

Dylan looked at the clock on the wall. "That gives us an hour and a half. Did they happen to tell you who it was they contacted?"

"Val LaBelle."

"So, he's surfaced sooner than I'd thought. How long will it take us to reach Copley Square?"

"This hour of the morning," Shawna said, "half-hour, forty-five minutes at most."

"Then we have time for more coffee," Dylan said.

"Shouldn't we go there now?" Catlin asked.

"We'd only foul things up," Shawna said. "Besides, it's fifteen degrees outside. Only a fool would stand around Copley Square in this weather, we would stand out like a sore thumb."

Dylan refreshed his coffee. He realized that he was barely able to function. Shawna had dropped him off around two that morning and he was feeling the effects of days with less than adequate sleep. His eyes burned and it was getting harder and harder for him to comprehend details.

"Either way," he announced, "If my butt was made of flint all you'd see would be sparks. As soon as I finish this coffee, we need to get going or I'll crash and burn."

Val parked their car in a public lot near Copley Place. "It's only a short walk to Copley Square," he said.

"How will we know these people?" Claudette inquired.

"I'm cold," Sandra said.

Claudette shivered in the cold and held Sandra's hand tightly. "We'll get someplace warm, honey," she said, trying to soothe the child.

"C'mon," Val said.

"You didn't answer my question," Claudette said, pressing her uncle for information.

Realizing that she was not going to back off, Val said, "He'll be wearing a red parka and she'll be in a fur."

"Fur?"

"Yeah, one of those coats they make from animal skin."

"Val, I know what a fur is—what type?"

"Damned if I know… one with hair."

Felicien Paradis and Wayne Cloutier were sitting at a window table in a restaurant across from Copley Square. "This *source* of yours, he's reliable?" Paradis asked.

"He knows better than to cross me."

"He's sure that LaBelle and Claudette are supposed to be here?"

"He called and said that Val had surfaced. He and the woman are supposed to meet with some rich guy and his wife."

"What's your plan?" Paradis asked.

"We do nothing today."

"Then what in hell are we doing here?"

"I got people waiting nearby… both in cars and on foot. We follow them, let them make the exchange, and then we take them—and the money."

Paradis sat back, smiled, and said, "I like it…"

A cold wind blew across the plaza and Claudette wrapped her arms around her torso. Sandra turned her back to the biting cold draft and whined, "I'm cold."

"Be quiet. We won't be here long." Claudette squatted beside the girl. "Now we're going to meet some people—very important people, so you better be good. You only speak when spoke to and then only answer their questions. If you mention Maine and your family, your mother, father, brother, and sister will be hurt. Do understand me?"

Sandra's face was rosy pink from exposure to the below zero wind-chill.

"Did you understand me?" Claudette said in a tone that supported her threat.

"They're here," Val said. He led the way to a tall man in a red parka and a woman in a long dark brown sable coat. As Val closed with them, he pulled the glove off his right hand and held it out to the man. "Mr. Douglas?"

The man followed Val's lead and removed his glove and shook hands with Val. "Call me Wilton." He turned and placed his hand on his companion's back. "This is my wife, Suzanna."

Val in turn introduced Claudette and added, "…and this is Sandra."

Suzanna Douglas squatted in front of the young girl. "Hello, Sandra," she said.

Sandra looked at Claudette who nodded once and then said, "Hello."

Suzanna lowered the toddler's hood, studied her for a few seconds, and then replaced the hood on the girl's head. She stood and said, "She's a darling." She turned to her husband and said, "I'll leave the arrangements to you. I'll be at Neiman Marcus." She walked to a limousine and got in, leaving her husband to walk the block and a half to the upscale retailer.

Douglas watched the limo drive into the city traffic and then sad to Val, "Looks as if you have a deal."

LaBelle glanced around the square and then asked, "You bring the cash?"

"No, I left it in a secure place—until I met with you and felt safe."

"You afraid we'll rip you off?"

"It happens," Douglas replied.

LaBelle said, "Claudette, you take the kid and go to the car while Wilton and I deal with the specifics of the exchange."

Cloutier glanced out the window and said, "They're here."

"So, all we do today is watch?"

"That's right. Once the exchange is made, we move on them."

"Makes sense we get the money and the kid and LaBelle and Claudette get what's coming to them."

"Hold on, forget about the kid. Once we got the dough, we don't need the heat takin' her will cause."

Paradis glared at Cloutier, he wasn't accustomed to being given orders, let alone following them. However, to get to LaBelle and Claudette, he needed Cloutier and his organization. "Okay, this is your turf and you call the shots."

Paradis saw Claudette and the kid walk toward the Copley Place Parking Lot. "Still," he said, "It don't make sense letting them walk away, we could take them right now."

"Use your head, Felicien, the customer would be a fool to make the exchange in a public place. We don't move until we're certain they got the cash."

The car's heater was beginning to have an effect on the freezing interior when Val returned. He got in and said, "We'll make the exchange tomorrow." He glanced at the three-year-old girl in Claudette's arms. The kid had removed her left mitten, was sucking her thumb, and clung tightly to his niece, he asked, "This is new.

When did she start doing that?"

"Doing what?"

"Sucking her thumb and holding on to you like that?"

"You just ain't around her enough. She's been sucking her thumb since Felicien took her. The clinging started when Felicien scared her. She and I both have that fear."

"Don't worry. He can't get to you without going through me."

"Just remember to take him serious."

Val put the car in gear and backed out of the parking slot.

"When do we get the money?"

"Douglas will call me later with a specific location," Val answered.

The plaza was visible over the short concrete wall and three police cars, their lights flashing, stopped near the sidewalk on Huntington Avenue. The cops exited their cruisers and ran into the plaza. It was obvious that they were looking for someone. For a brief moment, Val wondered if Douglas had set him up, but thought of how anxious the husband and wife seemed, made a mental note to exercise caution when they made the exchange.

When they exited the building, they didn't notice the white SUV that was parked near the exit ramp and pulled out behind them. Val drove past the two police cruisers, slowing down like the traffic jam that was developing as drivers slowed to gawk at the police activity. Once past the plaza, Val and the white truck drove onto the John F. Fitzgerald Expressway and drove to Quincy.

Dylan, Caitlin, and Shawna were driving toward the plaza when Shawna got the call. "Damn," she said, "They got there too late. The meet was over and Val and Claudette were gone when they arrived."

"What about the people your guys are monitoring?"

"They haven't made any calls, so we have no idea where they are at this moment."

"So," Dylan said, "we're back in a holding pattern."

"We could work this from another angle," Shawna replied. "We could check some places and try to locate Wayne Cloutier, the Beaupre woman's uncle on her father's side."

"What can he do for us," Caitlin inquired.

"Let me give you some history. Cora LaBelle married Louis Cloutier and had two kids with him, a boy, Claude, and a daughter, Claudette. The LaBelles and Cloutiers have been on the BPD radar for years. Louis worked as a baggage handler at Logan and, although he was never caught, it was believed that he was part of a major heroin smuggling scheme. During the Afghanistan War there was a group out of New York run by Frank Priddy…"

"I heard of him. He was smuggling smack in the coffins of dead soldiers."

"Yes, Louis Cloutier was on the fringes of the gang. Most of what Priddy did was centered in New York's Harlem, but the tentacles of his organization reached into Boston. The DEA and FBI believed that Cloutier was one of several people Priddy had getting the junk out of the coffins."

"Nice bunch of people, these Cloutiers."

"Aren't they?"

"I don't give a shit if they make you or not, stay with them!" Wayne Cloutier shouted into his cell phone. He broke the connection and said, "They're in Quincy. Head for Furnace Brook Parkway," he told his man who was driving. He turned so he could look into the backseat.

Felicien Paradis was smoking a cigarette and exhaling through the side window which was open about one inch. He seemed to be lost in thought. After several drags on the cigarette, he threw it out the window. "Tell me," he said, "what makes a man want to kill his niece, his own blood."

Cloutier was quiet for a few seconds and then said, "I guess you're owed an explanation as much as anyone. It goes back to her father, my brother. We were just kids, Louis, her father, was twenty and

I was eighteen. We were doing a job and it went south on us. The bastard took off and we were busted…"

"What type of job?"

"An armored car in Lawrence. It was taking the day's winnings from Rockingham Park race track to a bank in the city. It stopped to do a pick-up at First Essex Bank in Lawrence and we took it down. Like I said we was just kids and we didn't case the location. The friggin' police department was around the corner. In minutes the place was infested with cops and we knew we wouldn't have a chance in a gunfight, so we surrendered. Even then I knew better than to get nabbed for killin' a cop. As we was marched to the jail, I noticed that Louis was gone. They caught up with him a couple of days later. I never found out how they got on to him and it don't matter now. My older brother turned state's evidence and I did ten years of a twenty year stretch in Walpole.

"I heard of that place—it's a super-max, that's hard-time."

"Every fuckin' second."

"What happened to him? You get even?"

"He started working for some New York mobster named Frank Priddy."

"Him I heard of, too."

"Louis was handling baggage at Logan. Priddy was smugglin' smack in the coffins of dead soldiers comin' back from the war. Somehow Priddy got the idea that Louis was skimmin' smack and selling on his own. Louis got *disappeared*." Cloutier pointed at Dorchester Bay. "It wouldn't surprise me if my *big* brother is out there wearing cement shoes."

"But why the hard feelings against Claudette?"

Her mother always blamed me for Louis's disappearance and the kid and she have done anything they could to send me back to Walpole, only this time for life."

Cloutier's cell phone rang. He answered and listened for a moment and then said, "Stay there. We're on our way. We got them," he said.

Val stood off to the side of the window peering at the parking lot. He and Claudette had been in his room waiting for Douglas to call.

"What's out there that has your attention?" Claudette asked.

"A white van. I think it's been following us since we left Copley Plaza."

Claudette joined him near the window.

"It's the one parked on the other side of the street," Val said.

"What are we going to do?"

"Nothing right now, but have the kid ready to leave when I say."

Claudette left the window and walked to the bed where Sandra was sleeping. She stared at the three-year-old and said, "You know, there are times where I'm tempted to call all this off and take her back to her parents."

Val turned his head in her direction and said, "You better make up your mind because once we close the deal with Douglas, it'll be too late." He returned to his vigil and saw a second car pull off the road. He saw Wayne Cloutier and Felicien Paradis get out and cross the street to the van. "Wayne and your boyfriend are here. You better get ready, because we may have to move fast."

Val took his pistol out of his waistband and walked to the door. His hand was on the doorknob when Claudette asked, "Where are you going?"

"I'm fuckin' tired of being chased all over the city like I was a rabid dog."

"Think about this, okay? If anything happens to you how do I get in contact with Douglas?"

Val took out his cell phone and called a number. "Mr. Douglas? Val LaBelle. Be on the Esplanade, by Fiedler's Head at five tonight… bring the cash."

He broke the connection and tossed the phone to Claudette. "Douglas's number is in the *recents* menu under the telephone app. If I don't come back it's on you."

She nodded her understanding.

"You got the car keys?" Val asked.

"Yes."

"If I'm not back in fifteen minutes, get the hell out of here and meet Douglas."

"What is Fiedler's head?"

"Fiedler was the conductor of The Boston Pops Orchestra, which does the Fourth of July concert on the Esplanade, that's the park between Storrow Drive and the Charles River. There's this big goddamned statue of his head there. That's where Douglas will meet you. If it looks like you've been followed, call Douglas and arrange for another meeting place. Make it a public place, Claudette, if your boyfriend or Wayne get you off the beaten track, they'll kill you."

"I'll be careful."

"I don't think you'll have anything to worry about until after the exchange—they want the money, not the kid."

He opened the door.

"Val, be careful."

"It's too late for that."

"If we don't see each other again… thank you. I'd probably be dead if not for your help."

"Once this is over, check on your mother. She'll need help for a while."

"If this goes down okay, I'll take her with me when I leave."

"If I was you, I'd call a guy named, Raul Chavez—his name is in my contacts on the phone."

"Who's he?"

"An expert in helping people disappear. He owes me. Tell him what happened—don't tell him why though—and he'll help you."

Claudette kissed her uncle on his cheek and closed the door behind him.

Wayne and Felicien were talking with the driver of the van. "You're sure they're in there," Wayne asked.

"Look for yourself," the van driver said, "I believe that's Val LaBelle walking this way."

Wayne and Felicien turned to see Val walking across the hotel parking lot. "So it is," Wayne said.

"And he's carrying a piece," Felicien said.

Val reached the end of the parking lot and called out to Wayne, "What you looking for, Cloutier? If it's a hard time, you came to the right place."

"You talking to us or blowing hot air," Wayne responded.

Felicien stepped to the side so that Val couldn't cover them all at the same time. "You and Paradis been hounding us long enough. State your business and then get the fuck away from us."

"Our business is in the room you just left," Felicien said. "My woman is in there and she's got something that belongs to me."

Val stopped on the sidewalk across the street and said, "Way I hear it, she has as much right to the merchandise as you."

"Well," Felicien answered, "you was given bullshit information. Turn Claudette and the kid over to us and we'll leave you standing. Otherwise, do what you have to do to stop us."

Val turned toward Wayne. "If the shit hits the fan, Cloutier, You're going first, I got no use for a lousy piece of shit who turns on his own blood."

Val hoped that Claudette was in the car and ready to escape.

He saw Wayne and Felicien straighten up and their eyes went to the lot behind Val. "She's getting' away," Paradis shouted.

Val dropped to one knee and when Cloutier pulled a chrome-plated revolver he fired three shots in rapid succession. Two red splotches appeared in Cloutier's chest and Val spun toward Paradis. Before he could get a shot off Paradis fired, hitting Val in the side.

Paradis saw Val fall to one side and ran to the van. He saw where Val's third shot went; the driver lay on his side, a bullet hole in the side of his head. Felicien grabbed the obviously dead man and pulled him out of the warm van, dumping him on the frozen pavement.

Val struggled to one knee and fired a shot at the van. A metallic pinging noise told him that he'd hit the truck.

Paradis spun and fired two shots; the second hit Val in the torso and he fell back against the motel's road sign. Val's head rested on the icy cold metal and he knew he was hit bad; he was certain that the wound was most likely fatal. He watched helpless as Paradis put the van in gear, performed a screeching *U-turn* and sped down the street in the direction Claudette had gone. Sirens could be heard in the distance and Val relaxed and waited for death.

Claudette retraced the route she and Val had taken when they fled Boston. When she was on I-93 north she saw the white van careen off the exit and follow her. She accelerated and in minutes was flying through the O'Neill Tunnel.

The van fell back but she was unable to shake it. She took the exit for Route 28 which she knew would take her to Storrow Drive. She kept glancing in her rear-view mirror, looking for the white van. She was unable to see it for now.

Shawna got the call about the shootout in Quincy and she, Dylan, and Caitlin rushed there. When they arrived on site, Shawna showed the investigating detective her credentials and asked what the situation was.

"No situation, three of Boston's biggest assholes had some sort of disagreement and shot the shit out of each other."

"Three? What were their names?"

"Only two matter, Val LaBelle and Wayne Cloutier… the other guy was one of Cloutier's mob."

"You have any idea as to why?"

"Nope, but LaBelle was mumbling some shit about the Fiedler and five o'clock. The desk clerk called 9-1-1 and when the first responder got here the clerk said that LaBelle had a woman and kid with him. She took off in a car and a fourth shooter followed her in a white van."

Dylan was standing behind Shawna and he said, "Paradis."

"*Pair a* what?" the detective inquired.

"Not pair a, I said Paradis, Felicien Paradis, LaBelle's niece—she was most likely the woman with the kid—was his girlfriend until a week ago. They stole the child and are looking to sell her on the Child Exchange."

"Spell his name for me."

"P-a-r-a-d-i-s."

"Thought you said his name was pair-a-dee?"

"I did, it's a French name; Para-dis is pair-a-dee in French."

"Gotcha. Now suppose you tell me who *you* are," he said.

"I'm Dylan Thomas, the child's uncle and his mother's lawyer." He turned to Caitlin. "This is my sister, Caitlin Dufore. She's the child's mother."

The detective ceased writing in a notebook and he looked at Dylan. "That was Dylan Thomas—like the poet?"

Dylan tried not to let his irritation show when he said, "Yes, like the poet. Officer O'Reilly is assisting us."

The detective looked at Shawna. "BPD in the habit of letting officers run a personal investigation?"

"No, I'm using up a bunch of back vacation time."

The cop turned back to Dylan and Caitlin. "You folks gonna be in town long?"

"Depends," Dylan answered.

"Depends on what?"

"How soon we get Sandra back."

"How many dead did you find on scene?" Shawna asked.

"Two so far; Cloutier and his flunky—LaBelle is critical. Well, it's been nice talkin' to you folks, now I got to get to work. Good luck finding your kid."

When the detective left Dylan asked Shawna, "You got any idea what Fiedler and five o'clock mean."

Shawna was silent for a while as she ran possibilities through her mind. After several moments she said, "There are several statues and monuments to Arthur Fiedler, the former conductor of the Boston Pops. It has to be the Esplanade though. The niece doesn't know

Boston and the statue of Fiedler's Head is easy to find. All she needs do is get on Storrow Drive and she'll find it."

Dylan looked at his watch. "It's half-past three. If we're going to get there before the exchange we should get going."

Claudette was unfamiliar with The Esplanade and arrived early in the event she should have to find a parking place within walking distance. She found an open space on Mount Vernon Street and sat in the car staring out at snow flurries, even though the sun was shining.

Sandra had been quiet all afternoon. It was as if she knew something was going to happen and not entirely sure that she was going to like it. "Are we going to meet Mummy here?" she asked.

For some strange reason Claudette felt compelled to tell the truth. "Not today, honey, but we're meeting some nice people who are going to take care of you until I can get your mommy and bring her to you."

Sandra stared out the window for a second and seemed mesmerized by the snowflakes drifting through the bright sunlight. "How can it snow when the sun is out?" she asked.

"This is Boston… Boston is beside the ocean and the water is not frozen yet. When the wind blows off the water it brings moisture and when the moisture comes over the cold air on the ground it causes snow."

The child looked at the adult as if she wasn't sure whether she'd told her the truth or was teasing. "I don't understand."

Claudette laughed. "I don't either, Sweetheart, but I was told that's what causes it." She sat quietly for a second realizing that she was using terms of endearment when she spoke to the little one. She thought about what she was about to do—sell a child to two perfect strangers. All she had was Val's word that they were *really* looking for a child for their own and not to be sold as a white slave. She intentionally refused to look at Sandra because each time she did, accomplishing her task got harder and harder. *Even if I do it,* she thought, *I'll be running from Felicien for the rest of my life.* Her thoughts shifted. *Am I capable of killing him? He's capable of killing me, that's for sure.*

Realizing that if she didn't move, she'd lose her resolve, Claudette forced her mind back to the current situation. She got out of the car and opened the back door. She bundled Sandra's winter coat around her and took a tissue from her purse and spit-shined the girl's face. "C'mon kid, let's go meet these people."

"I don't want to stay with them. I want to go with you to get Mommy."

"Don't be difficult now. These are very nice people. It'll only be for a day or two and your mother will come for you."

Claudette lifted the three-year-old out of the car and placed her on the sidewalk. Snowflakes stuck to Sandra's hair and Claudette pulled her hood over her head; she tied the drawstring and said, "There you look great."

"I'm cold."

"This won't take long." Claudette glanced at her watch, four-forty. She had no idea how long it would take to walk to the Fiedler Head and hoped twenty minutes was enough time. A gust of wind raced down the street, bringing a burst of snow with it. She took Sandra by her hand. "C'mon honey let's get this over with..."

Felicien walked around the amphitheater, someone told him that it was called the Hatch Shell, as if he gave a damn. What he did care about was the statue of a big fucking head that was nearby. There were several small trees around it, nothing big enough to hide behind. He wished he knew from which direction Claudette would be coming. A gust of wind blew up the Charles, roiling the unfrozen parts of the river's surface with frigid whitecaps. He turned in a slow circle looking for someplace where he could watch and stay out of the wind. He saw several large oak trees and as he walked toward them, he thought: *I had no idea Boston got this friggin' cold.*

When he reached the trees, he checked his line of sight and was satisfied he had a good enough view of the shell and the statue to observe both. He was not concerned with confronting Claudette before the exchange; it was the after that worried him. He relished the thought of how she'd look when he took the money. *Who knows? If she doesn't give me any shit, I might give her enough money to get back to Maine.* He saw the familiar figures of a woman and small child walking toward the statue.

One of the advantages of having a Boston Police detective on your team was that she knew her way around the city. Even though it was the height of rush hour they were going against the traffic as they sped north, and didn't run into a traffic jam until they were in the Tip O'Neill tunnel. Shawna took the first tunnel exit and took city streets to Nashua Circle, where she took route 28 to Storrow Drive. They were on the Charles River Esplanade at four-thirty.

For fifteen minutes they strolled around the area near the Hatch Shell looking for Claudette and Sandra. Caitlin was getting anxious and said, "Do we grab her the minute we see them?"

"No," Dylan said.

"Why not?"

"Because we want to grab *all* of them, Paradis, the Beaupre woman, *and* the people willing to buy an abducted child," Dylan said, "Every goddamned one of them needs to go down for this."

"Caitlin," Shawna said, "If you go running to Sandra as soon as you see her who knows what will happen. These people have been involved in gunfights all over the area… there's nothing to stop them from killing you—and Sandra. You *have* to promise us that you'll do as we say or I'll send you back to the car."

"I understand," Caitlin said, although being talked to like an unruly child rankled her.

"It's for Sandra's safety as much as it yours," Dylan added.

"But what if the people buying my baby run with her?"

"We've passed four of my fellow detectives in the past five minutes," Shawna said. "Their job is to stop them, rescue your baby and arrest them."

"Okay. I promise to do it your way."

"We don't make a move until the exchange takes place… until it does the buyers haven't committed a crime—the money has to change hands," Shawna said.

Claudette held onto Sandra's hand and walked at a pace so fast that the toddler was being dragged along. The sun disappeared over the horizon and the snow flurries escalated into a squall. "Come on Sandra, we'll be late."

"I'm walking as fast as I can," the child protested.

"Oh, for Christ sake," Claudette swore as she hefted Sandra off her feet and carried her past the shell and toward the Fiedler statue.

She saw a well-dressed couple walking in the same direction. The man wore an expensive leather jacket and the woman at his side wore what was obviously an even more expensive designer fur coat. He carried a small tote and Claudette's heart began to race. Finally, she was to have financial security.

The couple saw her and stood beside the statue, waiting.

When she was within speaking distance, Claudette said, "Mr. and Mrs. Douglas?"

"Yes, is that our girl?"

Felicien saw Claudette appear before the statue. She was carrying a bundle which he assumed was the kid. She stopped before two people and said something he could not hear. He saw the man hand Claudette an overnight bag and take the child.

When Shawna saw the valise had changed hands, she raised a small two-way radio and said, "We got them. Move in."

Cops ran at the perpetrators from all four directions, each of them holding a badge in one hand and a gun in the other. They surrounded the Douglases and Claudette. "We'll take the child," Shawna said. She took Sandra from the woman's arms and turned to Caitlin. Before anyone could stop the enraged mother, she stepped forward and punched Claudette in the face.

Claudette fell back onto her buttocks and wiped at the blood that poured from her broken nose.

"You ever," Catlin said, "come within fifty miles of me or my children, I'll kill you." At that moment no one was about to deny her sincerity.

At the sight of her mother, Sandra leapt into her open arms, "Momma, you came—I knew you would!"

The police had Suzanna and Wilton Douglas leaning forward with their hands-on trees while they were searched. One of the detectives said, "I'll be goddamned." He handed Shawna a leather wallet. When she flipped it open, she saw FBI in large letters on an ID card and a badge. She looked at *Suzanna* and asked, "Her too?"

Wilton Douglas looked over his shoulder and said "My name is Brett Lynne—as it says on that ID. This is my partner, Suzanna Carlton."

Shawna looked at Dylan. "We nailed a couple of feds."

"Can we put our hands down now?" Lynne asked.

"What?" Shawna said and then she realized the federal agents were still in *the* position and she said, "Oh, sure, please do."

Carlton and Lynne straightened up, lowered their hands, and turned. "We've been working for a year to catch Valiant LaBelle and bust his adoption for hire business. We thought he'd be here."

"Val was shot in a gunfight earlier this afternoon. The last we heard he was in the I.C.U. at Quincy Hospital," Dylan said.

"Who are you?"

"Dylan Thomas…"

"Like the poet?" Carlton asked.

"Yes, like the poet," Once again Dylan was forced to hide his aggravation at having to answer that question. He wasn't entirely successful. "At any rate, our job isn't finished. Felicien Paradis is still loose."

Felicien watched the fancy dressed couple hand a valise to Claudette and she handed the kid to the woman. He was just about to step out of his place of concealment when the Esplanade erupted into an explosion of cops, all holding badges in one hand and guns in the other. He didn't wait around to see the final result. He cursed and walked to his truck.

Saturday: Day Fifteen

DYLAN MET SHAWNA FOR COFFEE in the hotel dining room.

"Where is Caitlin and the baby?" Shawna asked.

"I would imagine they're still in bed. It's going to be a long time before Caitlin lets that child out of her sight. Any word of the boyfriend?"

"Nope. It's believed that he's left Boston."

"Maine."

"I'm sorry?"

"Maine, he's headed back, running for familiar territory."

"Have you talked to Jean-Paul?" Shawna asked.

"That's the next item on my agenda. What's the latest on the Beaupre woman and LaBelle?"

"LaBelle lost his battle last night. I'm told he flat-lined just past midnight. She'll be arraigned on Monday. With the kidnapping charge that she's facing, it'll be a long time before she has a window without bars in it."

"I need to talk to her. Can you arrange it?"

"Don't see why not. You think she knows where Paradis ran to?"

"If anyone knows she will. My best guess is the Belgrade Lakes Region. His mother lives there. If anyone knows where he might be headed it'll be Beaupre."

"What are Caitlin's plans?"

"As soon as your people give her the okay, she's headed back to Maine."

Shawna picked up the phone and held up a finger telling Dylan she'd be right back and walked away. She returned in less than ten minutes. "We can see Beaupre at four this afternoon."

Dylan and Shawna sat in the interrogation room when Claudette Beaupre was escorted in by a female officer. Beaupre looked haggard and the blaze orange jumpsuit accentuated the bags under her eyes, which were bloodshot. The officer sat her across from her visitors and fastened her restraints to the heavy metal U that was welded to the table's surface. Claudette clasped her hands together and slumped forward staring at them.

Shawna got right to the point. "Rough night, Claudette?"

"I've had worse."

"I'll bet you've had better too," Shawna said.

Claudette didn't respond; she merely stared at her hands.

"Do you know who we are?" Shawna asked.

"I assume you," Claudette said without making eye contact, "are cops."

"Actually, I am a cop," Shawna said. "Mr. Thomas is not."

"Then why is he here?"

"He's a lawyer."

"If he ain't with the prosecutor, maybe he should be on this side of the table."

"The only problem with that," Dylan said, "is it was my niece you tried to sell."

"Why are you two here? Shouldn't my lawyer be here?"

"Do you have an attorney?" Dylan asked.

"Of course, Wilson Pettigrew."

Dylan saw Shawna shake her head, "I should have known," she said.

"Didn't we meet him last week?" Dylan asked.

"One and the same," Shawna answered. "We'll talk later."

Shawna turned to Claudette. "We aren't here to try and get you.

We just think it's a shame that you're going to take the fall alone for something your boyfriend was a part of."

Claudette's head snapped back and she stared at them. "What do I get if I roll over?"

"You get to tell Pettigrew that you're helping us on an open homicide investigation."

"You talkin' about the kid in Maine?" Claudette asked.

Dylan stared at her, his glare burning a hole through her. "Among others."

"What others?" She turned defiant.

"Your Uncle Val," Shawna said.

"I figgered as much. I knew he was goin' down as soon as he walked out the door."

"It was," Shawna replied, "a bad day for the LaBelle and Cloutier clan."

Claudette looked at the two people seated across the table. "Wayne dead too?"

Shawna nodded.

"He's no loss… never cared for me or my mother. How is she?"

"Out of the critical care unit. She's got a long road to travel, but she'll be all right."

"Now," Dylan said, "Where would Felicien Paradis run to?"

"Either of you got a cigarette?"

Both Dylan and Shawna shook their heads.

"Paradis?" Dylan prompted her.

"Only place he can run to is Belgrade Lakes. Check out a piece of shit named Vern Cole. Felicien was boosting cars for him."

Shawna and Dylan stood. "Anything I can get you?" Shawna asked.

"A pack of smokes."

"I'll ask if it's allowed. You should quit, this may be your best chance."

"I did quit ten years ago, stayed off them for four years, and then started again. If I quit there would be nothing to do in here."

Once Dylan and Shawna were in the corridor outside the

interrogation room, Dylan said, "Isn't Pettigrew the guy we thought was mixed up in this?"

"The same. We've been trying to connect him to the child exchange for years."

"Sly. Represent the one person that you know can connect you to the illegal adoptions."

"He's as slippery as a snake in water," Shawna replied. "Nevertheless, like all scumbags he'll screw up yet and we'll take him down. What are your plans?"

"Put Caitlin and Sandra on a plane to Presque Isle and head up to Belgrade Lakes."

"Want me to let Jean-Paul know you're coming?"

"That'd be good." Dylan held out his hand. "Shawna, we can't thank you enough…"

She smiled. "It was nothing that any other Maine-iac wouldn't have done."

Dylan shook her hand and said, "If you ever want to move back, contact me. A lawyer can always use a good investigator." He handed her a card. "Any time."

"You be careful now."

Sunday: Day Sixteen

DYLAN MET JEAN-PAUL THIBODEAU AT a coffee bar near the University of Maine, Farmington campus. "I hear that congratulations are in order." Thibodeau said.

"I'd have been lost without Shawna."

"That one was Boston's gain and Maine's loss."

"There's still work to be done though… Paradis may be back in the area. What do you know about a guy named Vern Cole?"

"Vernon Dwight Cole supposedly runs a logging business. The truth is he's the head of a car theft ring, although we've never been able to prove it. That big building of his is half garage, half chop-shop."

"We may be able to bring him down. Claudette Beaupre says that Paradis was boosting cars for Cole. She believes that Paradis has no place else to go and the only person who can help him is Cole. I don't know how much she actually knows—if anything. Nevertheless, it may be worth the time for you to send someone to Boston to talk to her."

"I'll make arrangements to send someone to see her in the morning."

Vern Cole knocked on the door leading into the small room in the far recesses of his *shop*. When he heard Felicien call, "It's open," he entered.

Felicien lay on the twin bed, smoking a cigarette, and watching a reality TV show on the small television. He saw Cole and sat up. "Hey Vern."

"I hate to break it to you like this, but you gotta get outta here."

"Why?"

"My sources say that I'm gonna get a visit from the staties tomorrow. You shoulda told me how hot you were… what the fuck you do—shoot up half of Boston?"

"I got caught up in a friggin' family feud between Claudette's uncles. It's over now, they both got killed."

"Yeah? Well right now you're hotter than a dry tree in a forest fire."

Felicien stood up and ground out his cigarette. "You want I should take off for a couple of days?"

"I want you should take off for good. You draw cops like a flame draws flies. I been operating outta here for over ten years without ever seeing a cop. Now I got every cop between here and Boston lookin' at me. I can't believe that you and your girlfriend were stupid enough to kidnap a kid. If that wasn't bad enough you took her across state lines, that's federal shit. If I was you, I'd be lookin' for the shortest route to Canada."

Felicien started shoving his few items of clothing into a small overnight bag. "I understand you man and I appreciate all you done for me."

"I'd also lose that goddamned van you drove up here. You carrying a gun?"

"No, I had to dump mine off the bridge between Portsmouth and Kittery—it was traceable to the shootings in Boston."

"I got one that's untraceable," Cole said. "C'mon, I'll get you the pistol. How you fixed for cash?"

"I'm strapped."

"I got some cash in the office, I'll stake you. Don't screw around, run for the border as fast as you can. If you're smart, you'll get out of Maine and you won't come back."

Monday: Day Seventeen

"WHAT YOU DOIN' HERE?" JEANINE Boutot asked her son. I thought you and that whore was settin' up housekeepin' in your uncle's shack."

"Things have changed."

Jeanine studied her son for a few moments. "What you do... kill her?"

"No, I did not kill her."

"Well, you should've. You get rid of the kid too?"

"Jeanine, I'm in trouble."

"No shit. In the past two days I've had the local cops, the Maine State Police, and the FBI here—every one of them wantin' to know if I seen you." She looked up and down the road. "You got any brains you'll get outta here right now. They probably got people watchin' us as we speak."

"I got nowheres else that I can go..."

"You shoulda thought about that before you let that woman talk you into this hare-brained kidnapping deal. You always was easily influenced by women."

Felicien lit a cigarette and paced around the small living room; he kicked discarded newspapers and magazines out of his path. He flopped into a worn easy chair and leaned forward, resting his head in his hands. "I guess I only got one choice..."

"You stopped having choices when you and that bimbo stole the kid. The cops told me you killed some kid up in Aroostook County—

what's wrong with your head? Kidnapping alone will get you twenty years—murder is life without parole."

Felicien ground his cigarette out and stood up. "I better get goin'."

"You never shoulda stopped in the first place."

Paradis pulled into the parking lot of the mall. He cruised through the aisles looking for a vehicle that was away from the building, but not so isolated that any activity near it would attract attention. He circumvented the massive building and saw a line of cars lined up along a deep ditch—an ideal situation. He slid the van into a vacant parking spot and entered the mall. He walked directly into a big box store and purchased an inexpensive set of screwdrivers.

He quickly removed the front license plate from the van and switched it with the car beside it. He was thankful that the snow and dirt from the road surface made both sets of plates indecipherable. He slid into the ditch and swapped the rear plates.

Back in his truck, Felicien blew on his fingers to ease the throbbing pain from them. As a teenager, he'd frozen his fingers while ice-fishing and since that day his hands quickly turned numb when cold. The rapidity in which it happened never ceased to amaze him. When feeling returned to his cold fingers, he started the motor, turned up the fan, and drove out of the mall.

Once he was back on route 27, he turned west and headed for the border crossing at Coburn Gore. He knew that it was over sixty miles to the border and that once he passed through the diminutive town of Eustice there would be a run of more than twenty miles through thick woods. He glanced at the truck's gas gauge, saw it was indicating the tank was a quarter full, and knew he had to fill up before he left civilization.

It started snowing as he drove out of Farmington.

By the time Felicien had traveled thirty miles, the storm had turned into a raging nor'easter. Felicien's shoulders ached from the strain of staring through the restricted view. The windshield wipers on the van were incapable of keeping up with the snow that stuck to the windshield and on several occasions, he had to stop and use his hands to wipe the glass. Snow had clustered between the wiper blades and their frames resulting in two narrow two-inch strips through which he could see. He banged the wipers against the glass so they were flush with the windshield and jumped back into the truck.

He cursed and twisted the heater temperature adjustment trying to get more heat out of the hopelessly over-matched defroster. He wished he was in a car with a much smaller interior to warm. A sudden gust of wind rocked the truck and sent it into a spin. Felicien steered into the skid and sighed with relief when the truck straightened and settled back on all four wheels.

Felicien pressed the accelerator pedal and the light rear end of the van began to fishtail. Once again, he slowed down until he felt the van stabilize. He cursed under his breath. The trip to the border should have taken about an hour; in this goddamned blizzard he'd be lucky to get there by morning.

Dylan and Danielle Stevens sat in front of the fireplace that covered one entire wall of the hotel lobby. They were sipping coffee and listening to the wind rattle the windows.

"I'm so glad that you were able to rescue your niece and capture that awful woman," Danielle said.

"On the negative side her boyfriend, who was the worst of the pair—he killed a teenage boy in Sherman—got away."

"He'll show up."

"Jean-Paul has notified every law enforcement organization in Maine, along with the RCMP, U. S. and Canadian Border people, and the FBI is looking for him too… taking a child across state lines for illegal purposes is a violation of the Mann Act, a federal offense."

The click of the snow and sleet hitting the window overpowered the relaxing snap and crackle of the wood fire.

"How much snow are they forecasting?" Dylan asked.

"Eighteen to twenty-four inches, then you have to deal with the drifting and sub-zero temperatures. The roads will be a mess tomorrow," Danielle answered.

The door opened and a gust of wind blew snow and sleet in behind the man and woman who darted inside. Dylan watched the fire dance as the moving air reached it.

"Time for me to go to work," Danielle said.

"What time do you get off?"

"Eleven… provided Earl can make it in."

"Well, you shouldn't be driving tonight," Dylan said with a lecherous smile.

"I know where to find you." She walked to the desk.

Dylan shrugged his arms into the sleeves of his parka and as he walked outside, headed for his room, he heard the woman say to Danielle, "Please tell us you have a room available."

The van's heater finally warmed the interior and Felicien began to sweat. He struggled out of his coat and tossed it into the passenger seat. The snowflakes flew at the van, coming out of the dark of the night like angry insects. In the headlights they looked as big as quarters and visibility was for shit. Suddenly the steering wheel spun madly to the right and the front tire left the road and dug into the soft snow of the shoulder. He tried to back up, but all he heard was the tire spinning. He hammered the steering wheel with his fists. "Why the fuck didn't Cloutier use a goddamned four-wheel drive!"

He looked in the cargo area for something he could use to put under the traction wheel, hoping it would allow the truck to pull out of the depression it was stuck in. He spied a canvas tarpaulin and thought that might do the trick. He got out of the truck and the wind slammed the door behind him. He heard the unmistakable *CLICK* of the doors locking. Felicien stared through the side window at his coat, which sat on the passenger seat in the warm interior.

He fought back the impulse to cry, lamenting to himself, *I am royally fucked. Only people out on a night like this will be cops and plow drivers.* He was fully aware that a cop would most likely have been given his description and a plow driver would immediately report his truck being off the road. He circled the van, trying every door as he came to it, hoping one of them was not locked. The effort was fruitless. He turned to the passenger side and squatted using the truck as a wind break. He saw smoke coming out of the exhaust pipe and moved as close to it as he could without burning himself. He couldn't help but notice the irony of worrying about burning oneself while freezing to death in minus forty wind chills. He wrapped the tarp around his arms around his torso and waited—for what he had no idea.

Tuesday: Day Eighteen

"I THOUGHT YOU MIGHT BE interested in knowing that we found Felicien Paradis," Jean-Paul said.

Dylan absentmindedly watched a pickup truck plow the parking lot of the hotel. "Where is he now?"

"The morgue."

"So, he went down fighting…"

"Nope. He was found on route 27, half-way between Farmington and the Canadian border. Apparently, he slid off the road and got stuck. Somehow or another he locked himself out of the truck and died from hypothermia."

"So, it's over…"

"Not quite. This afternoon we're raiding Cole's place. Beaupre has been a wealth of information about his operation."

The lawyer in Dylan's brain kicked in. "Are you working with actual knowledge or hearsay?"

"Hearsay, but enough to get a search warrant."

"Good luck," Dylan said.

"I'm confident we'll find something. Well, gotta run. I'll call later and let you know how it goes with Cole. By the way, the Boston PD says if we can't nail him, they have a witness that puts him in Mattapan the night of the shootout. It seems the dead guy on the stairs is a known associate of Cole." Thibodeau broke the connection.

Danielle came out of the bathroom, a bath towel wrapped

around her, and she was drying her hair with another towel and she asked, "Who was that?"

"Jean-Paul, they found Paradis. He's dead. I don't have all the particulars, but it appears that he froze to death."

"So, it's finally over?"

"It looks that way."

She walked to him and they embraced.

"You ever been ice-fishing?" Dylan asked. "We can drive up to my camp and spend a few days…"

Danielle let the towel drop. "Do we have to leave now?"

About the Author

VAUGHN C. HARDACKER is a member of the New England Chapter of the Mystery Writers of America and International Thriller Writers. Three of his novels, *Sniper*, *The Fisherman*, and *Wendigo* were finalists in the Crime Fiction category of the 2015, 2016, and 2018 Maine Literary Awards. His fifth novel, *My Brother's Keeper*, was released on July 2, 2019.

He is a veteran of the U. S. Marines and served in Vietnam. He holds degrees from Northern Maine Technical College, the University of Maine, and Southern New Hampshire University.

He lives in Stockholm, Maine, where he is working on his next crime thriller.